Dennis Marriott was born in Bicester, Oxfordshire, where he has spent most of his life. He started his working life as cinema projectionist, then joined the Royal Air Force on National Service. After which, he found employment in the Civil Service where he remained for the next forty-five years. He served in Bicester, Chilwell in Nottinghamshire and Donnington in Shropshire.

In his younger days he was a keen ballroom dancer and has been a member of a Camera Club, an Archery Club and a Judo Club, where he qualified as a Club Coach.

Now, his pastimes are reading, writing and listening to a wide variety of music.

THOSE PEOPLE
NEXT DOOR

Dennis Marriott

Those People Next Door

Vanguard Press

A CIP catalogue record for this title is
available from the British Library
ISBN 1 843860 42 2

Vanguard Press is an imprint of
Pegasus Elliot MacKenzie Publishers Ltd.
www.pegasuspublishers.com

First Published in 2003

Vanguard Press
Sheraton House Castle Park
Cambridge England

Printed & Bound in Great Britain

Dedication

To my late wife Rosemary, who, when she knew I had received yet another rejection slip, said quietly to me:

'Don't give up, don't ever give up.'

I am now so grateful to her that I didn't.

CHAPTER ONE

The tranquillity of the morning in Forsythia Avenue was faintly disturbed by the arrival of a removal van outside number twenty-five.

Someone was at last moving in.

Lieutenant Colonel (retd) Simon Hallett was busily engaged in trimming the front hedge of number twenty-seven, and was therefore keenly interested in the arrival of the removal van as this meant the arrival of his new neighbours.

Hallett paused in his clipping and pretended to inspect the top of the hedge, then turned his head as the removal men lifted a rolled carpet. As it was passed over some chairs, it became unrolled, and revealed to him that it was from a range of very expensive carpets that he had long admired but could not afford. He gave it a solemn nod of approval. What he had seen so far was obviously the choice of someone with taste, discretion and money. The tone of Forsythia Avenue was to be upheld.

Regarding his previous neighbour, Hallett had been only slightly sorry to see him go, and that was only because it left an empty house, and just about anyone might move in. Well, old Aubrey next door had been all right, but it was a pity that he had to be a sanitary inspector and as if that wasn't enough, he always seemed to be finding things to complain about and then he would organise petitions. After all, one had more things to do than keep signing petitions about petty complaints all the time.

What sort of chap would this newcomer be? Broker of some sort? doctor, solicitor or a company director maybe? Come to think of it, a doctor or solicitor next door could be very useful. Yes, pass the doctor a bunch of roses for his wife, and then ask him about that funny little pain in your knee. Or, if a solicitor moved in, he could advise you whether or not you had the legal

11

right to kick that detestable ginger cat from the house opposite off of your lettuce plants.

Hallett paused as two of the removal men walked carefully up the path carrying an expensive-looking antique hall stand. This time though, it was not the furniture that caught his eye; it was the removal men. Both in their early twenties, both with untidy hair, gaudy shirts and ragged jeans that looked as if they were regularly stored in a dustbin. A spell in the Army would do them good, he thought, that would put an end to their scruffy appearance; make men of them, instil some pride into them, show them – his reverie was interrupted by the sound of someone shouting.

'I said, could I use your phone, guv?'

Hallett then realised that this enquiry was directed at him. 'I beg your pardon, were you speaking to me?'

The driver of the removal van sighed. 'Your phone, mate, can I use it to call my boss, only the batteries have packed up on me mobile. I'll reverse the charges, all right?'

'Yes, I suppose so. Just knock on the door and tell my wife I have given my permission.'

'Ta, mate.'

The driver walked towards the house shouting to his colleagues to save some work for him and that he would not be long.

Hallett watched him go and he shook his head; it seemed a pity that here was a man old enough to show these young men the meaning of respect, of correct mode of address, of how to conduct oneself. Fancy saying 'ta, mate'. It really was not good enough.

Funny in a way, though, the driver looked a bit like someone he once knew. But who was it? I know; it was one of my soldiers, the one who was charged with a quite serious offence. What was his name; Private Chapple, or was it Chapley? But whatever his name was, he managed to spill porridge down the front of the Orderly Officer. Chappleton, that was his name, Private Chappleton.

Hallett's eyes narrowed as he recalled that day, not long after his promotion to Major, when it had been reported to him that Private Chappleton had spilled a whole plateful of porridge down the front of Lieutenant Jeremy Butterworth. It had been a tiresome business and he now recalled how it had all happened.

'Porridge, Sergeant-Major?'

'Yessir, seems a full plate of porridge was spilled on the Lieutenant's uniform.'

'But how could a thing like that happen?'

'Don't know, sir. All Private Chappleton has said is, he couldn't help it.'

'Couldn't help it? How the devil could he not help throwing porridge all over one of my officers?'

'Well, sir, it seems Lieutenant Butterworth was on duty in the cookhouse at 07.45 hours yesterday and he asked for any complaints; Private Chappleton said his porridge was lumpy and not cooked enough. The Lieutenant, on hearing the complaint called for a spoon, had himself a taste and said it was very good. Then he said he wouldn't mind some of that porridge himself.'

The Sergeant-Major paused and glanced at the Major.

'Go on, go on,' he said, his irritation at this event becoming evident.

'Well, sir, on hearing this, Chappleton stood up to offer his plate, and then it seems that the porridge was spilled all down the front of Lieutenant Butterworth.'

The Sergeant-Major paused again and looked uncomfortable.

'Is there something the matter, Sergeant-Major?'

'Well, it's like this, sir. Chappleton's complaint was that his porridge was lumpy and uncooked.'

'Yes, thank you, I think I understood that much.'

'Well sir, when the porridge was tipped down the officer's front, a lot of it was in big lumps, and when they hit the floor, they burst open and everyone could see the lumps were full of dry porridge.'

'Well?'

'Don't you see, sir? It proved Chappleton's point.'

The Major stared in disbelief. 'Sergeant-Major, you seem to be saying that just because of some culinary shortcomings, you believe that the men are entitled to tip their unwanted food onto my officers.'

'No, sir. I just think that we should proceed cautiously.'

'Now look here; I had better make myself clear. I will not tolerate this type of behaviour from anyone.'

'Normally I'd be the first to agree with you, sir. But this time I think we ought not to be too hasty.'

Hallett's expression was suddenly wary. 'What do you mean, too hasty?' he said, slowly.

'Well, if it got out that we, as it were, first provoked him by making him eat lumpy, uncooked porridge: then when the subaltern said it was good and he wouldn't mind some, Chappleton offered his plate. Well, sir, disregarding the unfortunate accident, it wouldn't look very good if we punished him for trying to do a kindness, would it?'

Hallett drummed his fingers on the desk. He was a relatively new Major, and there didn't seem much point in sticking his neck out for what may be nothing at all and might escalate into something that the more lurid daily papers could get a hold of. He looked up.

'I think that under the circumstances, I had better exercise a little caution here. After all, we mustn't make a mountain out of a molehill must we? I will hear this case tomorrow, Sergeant-Major, but in my opinion, no useful purpose will be served by making a fuss over what might be a trivial incident.'

'Whatever you think best, sir.'

Hallett leaned back in his chair and placed his fingertips together.

'It is my responsibility to look carefully at these matters and make sure that they are kept in perspective. It's all a matter of judgement.'

'Very good, sir. I understand.'

'By the way, who was with Mr Butterworth when this happened?'

'The Orderly Sergeant, Sergeant Shorthouse, sir.'

'Then kindly arrange for him to be here tomorrow.'

'Very good, sir.'

'Carry on, Sergeant-Major.'

The Sergeant-Major stepped back smartly and flashed up a salute that would have strained the elbow of a lesser man. His arm then snaked down to his side in a blurred flash. He about-turned and marched to the door, opening and closing it behind him with matchless military precision.

As he leaned back in his chair, Major Simon Hallett nodded in satisfaction. Really, one needed the wisdom of Solomon sometimes just to keep things in hand and prevent people taking problems and magnifying them into disasters. Yes, there was no substitute for training and experience, and if the Sergeant-Major was not so taken up with his football team and gave more thought to regimental matters, then he too might learn to handle cases like this one of Private Chappleton. Come to think of it, thought the Major, isn't Private Chappleton in the Sergeant-Major's football team? Idly dismissing that fact, the Major started to concentrate on the work that was now piling up in his in-tray.

Next morning in the Orderly Room, the ancient clock ticked slowly and loudly round to nine o'clock. The Sergeant-Major glanced in the wall mirror, made an infinitesimal adjustment to his cap, and turned to face Private Chappleton.

'Your 'at, lad, get it off.'

Briskly the hat was removed and placed on an adjacent table.

'Escort and accused, ah ten shun.'

Chappleton and the escort snapped to attention and stood as if awaiting delivery to Madame Tussauds. Sergeant-Major Bragge knocked smartly on the OC's door, opened it and announced that the escort and accused were ready.

Hallett indicated that he could proceed, but Bragge shook his head, frowned and tapped the top of his cap. Hallett looked puzzled and stared at his senior NCO standing in the doorway prodding the top of his cap.

'Something wrong, Sergeant-Major?'

'Beg pardon, sir. Your 'at.'

'But I'm not wearing – oh, I see what you mean.'

He reached out and took his hat from the top of a filing cabinet. Settling it firmly on his head, he looked briefly at Lieutenant Butterworth and Sergeant Shorthouse who were standing patiently awaiting the proceedings.

'Carry on, Sergeant-Major.'

'Escort and accused, quick march; left, right, left, right, left turn,' and as they approached the desk, he barked. 'Halt.'

Bragge saluted and gave the rather superfluous information: 'Private Chappleton, the accused, sir.'

'Thank you, Sergeant-Major. Now, 492426916 Private Chappleton, D Y, is that you?' said the Major, vaguely wondering what on earth the Y could stand for.

'Yessir.'

'Very well then. It is alleged that at 07.45 hours on the fourth day of March in the building known as 'B' Mess, you deliberately spilled a portion of food, namely porridge, onto the person of Lieutenant Butterworth. Now, did you comprehend that summary, Chappleton?'

After a few seconds of eyeball rolling thought, Chappleton replied. 'No, sir, it was an accident.'

For a moment Hallett looked at him in a sort of baffled silence.

'Chappleton, I am asking if you understood the charge.'

A look of relief spread over his face as the proceedings were made clear to him once more.

'Oh, yes, sir, I understood that, thank you.'

Hallett made a few meaningless marks on the papers in front of him. He looked up.

'Mr Butterworth, I intend first, to hear the evidence of Sergeant Shorthouse. Would you, therefore, please wait in the outer office and return on my summons.'

'Erse, of course, Medger…'

Butterworth had what the Major called a cut-glass accent and it was one that he found both irritating and difficult to understand. He particularly disliked the habit of drawling out his sentences as if next week would do.

At much the same pace at which he spoke, Butterworth sauntered to the door and disappeared into the outer office.

'Now, Sergeant. Your evidence, please.'

Sergeant Shorthouse was a small, dismal-looking man with a growling sort of voice that filtered through a ragged toothbrush moustache. His long Army experience, mostly with irascible commanding officers, had schooled him into punctuating his sentences with 'sir' more frequently than was usual.

'Sir, on the morning of March fourth, sir, I was on duty as Orderly Sergeant in 'B' Mess, if you see what I mean, sir. The Orderly Officer and myself had just stopped at the first table to ask for any complaints, if you take my meaning, sir. Private Chappleton said his porridge was lumpy and Lieutenant Butterworth asked me to get him a spoon, sir. I did this, and then I made my routine inspection of the tea-urns, if you are still following me, sir. On returning to the table I saw that the Orderly Officer had porridge tipped down the front of him, sir. He accused Private Chappleton, and I charged him under Section 69 of the Army Act. I hope I have made myself clear, sir.'

'Yes, Sergeant, thank you. Anything further?'

'No, sir.'

'Then you may go.'

'Sir.'

A rapid salute and Sergeant Shorthouse strode from the room.

Leaning back in his chair, the Major thought about the Sergeant's evidence. Nothing in it really. He admitted he didn't see anything, he didn't hear anything, and, apart from the fact that he had charged Chappleton, he might as well have not been there. Goodness only knows what he was doing here this morning mumbling his so-called evidence. He sighed; life could be very tiresome sometimes.

He looked towards his Sergeant-Major.

'Thanks for the use of your phone, guv.'

Hallett was jolted back to the present and stared at the removal man standing in front of him. 'I'm sorry, what did you say?'

'I said, thanks for the use of your phone.'

'Phone? Oh, yes I see. You're very welcome. Carry on.'

'You what?'

'I mean, if you need to use the telephone again, er, just carry on,' finished Hallett in an uncharacteristic fluster.

'Right, guv, ta.'

By now the hedge was in need of no further clipping, and

Hallett looked about for any other tasks he could potter with while he kept an eye on the unloading of the pantechnicon. The steady stream of tasteful furniture continued, and his hopes for a respectable, perhaps even a professional, neighbour were riding high. He felt satisfied that here would be a neighbour of one's own kind; the sort of people one could converse with intelligently. Not woolly headed dimwits like Jeremy Butterworth. He thought about Butterworth for a moment and again, his mind drifted back to that day.

'Sergeant-Major, ask Mr Butterworth to come in, please.'

Bragge strode briskly to the door, opened it and asked Lieutenant Butterworth to please come in.

He sauntered in, beamed genially, ambled across to the Major's desk and waved his limp salute.

'Would you please give your evidence, Mr Butterworth, and tell me what happened on the morning of the fourth of March in 'B' Mess.'

'Erse, Medger,' replied Butterworth and the Major settled back resignedly to interpret the languid flow of the Lieutenant's somewhat nasal sounding evidence.

'On the morning of March the fourth,' began Butterworth, 'I was on duty as Orderly Officer. I was inspecting 'B' Mess and asking if there were any complents and Private Chappleton complend that his podge was lumpair. I decided to test the podge to see if this was true.'

Hallett leaned forward feeling quite encouraged at this scientific approach by his subaltern. He picked up his pen.

'I see, and what was the result of your test?'

'It tested quaite naice eckchewly,' said Butterworth, 'I thought it needed just a little more sugar.'

A look of patient suffering passed across Hallett's face and he sighed. 'Please get on with your evidence, Mr Butterworth, and I would be obliged if you could hasten your delivery slightly.'

'Erse, Medger, quaite so. After I had tested the podge, I said it was very nice and I wouldn't maned some myself; whereupon Private Chappleton stood up and said "here, have mane" and spilled the whole lot down the front of my blues.'

Realising, because of the sudden silence, his subaltern had finished, Hallett looked up. 'Is that all?'

'Erse, Medger.'

'Thank you,' said the Major scribbling away busily, 'you may go now.'

Giving his limp wave that served as a salute, Butterworth turned and strolled once more into the main office.

'Right, Chappleton,' said Hallett, placing his elbows on the desk and lacing his fingers, 'you have heard the evidence of Sergeant Shorthouse and Lieutenant Butterworth. Now kindly give me your version of the incident.'

Chappleton fixed his eyes on the wall about two feet above Hallett's head. 'Sir, at 07.45 on the morning in question I was seated at a table in 'B' Mess and I had just taken a spoonful of porridge. On finding that the porridge was not to my liking, I decided to await the Orderly Officer, and when Lieutenant Butterworth came to the table to ask if there were any complaints, I described my porridge to the officer.' Chappleton's delivery was, by now, noticeably increasing in speed. 'On hearing my complaint, he called for a spoon with which to taste the porridge.'

Listening to Chappleton intoning his evidence, the Major found himself first marvelling at the man's newly found powers of articulation then idly wondering if the Y stood for Yves, but decided probably not.

'On the arrival of the spoon,' continued Chappleton, now in top gear, 'the officer tasted my porridge and said that he would not mind some more and, as I stood up to offer my plate to him, I slipped. Unfortunately, the porridge spilled down the front of the officer's uniform, and I apologised for the accident.'

Chappleton was now searching for the correct way to signify that his evidence was finished.

'Er, that is all, sir.'

'I see.'

Hallett considered this evidence and then thought carefully about the case. He glanced at the Sergeant-Major who was contorting his mouth at Chappleton.

'Something wrong, Sergeant-Major?'

Bragge looked startled then nodded towards the accused.

'Nothing wrong, sir, it's just that Chappleton wishes to say something more, don't you, Chappleton?' he said, raising his voice more to his parade-ground level.

'Oh, yes, sir, I forgot. I would like to make amends for my clumsiness by paying to have the Lieutenant's uniform dry-cleaned.'

Hallett received this rather touching gesture with some suspicion and felt that all was not what it seemed, but could not think why.

'That is very generous, Chappleton. However, I think it may be just a little irregular. But I'm sure it was well intentioned.' He tried to show that his tone was suitably sarcastic.

Chappleton, though, looked pleased. 'Well, sir, like the Sergeant-Major said, you couldn't very well…'

'Accused, keep silence!'

Sergeant-Major Bragge had evidently decided that the accused was having more opportunity to speak than regulations permitted.

In rather quieter tones he addressed Major Hallett. 'Er, that concludes Private Chappleton's evidence, sir.'

'Thank you, Sergeant-Major,' said Hallett, still wondering about the sudden outburst. He paused. 'I find the evidence lacking, case dismissed.'

Chappleton beamed and looked as if he was about to speak, but the Sergeant-Major again decided that enough talking had been done for one morning.

'Escort and accused, about turn, quick march, left, right, left, right, right turn; escort and accused, halt.'

He hesitated at the door. 'Will there be anything else, sir?'

'Yes, ask Mr Butterworth to come in, please.'

'Yessir.'

A few seconds later the Lieutenant's features made their appearance round the door.

'You wished to see me, Medger?'

'Yes, please come in.'

He sauntered in and as he stood blinking and beaming waiting for Hallett to speak, Butterworth noticed that the Major looked uncomfortable and was tapping a pencil in rapid tattoo on his blotting pad. Jeremy St John Butterworth was not the brightest of officers; in fact to all of his men he was known as Goofy. Whether this was because of his haw-haw style of laughing, his bumbling incompetence, or even because his front teeth stuck out slightly, may never be known. But in this unit he had always borne the name of Goofy. Now, even with the disadvantages of a woolly intellect and a general lack of awareness, Butterworth could see that Major Hallett was ill at ease.

'Look, er, Jeremy, I want to talk to you about this case. A most unfortunate affair.'

'Erse, Medger, good job the podge wasn't hot, what? Haw, haw, haw.'

'Jeremy, I will come straight to the point. I strongly believe that we should make our presence felt by our wisdom and foresight, our sagacity and discernment. Those are qualities men respect. You will find that the men are less likely to take advantage of you if you prove to them that you are alert and vigilant.'

'Quate so, Medger. Might one ask how you dealt with Chappleton after hearing the evidence?'

It suddenly occurred to the Major that he was still wearing his cap. Carefully removing this he placed it almost reverently on a small side table.

'As a matter of fact, I considered that there was a lack of evidence and I dismissed the charge.'

Butterworth stared at the Major, his face puckered in disbelief, his teeth protruding even more as they always did in moments of perplexity.

'You mean, sir, he got orf scot-free.'

'I mean, Mr Butterworth,' said Hallett, sharply, 'that I was not presented with enough evidence to prove the case. That is all I wish to say, except that I am somewhat distressed to find that I have expended a considerable amount of my time this morning and all to no purpose. I wish you to take more care in future.'

Butterworth's reply was predictable. 'Erse, Medger, thenk yaw.'

He was not offended nor hurt; he was feeling much as he always felt. Baffled by the way life never seemed to be straightforward.

Hallett stared at him as the limp arm waved in near salute once more and he turned and ambled out of the office.

'Excuse me, guv, is this yours?'

Hallett blinked as he found himself looking into the face of one of the removal men who was standing in front of him holding a ginger cat.

'Only he keeps getting in the van and he might get himself locked in. Yours, is it?'

Hallett instantly recognised the declared enemy of his lettuce plants.

'No, it is not mine. We do not own a cat and this one is a blasted nuisance. Please take it away.'

The man grinned. 'Where to?'

'It belongs to "The Larches" just across the road. I would deposit it in their garden if I were you.'

The man grinned again. 'Come on, puss. The man says you don't live here.'

Hallett watched as the man walked across the road carrying the cat and saying to it out loud. 'That man doesn't like you, puss, I think you've upset him.'

Hallett sighed and shook his head. Perhaps people like Jeremy Butterworth were not so bad after all. At least they showed some respect for you. But he recalled that even then, life was not as straightforward as it might have been.

As he sat back and thought about the case he had just heard, and of his subaltern's part in it, Hallett was wondering if he ought to do something about Jeremy Butterworth. He was a young officer who was a ready target for the men; it was a pity, but he was so gullible that the men could do as they liked with him. Perhaps if I had a word with him and put him wise to some of their conniving, showed him how to be on guard against their tricks. He sighed. It was no use. Really, there was no substitute for training and experience and Butterworth would have to learn the hard way. The way that he himself had learned. It was a long, rough road, but by thunder, it was worth it in the end. With a final shake of his head and another sigh he stopped his meditations and turned his attention to his in-tray.

After about twenty minutes of poring over wordy and obscure letters and circulars he felt the need of some refreshment. He pressed his buzzer twice to summon his chief clerk. About a minute later there was a tap on the door and Sergeant Eric Pridley put his head round the door.

'Did you rings?'

It was a practice of Pridley's, whenever he spoke to an officer, to finish off the last word with the letter 's' and thus it was difficult to say with any certainty, whether or not he had paid the proper respect and said 'sir'.

'Yes, Sergeant, I did ring. Are you busy?'

'Well, I haven't yet finished with that security file on my desks.'

Hallett looked suspiciously at his chief clerk. It seemed to him that very often Pridley spoke of things in the plural that quite clearly were singular. It was a most extraordinary habit and, at the moment, it seemed that he was claiming to have more than one desk.

'I beg your pardon, what did you say?'

'On my desk there's a file that holds a letter requiring a reply before I put the file back in the cabinets.'

Well really, this was quite ridiculous. How on earth could he put a file into a cabinets? It was a very sloppy way of speaking and one that must be corrected. Sometime, maybe, when the opportunity presented itself.

'Yes, very well, Sergeant. Now would you please clear these things from my out-tray and ask one of the clerks to bring me some coffee.'

Pridley nodded briefly. Ever since he had failed in his attempt to secure a commission he had resolved never again to call an officer 'sir'. He believed with a deep bitterness that he was far more fitted to be an officer than any of the chinless wonders drifting aimlessly round this Headquarters. He looked at his OC and mentally sneered at him.

Unaware of the waves of scorn being directed at him by his chief clerk, Hallett sat idly drumming his fingers on the desk.

This really had been quite a morning. What with the affair of Chappleton and the porridge, his oddly speaking sergeant and now all these letters and things to see to, his tasks seemed endless. And to make matters worse, the in-tray looked as if it contained even more work. Time for coffee and then get a break from the office. He was suddenly aware that Sergeant Pridley was still standing by his desk, frowning and peering into the out-tray at the few files there.

'Is this the lots?'

The Major stopped his finger-drumming and he too peered into the tray.

'Yes, that is the lots, er, that is all there is. Why do you ask?'

'Well, I was wondering if you had read that letter from District about food wastage; they want a reply by tomorrows.'

'Of couse I have read it, Sergeant,' said the Major, who had not yet disturbed the deeper recesses of his in-tray, 'but I wish to give a reply which has the benefit of lengthy cogitation, of deep enquiry into the wider implications of our comments.'

'They only want us to say on the tear-off strip how many "Don't Waste Food" posters we can exhibits.'

He stared tight-lipped at Pridley. 'Well just ask them for half a dozen, and now will you please arrange that coffee for me.'

'Right aways.'

What a surly wretch you are, thought Hallett. It's a good job we don't all take that miserable attitude, otherwise nothing would get done. Hallett promised himself that the very next time that Pridley used that idiotic mode of speech he would draw his attention to it. Really, it would be the kindest thing in the long run. After all, the Army had a responsibility to look after the needs of its men and this meant physical and mental needs. Yes, perhaps if he spoke to the Education Officer he may have encountered the problem before. He quickly rejected the idea when he recalled that Captain Binder, the Education Officer, had such an appalling stutter that would make it difficult to discuss vocal mannerisms with him. So, it looked as if this would have to be tackled face to face. It was just a question of waiting for the right moment.

A knock on the door preceded the entrance of Private Black

who shuffled in, precariously balancing a large white cup on a small blue saucer.

'Thank you, Partington, put it on the desk, please.'

'It's Black, sir.'

The Major peered suspiciously at the milky looking coffee that was now gently lapping in his cup having lost about a quarter of its contents into the saucer. What an extraordinary place this is, he thought. As if this morning wasn't bad enough, here was Private Partington making idiotic comments about the coffee. He looked up and recognised Private Black.

'Oh, I see. Very well, Black, that's all.'

Hallett picked up his cup and watched dejectedly as a trail of drips exploded into crazy patterns on his blotting pad. Typical, he thought. He sipped his coffee, lost in deep thought. Suddenly, he banged down his cup at the same time screwing his face into a mask of suffering.

'Ugh, no sugar.'

His hand reached for the buzzer, but he paused. Perhaps this was the time to get out of the office. Yes, that was it, meet the men, get to know them and their problems; let them see that you care. That was what being an officer was all about.

Just then the telephone jingled into life.

'Oh, blast,' he said picking up the receiver.

'Hallett here, who is this?'

'Dickie Bird here, Simon. Fancy a game of golf this afternoon?'

'Oh, hello, Dickie. Well, I really don't know. I suppose I shouldn't, but after all, we mustn't drive ourselves too hard, must we. I mean, I do a lot of work in the evenings and so on, so perhaps a little relaxation wouldn't hurt.'

'Good man, see you this afternoon, then.'

Hallett decided that perhaps he had done enough for one morning, and he walked from his office, settling his peaked cap firmly on his head as he strode into the main office.

'Oh, Sergeant, I'm just popping out for a while; in fact I may be gone for the whole morning. Anything for me?'

Pridley stared suspiciously at his Major. Quite clearly he was off on another dodge of some sort.

'All the files for your attention are now in your in-trays.'

Hallett frowned as Pridley once more demonstrated his plural-speak.

'Thank you. Well, carry on Sergeant.'

'Very goods.'

He left the office.

Outside he stood and looked at a squad of men being drilled on the square. The brisk, accurate movements, the precision, the sheer military efficiency of it all; these things appealed to him. He believed in the army and all its traditions. He disapproved of what he called the diminution of the British Empire.

Hallett saw the Sergeant-Major stride past the square yelling words of correction and encouragement. On noticing the Major watching the drill, Sergeant-Major Bragge marched smartly towards him, braked to a rigid halt just in front of Hallett, and snapped up his customary brisk salute.

'Did you want to see me, sir?'

'Not at the moment, Sergeant-Major. Oh, by the way, I'm away for the morning now, so just keep an eye on things would you.'

'Yessir. Oh, there was one thing I wanted to mention, sir.'

'What was that?'

'It's no good, guv, he keeps getting out again.'

Hallett found himself once more staring at the removal man who was still holding the ginger cat.

'I thought you were going to get rid of that creature.'

'I did. But like I said, guv, he keeps getting out again.'

'Very well. What I suggest you do now is to take it across the road to the house opposite, knock on the owner's door and ask them to please keep their cat inside the house before it gets hurt.'

'Right you are, guv.' He grinned and walked across the road carrying the cat and saying in loud tones. 'See, puss, I told you he didn't like you; he said you'd better go home before he hurts you.'

When he returned he saw that his colleagues had finished off-loading the pantechnicon and shouted that they should have left some for him. This was greeted with howls of derision from the men and a scowl from Hallett.

All three men then busied themselves folding blankets and

coiling bits of rope. Placing these in the van they closed up the tailboard and doors and made ready to leave.

At that moment, a large blue saloon purred quietly along the Avenue and pulled into the kerb behind the pantechnicon with practised ease.

The removal men suddenly quietened, and stood as if waiting the arrival of a Very Important Person. The car doors opened and onto the pavement stepped what was obviously, a family of four persons. Father, Mother and two sons.

The father spoke briefly to the men and Hallett's eyes widened as each was presented with a five-pound note. They expressed their thanks with much cap touching and smiling, then climbed into the cab of their removal van and chugged away.

On the pavement the family had paused to look at their new home and garden.

From his position, Hallett was able to observe the family, and was most impressed. The wife, an attractive woman in her late thirties was dressed in a neat, grey two-piece suit that fitted in a way that showed expert and individual tailoring. The two boys, one about eighteen and the other fourteen, were both smartly but not flashily dressed. The father was in his early forties; he looked pleasant and humorous. His clothes too, showed impeccable taste, and he wore them with the confident air of a man who knows that he is well dressed.

As the family walked slowly up the drive, Hallett decided he would speak to them. His speculation that a doctor or solicitor might move in, was, it seemed, well-founded. He judged his timing to meet the new neighbours over the low hedge that separated their drives. He moved forward removing his gardening gloves.

'Hello there, good morning. My name is Hallett, Colonel Simon Hallett. May I be the first to welcome you all to Forsythia Avenue, and express the hope that you will find it agreeable in every way.'

The new neighbours stopped and smiled. The father stepped forward with outstretched hand.

'Allo, mate, pleased to meetcha. I'm Fred Root and this 'ere's me family.'

CHAPTER TWO

Lieutenant Colonel (retd) Simon Hallett stared at his new neighbour in stark disbelief. It was as if the man had spoken to him in Swahili. Had he heard correctly? Had he really been addressed as mate? And did he hear him say, 'this 'ere's me family!'

But, with the training of years behind him, he recovered himself and shook the outstretched hand of Fred Root.

'How do you do,' he said, with as much formality as he could muster.

'Not too bad y'know. This 'ere's me better 'alf, Gladys. Glad, this is Colonel Hallett, our new neighbour.'

Gladys Root stepped forward nervously, looking as if she was about to bob a curtsy.

'Pleased to make your acquaintance, Mr Hallett, I'm sure.'

Momentarily, Hallett's mouth tightened into a straight, humourless line at this civilian habit of ignoring his rank.

'My pleasure, Mrs Root.'

'And my two lads, David and Gary,' said Fred, completing the introductions.

The two boys nodded a brief greeting which Hallett acknowledged with an even briefer return nod.

'Yes, well, must leave you now; ah, lots of things I ought to be doing. I hope you settle in all right.'

'Ta, squire. See you later if we need a cup of sugar or something, eh?'

Hallett's tight, polite smile became fractionally tighter.

'Pleased to have met you all, and now, if you will excuse me.'

With this final social requirement completed, Hallett turned and strode briskly to the door at the side of his house.

Giving his shoes a quick strop on the mat outside his door Hallett walked into the kitchen.

Behind the kitchen door, Elizabeth Hallett was busily sponging the leaves of a huge rubber plant. She was an attractive and pleasant woman in her early forties and, though her dark brown hair was faintly streaked with grey, her eyes twinkled continuously giving her face the look of a lively young girl. She loved her indoor plants and spent many hours caring for them and fretting over their health.

For some moments Hallett stood in the doorway and then he bellowed. 'Elizabeth, where are you?'

'Here, dear.'

At this instantaneous response to his shout, Hallett spun and almost overbalanced.

'Elizabeth, why are hiding behind that door?'

'I was just sponging this rubber plant, dear. Were you looking for me?'

Hallett solemnly laid his gardening gloves on the kitchen table. 'Our new neighbours have just moved in.'

At this point Mrs Hallett noticed an unsponged leaf on the rubber plant and started to attend to it. 'Really? That's nice.'

'No'. His voice was doom-laden. 'It is not nice, Elizabeth. In fact it could well be catastrophic.'

She answered over her shoulder. 'Well, if you say so.'

'Elizabeth, would you please leave that confounded plant and pay a little attention to what I am saying.'

Turning from her plant, she smiled pleasantly. 'Have you finished the hedge already?'

'Blast the hedge. I am trying to tell you something important.'

'I'm sorry, Simon, what were you saying?'

Hallett's voice was coldly patient. 'I was telling you of our new neighbours in number twenty-five.'

'Yes, I know. What about them?'

'Elizabeth,' now the voice was grave. 'I have just met them and would you believe it; they are Cockneys.'

There was something in Hallett's tone that suggested that to be a Cockney was broadly equivalent to suffering from something unpleasant and socially unacceptable.

Elizabeth was not concentrating fully on the conversation and her attention was partly on the rubber plant and a glacier ivy that seemed to be a little undernourished.

'I see. How many are there?'

'For goodness sake, it surely doesn't matter how many there are. I have just told you that they are Cockneys; can't you see what that means?'

During the course of their married life Elizabeth had weathered many such outbursts and was never upset by them.

'Well, I suppose it could be worse.'

'Pah!'

There was a long silence and Hallett stared out of the window.

Suddenly, he crashed his fist into his palm and quickly turned round. 'Do you realise what this could do to house prices?'

Elizabeth smiled, 'Oh really, Simon, I'm sure you are exaggerating. I expect that they are really quite nice people.'

'Well, we shall see, Elizabeth; we shall see.'

Before their conversation could proceed any further there was a sharp rap on the front door.

'Who on earth can that be,' said Hallett, the irritation still clearly detectable in his voice.

'Shall I answer it?'

'No, thank you, I will see to it. And, if it is one of those religious fanatics, or a double-glazing salesman, they will hear from me in no uncertain fashion.'

As he stamped his way down the hall he was preparing a speech to deliver to whichever nuisance was banging on his front door.

Swinging the door wide open he was surprised to see a smiling Fred Root waiting on his doorstep.

'Allo, squire, we meet again.'

'Ah, yes. It's Mr Root isn't it?'

'Right first time, squire. Can I see you a minute?'

Hallett frowned. 'You had better come in.'

He led the way to the kitchen where Elizabeth was waiting.

'Nice place you've got here, squire, very comfortable.'

'Thank you'.

Hallett walked forward and stood by his wife. 'Elizabeth, my dear, may I present our new neighbour, Mr Root. Mr Root, this my wife, Elizabeth.'

'I'm very pleased to meet you, Mrs Hallett.' said Fred, warmly.

Elizabeth took an immediate liking to Fred with his cheerful, friendly manner but as her husband was staring at them she thought that she had better be a little formal. 'How do you do, Mr Root.'

'Never better. You know, you must come round and meet my better 'alf.'

'Thank you, we'd love to, wouldn't we, Simon?'

'Yes of course we would; sometime. Have you finished with my wife's hand, Mr Root?'

'Eh? Oh, sorry, got carried away.'

'Mr Root, is there perhaps something I can do for you?' said Hallett in his 'what do you want, corporal' voice.

'Yes, as a matter of fact that's what I called about. How are you off for Rosie Lee?'

'I beg your pardon?'

'My fault, squire, I meant tea. You know, Rosie Lee, tea, see?'

'Not entirely, no. But I think we may be able to help you. What sort of tea do you like?'

As far as Hallett was concerned, to ask this sort of question of someone like Fred Root was merely rhetorical. One really did not expect an answer. The question had been put merely to inform Root that tea was a cultured drink and not something to be degraded with the title of Annie Lee or whatever it was he called it.

'I'm not fussy, squire. What sort have you got?'

'Well, we have a rather nice Darjeeling.'

'Darjeeling, eh? Well thanks all the same, squire, but it's never been quite to my taste and then there's all those big leaves you get left with at the end. No, thanks very much anyway. You haven't got a nice aromatic china tea, have you?'

'The only other thing we have is a packet of PG Tips,' said Hallett, sharply.

'Thanks, that'll do a treat.'

Fred turned to Elizabeth. 'Can't beat a nice cup of tea, can you?' He smiled. 'We were both sure that we packed some ready to brew up when we arrived, but we still can't find it.'

She found his smile very easy to return. 'I'm glad we were able to help.'

'Elizabeth, I cannot seem to find the tea anywhere, perhaps you could help.'

Hardly taking her eyes off Fred, Elizabeth stretched out a hand to the larder and withdrew a packet of tea.

'Thanks Mrs Hallett, do the same for you sometime.' He turned to Hallett. 'Thanks for your help, squire. Must go and help with the unpacking. See you again.'

Hallett nodded curtly and Fred walked out of the door shouting to his wife to put the kettle on.

Hallett frowned. 'What an extraordinary man.'

Elizabeth was still smiling. 'Yes, wasn't he.'

'How do you suppose he knew so much about tea,' said Hallett, who felt irritated that his attempt to humble Fred Root seemed to have had the reverse effect.

'Perhaps he's had experience in the tea industry.'

'Nonsense. Probably read it on the back of a packet of tea.'

Elizabeth smiled again. 'Well I thought he was quite charming.'

'Oh, really, Elizabeth, how can you say that?'

She laughed. 'It's very easy. He seemed to me a very pleasant person; don't you agree?'

Hallett gave his well-known snort of indignation and allowed that to stand as his final contribution to the conversation.

Having given his opinion of Fred Root, Hallett saw that his wife had returned to her house plants and so, decided to continue with his gardening. He marched stiffly out of the door carrying his gardening gloves as if on the way to inspect his troops.

Elizabeth paused in her inspection of Emily, the name by which she affectionately referred to her rubber plant, and stood looking thoughtfully at the primrose coloured kitchen wall without really seeing anything. She couldn't remember when she had last spoken to someone as friendly and natural as Fred Root.

She gave a little smile and walked to the mirror in the hall. She looked carefully at her reflection. Not too bad, she thought, not too bad for a forty-two-year-old. She turned sideways and, watching the effect carefully, took a slow, deep breath and stood for some moments feeling satisfied that she had retained her trim figure.

At that moment Valerie Hallett came downstairs to ask if her friend Myra had telephoned. Seeing her mother in that yoga-like pose before the mirror, she stared at her with a mixture of amusement, wonder and affection; three emotions which Valerie experienced frequently in her dealings with her mother.

'Are you all right, mother?'

'Oh, you gave me quite a start, dear. Yes, I'm fine thank you. I was just seeing, er, if this hairstyle suited the shape of my face.'

Valerie smiled affectionately but looked slightly puzzled.

'Well, it seems to have suited you for the last two or three years.'

'Does it? Oh good.'

Humming happily to herself, Elizabeth returned to her rubber plant and continued with her task of caring for its well-being. Valerie smiled again and continued on her way to the kitchen.

In the Root household Fred was surveying their moving in progress over the rim of a large cup of tea. He set the cup down and started to stuff into a tea-chest some old some newspapers that had been used for packing. The door opened and Gladys walked in carrying her cup of tea. Fred stopped disposing of newspapers and walked to meet her picking up an empty wooden case as he did so.

'Here you are, Glad, park yourself on that.'

'Thanks, Fred.' She sipped her tea and sighed contentedly. 'Ooh, I needed that didn't you? I can't think where I packed that tea, but I expect it will turn up somewhere. But it was very nice of next door to lend us some and we must return it as soon as we can.'

'Yes, I'll take a packet round as soon as we get organised.'

Gladys looked thoughtful. 'What sort of people are they, Fred?'

'Oh, they're all right. Colonel's a bit prim, but I think we'll get on OK. His wife seems very pleasant.'

'I noticed you bringing out your Cockney voice again when we first met them. You always seem to do that whenever we first meet someone or when you start talking about the old days.'

Fred grinned. 'I only do it so as people know where they are with me. Then when I get to know them better, I can relax and be myself.' His eyes twinkled as he looked at Gladys. 'Cor stone the crows, missus, you don't 'alf rabbit on. Gets me in a right two and eight, you do.'

They both laughed at Fred's recall of the Cockney voice that he had all but lost over the years.

'Tell you what, let's invite them round as soon as we get straight.'

'All right, but not too soon, Fred. I mean, let's get settled in a bit first. You know, let's get a bit organised before we start entertaining.'

'Right you are, Glad, whenever you say.'

Fred looked round the room and was struck by the silence. 'Where are the boys?' he asked.

'They've just gone down to the shops and then they are going to have a look around.'

'Oh, well, we'll enjoy the peace while we can.'

Having finished her tea, Gladys was now down on her knees by a packing case, rummaging through it and strewing the contents around her in muddled heaps.

'Lost something, Glad?'

'It's the electric carving knife. I can't find it, but I am sure I packed it in this case.'

'Well, don't worry about it, it'll soon turn up.'

'But it should be in this case, Fred.'

'I daresay it should, but leave it alone and it'll turn up later.' He was thoughtful for a moment. 'It makes you think, though. We've come a long way together, Glad, you and me. I don't think we used to worry much about electric carving knives when I had my stall in the market. Wouldn't have done much good anyway.

34

We wouldn't have had much to cut with it, would we?'

'Well, maybe we wouldn't then, but we have now. And let me remind you, Fred Root, that not every market trader goes from selling fruit and veg from a stall in the market, to opening four fruit shops of his own, now do they?'

Fred smiled. It was always pleasant when Gladys showed him how proud she was of his success, and at times like this, he remembered how easily he had fallen for the pretty little waitress from the Unicorn café. He recalled, as he often did, how thrilled he had been when she agreed to become his wife.

He leaned forward and kissed her. 'Well, not every market trader has got Gladys Root for a wife, have they?'

'Oh, get on with you, I've got work to do even if you haven't.'

Fred laughed, picked up the cups, walked out to the kitchen and put them in the sink. As he glanced through the window he could see his neighbour standing in the garden pulling on his gardening gloves and it seemed to Fred that he looked a bit severe. He decided that he might as well go out and talk to him. He called to Gladys that he would be in the garden if he was wanted. He strolled out and across to where his neighbour was snipping viciously at a tall bush.

'Making a peacock, squire?'

The snipping stopped and Hallett slowly turned round. 'I'm sorry to appear stupid, but I don't think I quite follow you.'

'A peacock. You know, like they shape out of hedges.'

Hallett gave condescending smile. 'I'm afraid that one of the things I have never studied is…'

Hallett's voice tailed off as he realised that he couldn't recall the horticultural term for shaping birds and things out hedges.

'It's called topiary,' said Fred, helpfully.

'Is it,' came the cold reply. 'Well, I have never studied it.'

With this he turned back to his clipping.

'Nice crop of roses you've got there.'

The clipping stopped again and this time the response was a little less frosty. 'Thank you, I am rather proud of them. Do you like roses?'

'Yeah, smashing flowers I reckon. You've got some nice

varieties I can see.'

Putting the garden shears to one side, Hallett, now thawing noticeably, walked over to join Fred.

'Do you intend to grow roses yourself, Root?' he said, showing his customary use of a surname to anyone he considered to be 'not one of us'.

'Might do. 'Ave to wait and see after I plan me layout of the garden and complete me soil test.'

The Hallett eyebrows were raised a little at this professional sounding approach to gardening.

'Have you any favourites among roses?' said Hallett, ever eager to show off his mastery of the names of his roses.

'That's a nice little bloomer there,' said Fred, indicating some attractive tea-roses.

'Ah, yes, that is called Fandango.'

'Yes.' said Fred. 'It's one of your hybrid tea-roses. Pity about it.'

Hallett was immediately ready to defend his precious roses. 'What do you mean, pity about it?'

'I mean it's a pity about the disease it's got.'

Swiftly Hallett plucked a rose and stared at it. He looked at Fred. 'I have been growing roses for the past ten years and this Fandango is one of my prize blooms. Look at it, how can it be diseased?'

'It's been attacked by phragmidium mucronatum,' said Fred, patiently.

Hallett was now looking worried. 'It's been attacked by what?'

'Phragmidium mucronatum. The more usual name for it is rust.'

'Rust? I think not. Perhaps you would care to show me.'

'Look *under* the leaves, squire.'

Cautiously he turned the rose over and stared aghast at the rust-coloured swellings on the underside of the leaves. 'My God! This means that I will have to destroy my entire crop of Fandangos.'

Fred smiled. 'No, no, it's not as bad as all that.'

'I feel I must correct you there. I remember reading that the only cure for rust is to dig up the whole crop and burn them.'

'Not nowadays you don't. All you have to do is to examine each rose, cut off any affected parts, put them in a paper bag and burn them.'

'Are you quite sure?'

'Course I am. Do it for you if you like.'

'Really? that's very civil of you.'

'My pleasure, squire.'

Fred stepped over the low hedge. 'Got some secateurs, 'ave we?'

'Yes, of course. I'll get them for you now.' He went to his garage and when he returned, Fred was examining the roses.

'Have you a great deal of experience with roses then, Root?' he said, as he handed Fred a pair of secateurs.

'A bit. I suppose it's a sort of professional interest, really.'

Hallett was wary once more. 'Professional?'

'Well, not really professional. It was involved in my job; I used to sell a lot of roses from my market stall.'

The Hallett mouth hung open for a few seconds. He gulped. 'Your market stall. Is that what you said?'

'That's right. I used to have a pitch in town some years ago now.' He smiled. 'Cor, to think of it now; up at the crack of dawn, out in all weathers, standing about for hours some days just waiting for customers. Things have certainly changed now.'

While listening to this explanation, Hallett had been glancing anxiously over Fred's garden. 'What happened to your, er, stall?'

'Well, I had a bit of luck, didn't I?'

'Did you?'

'I'll say I did. I won a few hundred pounds on the dogs, put it with what I already had and I opened up a fruit shop.'

'I see; and does this mean you are a shopkeeper?'

From his tone it could be felt that Hallett placed shopkeepers only a notch or two above labourers and odd-job men in his personal version of the social strata.

'Well, indirectly I suppose I am, yes. You see, my first shop was such a success that I soon opened another, then another and another until, in the end, I've got four fruit shops, all doing well and a manager in each one of them.'

Hallett stared, hardly able to believe what he had just heard. 'You own four fruit shops?'

'That's right, squire.'

This was certainly an improvement. To be a shopkeeper was barely acceptable, but to be a shopkeeper four times over, that was a different matter.

'With a manager in charge of each, you say?'

'Right again, squire. The name's handy, don't you think?'

'Handy? In what way do you mean?'

'Well, they're fruit shops, see, and the name on the shop front reads "F Root", get it? Fruit. Lucky for me wasn't it?'

'Yes, singularly fortuitous.'

'My words exactly, squire.'

Hallett received this claim very coldly and turned once more to his roses.

Fred smiled. 'Say no more, I'll get cracking on your roses. Where did I put the secateurs?'

Meanwhile, in the sitting room of the Halletts, Valerie was sitting in a large leather armchair reading a women's magazine. The room was furnished in a distinctly military style and the walls were dotted with photographs of various military figures all sporting luxuriant moustaches. Over the mantelpiece the wall was decorated with a primitive African shield with two spears crossed behind it. The warlike effect was rather spoiled because someone had tucked a television licence reminder behind the thongs criss-crossing the front of the shield.

Elizabeth entered from the kitchen and walked to the window pausing on the way to pick up the end of a piece of trailing ivy and wind it round a stick in its flower pot.

Glancing out of the window she saw her husband talking earnestly with their new neighbour. 'Look, there's your father talking to Mr Root.'

Valerie was absorbed in her magazine and had just arrived at a particularly exciting love scene. She answered without looking up. 'Really?'

'Yes, Mr Root is cutting off your father's roses and putting them in a paper bag.'

The love scene quickly faded as Valerie came back to reality. 'Who did you say Mr Root was?'

'He's Frederick Root, our new next door neighbour.'

Valerie decided that the love scene would have to wait for a moment and, discarding the magazine, she moved over to the window.

'I must say he looks very pleasant. Have you met him yet?'

'Only briefly; and yes, he certainly seems very pleasant.'

'Well, he seems to be getting on with father, doesn't he?'

'Yes, they're chatting like old friends. I wonder if they have settled in all right or if there is anything that they need.'

Valerie shrugged. 'I expect they will ask, won't they?'

'I don't know, maybe they wouldn't like to. Do you think that they would have their cooker and things connected yet?'

'I don't know Mother, should you ask them?'

'That's a good idea. You could go ask Mr Root. No, better still, ask your father to ask him and, if necessary, he can use our telephone to speak to the Gas Board or someone.'

'All right, Mother, I'll go now.'

'Thank you, dear, otherwise they might not be able to cook their dinner. And that reminds me, I must start thinking about what we are to have tonight.'

She tripped off happily to the kitchen. pausing only to pull a dead leaf off Hannah, an especially healthy looking glacier ivy.

Casting a longing glance at her magazine, Valerie started for the door just as the telephone rang.

She called out. 'I'll get it, it's probably Myra.'

First sitting herself comfortably in an adjacent chair and tucking her feet under her, Valerie picked up the telephone. 'Hello.'

'Hello, Valerie, it's me. Guess what? I passed!'

'Oh, well done, Myra, was it difficult?'

'Well, you know, not too bad. I did well on my Highway Code. But how about coming for a drive this evening?'

'Great. Where shall we go?'

'You tell me and we'll go there. Now let me tell you about the examiner I had.'

'Just a minute, Myra.'

Valerie had just noticed her brother Richard wander into the room reading one of his favourite science fiction books. He was a pleasant, unusually clean and tidy looking boy with a very serious air about him.

'Richard.'

He looked away from his book where there was an exciting confrontation between an interplanetary space patrol and a damaged Plegetorian space ship.

'Yes?'

'Look, be a dear and take a message to father. He's in the garden with Mr Root.'

'Who's Mr Root?'

'He's our new neighbour. Now tell father that mother said to ask Mr Root if their arrangements for dinner tonight are all right.'

'Now?'

'Yes, now, please.'

Richard sighed, strolled off through the door and, still reading, he made his way out of the front door and over to where his father was speaking to their new neighbour.

Inside the sitting room Valerie settled back to hear Myra's description of her driving examiner.

The door to the hall opened and Elizabeth came in carrying a small plastic watering-can. She started on a systematic tour of her plants, carefully measuring a steady stream of water onto each one.

'Valerie, dear, did you give my message to father?'

Covering the mouthpiece with her hand, Valerie replied. 'No. Richard has just taken it.'

'Good, that will give him a chance to meet Mr Root,' said Elizabeth and crossed the room to look out of the window.

In the garden Fred was busily cutting off the diseased parts of the roses and placing them in a paper bag. Hallett stood by watching carefully, but ensuring that he maintained control of the operation and had placed himself in charge.

'Don't miss that one there, and look, another one there at the bottom.'

'Right you are, squire.'

At this point Hallett noticed Richard standing close by

absorbed in his book and he frowned as he observed that the book was entitled "Invasion of the Plegetorians".

'Yes, Richard?'

'Oh, message from mother.'

'Just a moment.' He turned to Fred. 'Mr Root, this my son Richard. Richard, this is our new neighbour, Mr Root.'

'Hello, Richard.'

'How do you do, Mr Root.'

The introduction having been completed, Hallett took Richard by the elbow. 'Please excuse us. Come with me, Richard.'

They walked a short way, then Hallett looked sternly at him.

'Richard, when you have occasion to bring a message to me, I would be obliged if you would not bring your lurid literature with you.'

'Sorry, Dad. I got carried away with a confrontation with a Plegetorian space ship.'

'Yes. Now will you please return to the house, and in future, try to concentrate on what is going on around you.'

Satisfied that he had once more restored his son to the path of reasonable and sociable behaviour, Hallett turned to go.

'Dad?'

Giving vent to an unnecessarily deep sigh, Hallett turned back. 'Yes, Richard?'

'Don't you want to hear the message from mother?'

Hallett's face registered the fact that Richard had just scored a point. 'Well, of course I want to hear it; what is it?'

Richard screwed up his face in an effort to remember the message he had to deliver. 'Mother says have you made arrangements for dinner with Mr Root yet?'

'Dinner? Mr Root? Do you mean that I am to extend an invitation to the Roots to have dinner with us?'

'I don't know, but that was the message.'

'Well, in view of the brevity of our acquaintance with Mr Root, I find that more than a little strange.'

'Well, that's what I was told.'

Hallett took a deep breath and prepared to hold forth on the modern lack of education, the absence of comprehension and the deficiencies of the young in general, when he noticed Elizabeth looking at him from the sitting room window.

He frowned to indicate how baffling he found her request and Elizabeth, unable to see why he was not asking Mr Root about his cooking arrangements, waved him away and indicated that he should turn and speak to Mr Root.

Hallett shrugged and turned away.

Meanwhile, Richard resumed his encounter with the invaders from outer space and read his way quietly back to the house.

Hallett walked back to Fred who was straightening up from the roses holding the paper bag.

'There you are, squire. Just burn that lot and everything is as good new.'

'Thank you, I'm very grateful.'

There was a good deal of fidgeting with the paper bag before Hallett could bring himself to mention the subject of dinner.

'Ah, Mr Root, would you and your family care to have dinner with us this evening? Unless you have already made other plans,' he added, hopefully.

Fred smiled. 'Well, that's very nice of you, we'd love to. It'll only be the wife and me, though, the boys are going to visit their Auntie Myrtle. She only lives just down the road. What time would you like us to pop round?'

'Shall we say seven-thirty for eight?' said Hallett, hoping that the mention of two times would throw Fred into confusion.

'Right you are then, seven-thirty it is and nosebags at eight.'

If Hallett had any lingering doubts about the inadvisability of inviting such people as the Roots to his dinner table, they were now swept away. Of all the nerve, nosebags indeed! However, good manners insisted that he must reply to the acceptance even to such a neighbour as Root.

'Ah, yes, thank you. We shall look forward to it.'

'Right then, squire, see you later.'

So saying, Fred strode off briskly to his house.

Hallett stood glaring at the Root house, then decided that it was time he asked Elizabeth why on earth she had found it necessary to invite those dreadful next-door people to dinner. There was no doubt about it, Elizabeth must be warned that she should take a more responsible attitude to her duties. After all, he thought, how would it be if I went around inviting every person I met to come and have a meal with us. We would pretty soon be the laughing stock of the district. Even as he thought this, he was aware of the wild exaggeration of his complaint, but he was still determined to speak to his wife and demand an explanation.

He marched in at the back door and found Elizabeth holding a pot plant with white veined leaves and was deliberately pinching out the flowers and discarding them.

'What on earth are you doing, Elizabeth?'

'Oh, hello, Simon, how's Mr Root?'

'Never mind Mr Root, why are you destroying those flowers?'

'But this is a fittonia. You only grow it for the leaves. Pretty, isn't it?'

Hallett had little patience with the practice of growing pot plants, and regarded it as having almost no connection with gardening. Imagine, growing plants just to look at the leaves.

'Yes, yes, I'm sure that it is quite attractive, but there is something I want to ask you. Why have I had to invite the Roots to dinner tonight?'

'Have you invited them for dinner tonight, then?'

'Well, of course I have. I am just asking you why did I have to?'

'I'm sorry, Simon, but I seem to have lost the thread of this somewhere. Why did you have to invite them?'

Taking a deep breath to control his impatience, Hallett replied with icy calm. 'Elizabeth, I invited them because you asked me to do so.'

She guessed that there had been a mix-up somewhere, but decided not to pursue it.

'Oh, I see. Well, what time did you arrange?'

'I thought that seven-thirty for eight might be convenient.'

'Eight o'clock? That's fine. I had better start thinking what we can have.'

Elizabeth had no idea how Simon could have been so

confused as to think that she wanted him to invite their new neighbours to dinner, but long experience had taught her a sort of judo-like mental reaction to her husband's temper. She moved in whichever direction she thought he was trying to push.

'Simon, is there something special that you would like me to serve?'

Hallett's face twisted into something resembling a cross between a frown and a sneer. He was tempted to suggest that beans on toast might be appropriate. 'Under the circumstances, I think that we had better keep it unpretentious.'

But, even as he spoke, Hallett's eyes lit up. This could be his chance. Where better to prove one's superiority over the Fred Roots of this world than at a splendid meal with all the attendant trimmings. Not an opportunity to be missed, he thought.

'No, no. On second thoughts, perhaps we ought to give them something special. In fact, I fancy something quite Epicurean. I may even decant one of my bottles of the '83 claret; you know, the St Emilion Ripeau. Also, could you prepare that Portuguese dessert you do so well. What is it called?'

'You mean, Sonhos de Morangos, Strawberry Dreams?'

'Yes, that's it. First class.'

'What about the rest of the meal?'

'Well, could you manage Fillet de Boeuf en Croute?'

'I think so.'

'Splendid.'

'Very well, I had better get started then.'

Elizabeth busied herself round the kitchen and Hallett felt that he was now more in the mood for his gardening chores.

With a noticeably sprightly step he walked out of the kitchen and strutted down the path towards his garden. From the doorway of his kitchen, Fred raised his hand in friendly greeting.

Hallett smiled and waved. Just you wait, he thought, you are soon to find out that there is more to good living than flashy cars and expensive suits.

He looked forward to dinner that night with an eager anticipation he had not known in years.

CHAPTER THREE

The newly unpacked clock on the Root's mantelpiece showed that the time was almost seven-thirty. Fred was busy adjusting his tie and generally checking his appearance in the mirror. Gladys walked into the room wearing a simple but smart dress in petrol blue.

'Fred, we'll have to hurry.'

'Relax, we'll be there on time.' He turned from the mirror. 'Cor, you look a treat and no mistake.'

'Give over, Fred. You've seen me in this old thing before. Anyway, I'm not sure that it does anything for me, now.'

'Well, if it doesn't do anything for you, it sure does plenty for me. Makes me sorry we're not staying in.'

'Fred Root, you're shocking; I'm glad to say.'

They laughed and Fred turned back to the mirror. 'I'm just about ready, so, next door, here we come.'

For a moment Gladys looked worried. 'Are you sure they wanted us tonight, Fred?'

'Course I am. Asked me earlier, didn't he?'

'Well, it does seem funny.'

'Does it? Well, we'll have a good chuckle over it and then let's go.'

Fred glanced round the room which was really quite well organised considering that this was their first day in the house.

'Y'know, I think I'm going to like it here if everybody is as friendly as Hallett and his wife.'

Gladys nodded but still looked a bit worried.

In the living room of the Halletts, he and his wife were awaiting the arrival of their guests. He was dressed in a dark blue suit and she in an attractive white dress.

'Well, as they are not yet here, Elizabeth, we may as well sit down and have a drink.'

'Thank you, Simon. Will you mix a pink gin for me, please.'

'Elizabeth, I think you are aware, that while I don't mind pouring drinks, I do not like mixing them. It makes one feel like a barman.'

'But all you have to do is to take the Angostura bitters and…'

'I know perfectly well how to create a pink gin, but that is not the point. It's just that I do not like fiddling with drinks. Why can't you drink sherry or something?'

'Oh, very well then, I don't want to be a nuisance. I'll have a whisky and ginger instead.'

Hallett gave an impatient snort and marched towards the cocktail cabinet muttering that one might as well talk to oneself. Elizabeth watched him with just a trace of a twinkle in her eyes.

There was a prolonged clinking of bottles and glasses before Hallett walked back carrying a glass of whisky and ginger and a small glass of whisky for himself.

He handed his wife her drink.

'What time do you expect Valerie to return tonight?' he said, adopting his favourite back to the fire stance.

'I'm not sure, but they will have so much to chat about now that Myra's passed her driving test. About eleven o'clock, I dare say.'

'Hm, that's plenty late enough.'

Hallett had yet to decide whether or not he approved of women drivers.

'Simon, are you sure you don't mind Richard going to that Science Fiction meeting?'

'It's not so much that I mind, Elizabeth; it's just that I regard it as so much nonsense. However, one just hopes that one day he will see sense, though goodness knows when. If only they hadn't stopped National Service conscription we might find that the young people of today…'

'Was that the door, dear?'

'What? I didn't hear anything.'

'Must be my imagination, sorry.'

Elizabeth was contented that her little diversion had neatly

46

stopped Hallett's flow which, had it reached full flood, would undoubtedly have included the lack of ambition in the young, the tendency of modern teenagers to become criminals, the lack of proper respect for the old and so on, until Elizabeth, who had heard it many times over the years, would have felt tempted to recite it silently with him.

As Hallett was searching his memory to find what he had been saying before he was interrupted, there was a knock on the front door.

Elizabeth started up. 'Good heavens, there really is someone at the door.'

'That will be the Roots, I expect. I'll go.'

He walked to the front door and opened it to find Fred and Gladys Root smiling at him.

'Good evening. So glad you could come. Please come in.'

'Ta very much, squire. After you, Glad.'

They walked through the hall and into the sitting room where a smiling Elizabeth met them.

'Now, my dear, you have met Mr Root. Allow me to introduce you to Mrs Root. Mrs Root, my wife, Elizabeth.'

Elizabeth smiled and shook hands with Gladys. 'I'm so pleased you could come. Tell me,' she said, as they walked towards the settee, 'what do I call you?'

'I'm Glad.'

To Elizabeth this seemed a simple and happy statement of fact, even if a little out of place.

'Good, so am I.'

Gladys looked puzzled. 'I thought you were called Elizabeth.'

Elizabeth began to feel that she was losing her grip on this conversation and felt that she ought to make an effort to regain it.

'Most people call me Elizabeth and others call me Betty.'

It was obvious from Mrs Root's reaction to this information that, far from helping to clear the situation, it had added to the confusion.

Gladys looked uncertainly at Elizabeth. 'Why on earth do they do that?'

With an effort that was almost desperate she tried to change the subject.

'Would you like to see the rest of the house?' she asked, waiting in suspense to see if Mrs Root would now deliver a meaningless reply and so bring the conversation to an awkward, confused silence.

'Thank you, I'd like that.'

Elizabeth almost laughed with relief at this and escorted Gladys from the room, cheerfully describing the house and its history as they made their way down the hall.

While the ladies were talking, Fred Root and Hallett had been walking round the room looking at the photographs and trophies adorning the walls.

'That is a picture of me passing out at Sandhurst.'

'I see. Been on the booze, had you?'

'By passing out I meant…'

'I knew what you meant, squire, it was just me little joke.'

'Really. Well, I'm sorry I didn't see it.'

Not put out by the cool response to his humorous attempts, Root continued his cheerful progress round the room while his host wore his 'I wish I'd had you in my regiment' look.

Eventually, they stopped by a small table where Hallett's 1983 St Emilion – Ripeau sat glowing warmly in its decanter.

'Would you care for a drink, Root?'

'Ta, squire, don't mind if I do.'

With the reverent care of an explosives expert handling nitro-glycerine, Hallett slowly poured the precious claret into two expensive looking glasses.

He handed one to Root. 'Perhaps you would care to give me your opinion on this.'

Root took the glass. 'Ta. Bottoms up then,' he said, cheerfully.

Hallett's frown at this casual reception of his prize claret changed to a look of horror as Root, without ceremony, downed almost half of the contents of his glass in one gulp. He smacked his lips. 'Very fair,' he said, 'very fair drop of plonk is that.'

'Thank you,' said Hallett, expressing as much sarcasm as he dared to use on a guest. 'I'm so glad you like it. It's not often one has the chance to share the contents of one's modest cellar with a connoisseur.'

'Well, you can't help liking it, can you?' said Root, taking another small sip. 'I mean, that was a classic year for claret, that was.'

A small warning bell sounded in Hallett's head, but he felt that he had to proceed. 'What was?' he said, his voice now less firm and confident.

'Well, 1983 of course.' He took one more sip and nodded in satisfaction. 'Classic year. I should say it's St Emilion Ripeau. Am I right?'

Almost imperceptibly, Hallett nodded.

He asked himself how could this have happened. How could a man like Root identify all those details and without even having the decency to observe the formalities of wine-tasting. It struck at the very roots of the system. It was not natural.

He stood there, his own glass of claret still untasted, feeling the world had let him down badly.

'Come on, squire,' said Root, indicating the untasted drink, 'get it down you.'

Without realising what he was doing Hallett lifted the glass to his lips and downed most of the glass in one gulp. There was a brief pause, then his eyes bulged, his face deepened in colour and he clutched his throat.

'My God, what on earth came over me?'

Root laughed and took his glass. 'You'll have to go steady, old son, or we'll be getting you up to bed in a wheelbarrow.'

Hallett struggled to recover himself and was soon once more in command. He now felt more than ever that it was his duty to establish the correct relationship between Root and himself. He considered that he had been unlucky over the wine and, merely because of a lucky shot in the dark by Root – he disregarded the odds against this happening – he had been unable to demonstrate the real skill and artistry of wine-tasting. Very well, he thought, we will keep to areas of conversation where I am the undisputed superior. In other words – the Army.

They walked, carefully steered by Hallett, to a reproduction of an engraving of a 19th century battle scene. Together, they gazed at the picture with its mounted and foot soldiers, billowing smoke and dying men and horses. There was more than a trace of reverence in Hallett's voice as he offered his praise of soldiers of the past.

'By George, those fellows certainly knew how to fight,' he said, 'and how to die.'

'You're right there, squire; and that was a nasty affair that was.'

The warning bell sounded again. 'You know something about this particular battle?'

'Well, not much really. It's the battle of Talavera, isn't it?'

Hallett's eyes closed momentarily in silent suffering. His voice was unusually quiet. 'Yes, it took place in the early eighteen hundreds.'

'Yes, 1809 if I'm not mistaken.'

Hallett nodded and decided on an attempt to establish his superiority once more.

'The British Commander was a Major-General Howorth,' he said, with the authority of a military historian.

Fred looked slightly embarrassed. 'Er, I think you'll find that Howorth just commanded the Artillery. It was Lieutenant-General Wellesley who commanded the British and Allied Army.'

'But of course. As I said, Howorth was British Commander of the Artillery, and you are quite right that the overall Commander of the British and Allied Army was Wellesley.'

'They certainly were great days, squire.'

'Quite so, quite so,' said Hallett, feeling that his excursion into military matters had not been quite the success it should have been.

Root turned away and looked round the room at the impressive collection of militaria, photographs and trophies.

'Quite a collection of mitlitaria you've got here.'

Seeing that his attention was diverted, Hallett quickly took a close look at his engraving of the Battle of Talavera, and read the name of the engraver. He then led Root to the middle of the room.

'Thank you. It has taken me a long time to acquire them.'

He looked back at the picture he had just left. 'You know,

Root, I am really proud of that engraving of the Battle of Talavera, even if it is only a reproduction. The engraver, of course, was…'

His voice faded as he realised that he had forgotten the name he had only just read at the bottom of the picture. He snapped his fingers impatiently.

'I think you'll find it was Voudramini,' said Fred, thus filling Hallett's cup of bitterness to overflowing.

He looked at Fred with a sort of defeated expression and sighed. 'Yes, I'm sure you are right. However, I think it is time we joined the ladies.'

Together they walked from the room, Hallett looking slightly less upright and military than he did earlier.

In the kitchen, Elizabeth and Gladys were busy loading dishes onto a trolley.

'It was very nice of you to help me finish preparing the dinner, Mrs Root.'

'You're very welcome I'm sure, and I'm Glad.'

Pleased though she was to learn of this state of perpetual happiness, Elizabeth found it a little baffling, but decided to reply in kind. 'Yes, of course, so am I.'

'I know, but I still don't think I understand it.'

With the distinct feeling that the conversation was again slipping away from her, Elizabeth searched for something appropriate to say. She was saved from further thought on the subject, as the door opened and in walked the two men.

'Dinner almost ready, Elizabeth?'

'Just about, Simon.'

'Good, good. Are you fond of cooking, Mrs Root?'

'Not Mrs Root, squire. Her name's Gladys, but we call her Glad.'

Elizabeth glanced quickly at Gladys and, as their eyes met, the mix-up of the last few minutes became clear to them simultaneously.

Together they smiled, then they laughed together.

Hallett and Root looked at each other, the perplexity showing on their faces.

'What can we possibly have said to provoke that?'

Fred shook his head. 'Search me, squire, but it must have been something good.'

The two ladies subsided and started to move the trolley towards the door to the dining room. Still looking puzzled, their husbands followed them.

The dining room was furnished in heavy, comfortable furniture and the walls carried the inevitable reminders of military life.

They seated themselves round the table although Hallett found that his appetite, like his enthusiasm for this meal with his new neighbours, had waned a little. But, he consoled himself, he still had a few shots to fire yet. Perhaps after the meal he could steer the conversation a little.

As Fred put down his fork and spoon he sighed contentedly. 'Well, I've got to hand it to you, Elizabeth, you certainly can cook.'

'Thank you, Fred. More dessert?'

'I don't think I'd better, thanks. But that really was a smashing pudding.'

Hallett smiled although he wasn't too pleased at hearing his favourite dessert described as 'a smashing pudding'.

'I'm glad you like it,' he said, 'because this particular dessert happens to be one of my wife's specialities. It's a foreign recipe.'

'And very nice too. Portuguese isn't it?'

This time Hallett could only just bring himself to nod.

'Thought so. It's the old Strawberry Dreams. Sonhos de Morangos.'

Elizabeth smiled. 'Isn't that clever, Simon? I thought that we were the only ones to know about that particular dish.'

It was evident from Hallett's face that he held this belief even more fervently than Elizabeth.

'Yes, Elizabeth. Now may we have the cheese and biscuits, please.'

'Certainly. How about you, Gladys, would you like some cheese and biscuits?'

'Oh dear, I think I shall burst if I do.'

'Fred?'

'Well, I thought I was full up, but I must admit, I do like a bit of cheese.'

Elizabeth walked to the sideboard and returned with a well-filled cheese-board and a small basket of biscuits. She placed them on the table and Hallett offered the board to Fred.

'Is there anything you particularly care for?'

Fred looked at the cheeses on display. 'Cor, that's quite a line-up for you. Roquefort, Camembert, Cantal, Pecorino; it's a bit difficult to decide, isn't it? I think I'll try a little Camembert, one of my favourites.'

Hallett felt that he could no longer tolerate the mystery of Fred's knowledge of such a variety of things, without some sort of explanation.

'I must say you seem remarkably well informed about cheese and wine and so on. How did that come about?'

'It's no mystery, squire. You see, when I opened up these fruit shops of mine, I found myself with time on my hands.'

Elizabeth looked up. 'Do you have more than one shop, then Fred?'

He nodded. 'Afraid so. I was telling the Colonel about it earlier. There are four shops each with a manager installed. It means that I have time to read, listen to music, visit places of interest, travel and so on. It gives me something to do.'

'I see,' broke in Hallett, 'highly commendable, I'm sure. But then, one could hardly tolerate a life of total lethargy, could one?'

'Well, here's one who couldn't.'

'Nor I. For my part I keep myself busy with the garden and various other pastimes, one of which is heraldry.'

'Heraldry, eh? That sounds interesting.'

Hallett was recovering from his earlier setbacks and was now preparing to move into top gear.

'Yes, it's absolutely fascinating. In fact, I have traced my own family crest and our family motto.'

Elizabeth paused in the act of buttering a very brittle cream cracker that threatened to shatter at every touch of the knife. 'I didn't know that, Simon. What *is* our family motto?'

'I feel it is very apt,' said Hallett and continued with obvious pride. 'I Live By The Fruits Of Fortune.'

Fred nodded approvingly. 'I Live By The Fruits Of Fortune,

eh? I like that; very profound.'

'Yes, it makes one proud to know that the family history includes a motto that, if I may say so, is an inspiration to us all.'

Hallett treated Root to a lofty, condescending smile. 'How about you? Do you know whether you have a family crest?'

Fred laughed. 'I shouldn't think so, squire.' He thought for a few moments. 'But, if we have, it ought to be; let me see now.'

Root paused and looked thoughtful. 'It ought to be an argent field with carrots, pilewise proper. In chief, a cash register, gold. In base, a greyhound, salient, sable.'

Gladys looked puzzled. 'Why a greyhound, Fred?'

'Don't you remember, Glad? I got my start with a win at the Greyhound Derby, didn't I?'

He turned to Hallett. 'That's why a greyhound salient. About to jump; see?'

No words could express Hallett's exasperation at Fred's knowledgeable display of the hobby, which he had, up to now, regarded as somewhat exclusive to the higher echelons of society.

Quietly, Hallett asked, 'I don't doubt that you also have in mind a suitable motto?'

Fred's smile broadened. 'How about; I Live By The Fortune In Fruit?'

CHAPTER FOUR

It was now over two months since Fred Root and his family had moved into number twenty-five. Their relationships with the Halletts had been agreeable, even if sometimes a little formal. The Roots had quickly settled into their new home and were finding life comfortable. Hallett's attitude, though, had not changed greatly, and he still referred to them as 'the Roots' or 'those people next door'.

It was Saturday morning at about eleven o'clock and Hallett was seated at his desk in a converted back bedroom he called his study. There came a sharp, efficient sounding rap at the front door. There was a long pause and the rap was repeated, only louder.

Feeling that there was surely someone in the house capable of carrying out the simple task of answering a door, Hallett continued working. On hearing the rap for the third time, he slammed down his pen, scraped back his chair and stamped noisily out of his room and down the stairs.

He had just reached the third stair from the bottom when Elizabeth came out of the kitchen and shouted. 'Simon, there's someone at the door. Oh, there you are, dear, there's someone at the door.'

'For heaven's sake, Elizabeth, I know that. In fact, I should think that by now, the whole street knows there is someone at our door. And in any case, why didn't you answer it yourself?'

'I had flour all over my hands and I could hardly touch the front door like that, could I?'

Hallett sighed with a volume loud enough to demonstrate that his patience was all but exhausted. He stamped down the last three stairs, strode to the front door and flung it open.

Standing outside was a smartly dressed man in a dark, well-cut blazer, dazzling white shirt with striped tie, sharply creased grey trousers and black, hand-made leather shoes. His dark hair, sleekly brushed back was streaked with grey at the temples. His small moustache was neatly clipped and he gave an overall impression of neatness and efficiency.

'Good morning, sir. I'm sorry to bother you like this, but could I please trouble you for some water. My radiator has run dry.'

His clear, even voice was pleasant and, despite his calling Hallett 'sir', he had an air of authority about him. Hallett was impressed. 'But of course, my dear chap, please come in.'

The stranger smiled and stepped inside. 'That's very good of you, I'm most grateful. Please allow me to introduce myself. My name is Porch, Martin Porch. How do you do.' He extended a hand.

Hallett shook his hand warmly. 'Hallett, Simon Hallett. Delighted to be of service to you. Please come this way.'

He led the way into the sitting room and invited Porch to sit down.

The door opened and Elizabeth walked in, drying her hands on a small towel.

Porch stood up.

'Mr Porch, this is my wife, Elizabeth. Elizabeth, this is Mr Martin Porch, he's having a spot of trouble with his car.'

'Mrs Hallett, how very nice to meet you. I must say you keep a beautiful home here. I suspect some previous training in interior design, what?'

'I'm pleased to meet you Mr Porch and you're very kind to say those nice things about our home.'

Porch smiled. 'I assure you I meant every word of it. It's not every day one gets to see such taste and flair.' He turned to Hallett. 'You're a very lucky man, sir.'

He beamed. 'That's very nice of you to say so. Now let's see about that water for your car.'

'Thank you. In a watering-can if you don't mind.'

Together they left the room leaving Elizabeth looking thoughtful and a little puzzled. When Porch had smiled at her, she felt that it was a switched on smile, showing very little sincerity.

Outside in the garage, Hallett eagerly plied his visitor with questions. 'Live locally, do you?'

'No, sir, wish I did. Actually, I'm from the Midlands.'

'What line of business are you in; anything interesting?'

'Well, some people might say so. I'm a representative with a property dealer and we specialise in restoring country houses to their former glory and selling them to suitable clients. Quite a profitable line, actually.'

'Been in it long have you?'

'About two years. In fact, ever since my release from the Army.'

The Army, thought Hallett. Of course. Only the Army could produce neat, efficient, friendly chaps like this. It was all to do with the training and the discipline, of course. Proved it time and time again.

'The Army, eh? That's a coincidence; I'm an ex-military man myself.' He became fractionally taller. 'Lieutenant Colonel, Second Battalion, Queen's Own Birnshires.'

Porch almost stood to attention.

'Well, this is an honour, sir. Been a great admirer of the Birnshires for many years. I was in the Royal Hamlington Regiment myself. Well, well, Colonel, I had no idea I was talking to an ex-soldier. I must say it's given me a great surprise to find a distinguished soldier like yourself bothering to help a mere ex-major with his motoring problems.'

When Porch came through the front gate he evidently missed the fact that the house was called "Mafeking" and in the sitting room he must have failed to see the military pictures, the two pairs of crossed swords and the African shield with its two spears.

'My pleasure, Major. Now let's find that watering-can for you.'

In a very short time, they were both out by the Porch's car carefully pouring water into the radiator.

'There, that should do it. Start your engine.'

Porch climbed into the car and turned the ignition key. The engine whirred and spluttered but refused to start.

'All right, turn off, no sense in wasting your battery.'

Porch climbed out of the car and stood with Hallett staring at the engine. 'Any idea what the trouble might be, sir?'

Hallett peered thoughtfully at the ignition coil. 'It's probably this, your petrol pump.'

'Oh, this really is a nuisance. I wonder if I might impose further on your kindness and ask if I might use your telephone, please. I rather stupidly left my mobile in my desk.'

'But of course, my dear chap. Come with me.'

As they walked back up the drive the Colonel described in detail how he was once in a similar position in the desert on exercise with a half-track that refused to start. They approached the kitchen door. 'And so, I stripped it down, cleaned out the sand, re-assembled it, and off we went. Damn close call, though; we had to get out quickly.' He didn't trouble to explain why speed, on an exercise had, apparently, been so vital.

'A truly memorable experience, sir.'

'Oh, just one of many, Major, just one of many.' He looked thoughtful. 'Look, it's getting close to lunch time. Why don't you have a bite to eat with us, and meanwhile, you can contact a garage to fix your car.'

'That's very generous of you. If it's not too much trouble I'd love to stay for lunch. Are you sure Mrs Hallett won't mind?'

'Elizabeth? Nonsense, she's a soldier's wife. She's learned to take it all in her stride.'

They entered the kitchen and the Colonel was a little dismayed to find Fred Root talking to Elizabeth while she searched in a cupboard.

'Mornin' squire, 'ope you don't mind but Elizabeth is tryin' to find some vinegar for me chips. I always say that chips ain't the same without vinegar, don't you?'

Hallett wondered if it was his imagination but Root seemed to be rather more Cockney some times than at others. He decided not to give an opnion on the subject of vinegar on chips.

'Good morning. Er, may I introduce Major Porch, late of the Royal Hamlington Regiment,' he turned to Porch. 'This is Mr Root,' he hesitated, 'he lives next door.'

'Mornin',' said Fred, beaming at Porch.

'Pleased to meet you,' said Porch, looking slightly baffled.

Hallett took his new guest by the arm. 'Through that door and you can use the telephone to get a garage to come round and fix your car.'

'Thank you, sir.'

Porch walked into the hall and dialled a number. He could be heard talking to someone about the car and requesting in his authoritative way, that they get someone round and fix this fuel pump at once, and never mind someone's lunch-time, get him here. He replaced the receiver and rejoined them in the kitchen. 'There, that's fixed that. They will send someone round straight away.'

Hallett beamed. 'Well done, that's the way to get some action. By the way, Elizabeth, could you lay another place for lunch? Major Porch will be dining with us.'

'Yes, of course. I hope you like salmon salad, Major Porch.'

'It sounds delightful, Mrs Hallett, and please call me Martin.'

'Yes, of course, and please call me Elizabeth.'

She turned and smiled at Fred. 'Here's your curry-powder, Fred.'

Hallett stared. 'Curry-powder? I thought you wanted vinegar.'

Fred grinned. 'Little joke, squire. Thanks for the curry-powder, Elizabeth.'

With that he strolled from the kitchen.

After lunch was over, Elizabeth was in the kitchen, while the Colonel and Martin Porch were chatting in the sitting room. The Colonel was just describing some of his Army experiences.

Porch sat back in his chair with a look of admiration on his face. 'I must say, Colonel, you certainly have seen some action in your time.'

'It's all part of the job, Martin, all part of the job.'

'Don't you find civilian life rather dull after all that, though?'

'One gets used to it, you know. But what about you. Don't you find life a bit dull now?'

'Not as much as I feared. You see, I have the excitement of helping to select large old properties and then the pleasure of seeing them restored to make fine, stately homes, but with all the conveniences of modern life. It's very satisfying.'

'Yes, I recall you telling me about it. What happens to it once a property has been restored?'

'Well, there's quite a big demand for them. In fact, whenever I choose an investment project, we have no trouble in getting the financial backing, because it's such a good investment; even if it does take a few months.'

'Investment project. What's that?'

'My apologies, Colonel; trade jargon. An investment project is the term we use for an old property with restoration potential. To spread the cost of the restoration we sell shares in the project, and then, when the house is sold, we pay out a handsome profit to our investors. Naturally, we make a good profit ourselves, but without too much outlay.'

'Sounds interesting. But I don't remember ever seeing any advertisements for this, though.'

'That's because we don't need to advertise. It's all done by personal contacts and through brokers. We call it one of the City's little closed shops.'

'Hmm, I see. How does one see about getting in on one of these projects?'

Porch looked worried. 'I'm afraid you place me in rather an embarrassing position, Colonel. After accepting your hospitality, I have to say that it's virtually impossible to get in, unless you are in the know, if you see what I mean.'

'Quite, quite. A nod's as good as a wink. But couldn't you put me in touch with someone?'

Once more Porch looked worried. 'I wish I could get you a contact, Colonel, but it's a sort of unwritten rule of my company that new investors are generally selected by Head Office staff.'

'I quite understand, Major, say no more.'

'Look, you've been jolly kind to me and I'd like to repay that kindness. Please let me talk to my MD in London, and see if I can arrange a meeting.'

'M D?'

'Managing Director.'

'I see. Well, that's very kind of you, Martin.'

'I am sure you understand that I can't promise anything, but I'll do my best.'

'Good man. Now, would you care for a drink?'

'Thank you, Colonel, that would be rather nice.'

He walked to a small table, picked up a decanter, poured two glasses and handed one to Porch. 'There, try that, then you may care to give me your opinion.'

Porch took his glass by the stem and looked at the wine against the light.

'From its colour it's probably a sweet dessert table wine, possibly Italy or maybe Spain. Or, of course, it maybe just very old wine from a cask.'

Hallett's face was wreathed in smiles at this display. 'Please go on.'

Porch passed the glass beneath his nose several times, sniffing delicately. 'Well, the bouquet is rich, so definitely a dessert wine, possibly a sweet Bordeaux or maybe a sweet Loire.'

He sipped a little and savoured the taste with obvious pleasure. 'Yes, it's as sweet as I thought. A medium-sweet dessert wine. Rules out a sweet Loire, though. Not acid enough and rather too much body for that. A good, clean, down-to-earth flavour, even if a bit short. I would say a medium sauterne of bourgeois quality, about 1984.'

Hallett could hardly contain his excitement. 'You're absolutely right. That's marvellous.'

'Thank you, Colonel,' he said, looking modest. 'You surely must have an extensive cellar.'

'Oh, moderate, you know. One likes to feel that there are still things in life worth enjoying.'

Porch glanced out of the window and saw a man in overalls closing the bonnet of his car.

'Oh, good, it looks like they have sent a man from the garage and he has fixed my car.'

They slowly finished their drinks and walked outside.

The man in overalls walked towards them and spoke to Porch in a gruff, Cockney voice.

'It's all fixed, Guv. It was your fuel pump.'

'Thank you. How much do I owe you?'

The man handed him a bill, and while Porch was settling this, Hallett saw to his annoyance that Fred Root was standing in his garden, watching the proceedings. Fred waved in a friendly way.

'I see you got the car fixed then, squire.'

He nodded curtly. 'Yes. It was the fuel pump, just as I suspected.'

The overalled man walked off down the drive leaving Major Porch replacing his wallet in his inside pocket.

'Well, Colonel, I must not impose on your hospitality any more, and I really must get back to my end of the country. I feel a bit of a stranger here.'

They shook hands.

'I'll be in touch just as soon as I've had a chance to contact my MD. But quite honestly, I mustn't hold out too much hope. The last I heard, there was a long waiting list.'

'I quite understand, Major. You now have my telephone number and I'm sure you will do whatever you can.'

'You may depend upon it, Colonel. Well, good-bye, and thank you again for all your help.'

'Not at all. Good-bye, and safe journey home.'

'My regards to your charming wife. Good-bye, sir.'

With a cheery wave, Major Porch strode down the drive, climbed into his car and drove off down the Avenue.

As he watched him go, Hallett felt almost a pang of regret at their parting. It was good to know, though, that there were still officers and gentlemen about, even if they were in short supply.

He turned to go to the house but Fred Root evidently wanted to chat. 'Friend of yours, squire?'

'As a matter of fact we met only this morning, but we quickly found that we have a lot in common.'

'Ex-Army is he?'

The Colonel felt that this made his new acquaintance sound like a pair of government surplus boots. 'He is a former military officer, yes.'

Fred nodded. 'Thought so.'

'A man after my own heart is Major Porch. You should have seen him sample one of my wines. He identified it in minutes.'

'Seemed a nice sort of bloke. From what I heard you'll be keeping in touch.'

Hallett hesitated. 'Look, Root, he's going to try and cut me in on the ground floor of an investment scheme he's involved with. He can't guarantee to include me, but he's going to try. Damned decent of him, what?'

'Sounds OK. Room for any more?'

'Well of course, if you don't mind speculating, I'll try to get you included as well. Obviously, I can't make any promises, but if we can get in, there's a small fortune to be made.'

'How does it work, squire?'

They walked slowly towards the house and Hallett explained the scheme in detail.

CHAPTER FIVE

'What are you thinking about, Fred?'

'Eh? Oh; sorry, Glad, I was miles away.'

'I know you were. What's the trouble?'

'Nothing for you to worry about, love; honest.'

It was late evening and Fred was sitting on the sofa sipping his usual night-cap, a mug of cocoa. He set the mug down on a small table and sat staring into space, looking very thoughtful.

'You can't fool me, Fred Root, there's something on your mind.'

He looked at her and grinned. 'No, I can't fool you, can I, Glad. But really, it's nothing for you to get concerned about.'

'If there was something wrong you would tell me, wouldn't you?'

'There's nothing wrong, Glad. It's just that I've been talking to the Colonel and he has told me about a little investment plan and I'm thinking about it.'

'Is it a good one?'

'Oh, it's a good one, all right. Your investment guaranteed to double or triple itself in months.'

They talked together quietly for a while and, as they talked, it became clear to them what they should do.

'You're sure you don't mind the risk, Glad?'

'There's not much risk according to what you've told me, is there?'

'Right. That's what we'll do then.'

Gladys hurried off to the kitchen and Fred could hear the noises of crockery and cutlery being laid out for the next morning's breakfast. He leaned back on the sofa with his hands behind his head. He had that feeling of contentment that comes with knowing that the one you have chosen to be your life's partner, has proven to be the right one. There had been ups and downs, and, no doubt, there would be more. But Fred knew that if he had to choose again, he would still choose the pretty little waitress he had courted and won in his market stall days when he called in the Unicorn Cafe every day for his dinner. Funny, he thought, how they had now accepted that as lunch. Gladys managed very well and, although she wasn't as relaxed in company as he was, she was doing all right.

The noise of the telephone woke Hallett from his after-lunch nap in the sitting room.

Its persistence was irritating and he waited to see if someone would answer it in the hall.

It shrilled again.

'Oh, blast. If it's another wretch asking if this is the bus station, I'll soon put him right.'

He heaved himself from his chair and shuffled across the room still feeling sleepy. He had just reached the telephone as Elizabeth opened the door and said, without looking in. 'Don't disturb yourself, dear, I'll take it in the hall.'

She closed the door.

Hallett snorted. He knew from experience that to pick up the telephone and explain that he might as well take the call himself and, at the same time try to announce his name to the caller, could only lead to an unbelievable confusion of voices.

He waited. The door opened again and Elizabeth came in. 'Simon? Oh, you are awake now. You're wanted on the telephone.'

'Who is it?'

'It's that Major Porch. He wants to speak to you and he says it's important.'

'What? Well, why didn't you say so at once; it's most important that I speak with him.'

He reached for the telephone and, surprisingly, Elizabeth laid her hand on his to stop him. She looked at him with the serious expression she wore only when she was really worried. 'Simon; this Major Porch. Is he involving you in some sort of financial deal?'

'What Martin Porch is trying to do, Elizabeth, is to allow me to get in on an investment that is not available to everyone, and gives me the opportunity to make a considerable profit. Now, if you don't mind, I think that I had better speak to him.'

He lifted her hand away and picked up the telephone. 'Hello, Martin. Simon Hallett here. How nice to hear from you so soon.'

He listened carefully. 'I see. Good man. I'll meet you in London then on Tuesday next. Right. Yes, I think I know the place you mean. But you'll send details of how to get there? Good. Oh, by the way, I hope you won't mind but my next door neighbour has also expressed an interest. I don't wish to complicate things, but he has a few pounds he'd like to invest. You think you can arrange that? That's splendid. Till next week, then. Good-bye.'

He replaced the receiver and rubbed his hands together. 'There, Elizabeth, that's the way to do business. In about six months we could be looking at a profit of double or even triple our outlay.'

'But how much are we investing, then?'

'They have to restrict it, but I will be allowed to put up four thousand pounds.'

'But Simon, we can't afford to do that.'

'You mean we can't afford not to. I believe that this is a golden opportunity for us and this is no time to be timid.'

'Did I hear you say Mr Root is interested?'

'He is and very much so. In fact, he's prepared to put up the same amount as I.'

'Simon, are you sure that he's interested?'

'You can take it from me that Root is no different to anyone else when it comes to money. He knows a good thing when he sees it.'

Elizabeth still looked worried and a little puzzled.

Hallett clapped his hands together. 'Well, I no longer feel the need for a nap. I think I'll expend a little effort on the back garden.'

Humming tunelessly but happily he walked out to the kitchen and Elizabeth could hear him opening drawers looking for his gardening gloves.

Quietly she picked up the telephone and dialled a number.

In number twenty-five, Fred was reading when the telephone shrilled.

'All right, Glad, I've got it.' He picked up the telephone. 'Hello, Fred Root here.'

'Fred, this Elizabeth Hallett and I must talk to you.'

'Hello, Elizabeth. Why the formal title all of a sudden?'

'Please, Fred, I must talk to you, it's urgent.'

Fred could clearly sense a pleading note in her voice. She sounded as if she was in some sort of trouble. 'All right. When and where?'

'Can you come round right away on the pretext of looking at one of my pot plants?'

'I'm on my way.' Within a few minutes Fred was tapping on the kitchen door and being admitted by Elizabeth.

He sat himself down at the kitchen table and she placed a thorny, red flowered potted shrub in front of him.

'In case Simon comes in,' she explained.

'That's a nice euphorbia,' he said, and looked closely at it. 'Not doing too well, though, is it?'

'No, but let's talk about that later. What about this scheme you and Simon are in to make money, Fred. What's it all about?'

He smiled. 'I don't think that it's anything for you to worry about, Elizabeth. It's really not such a bad investment. But why don't you want him to know that you're talking to me about it?'

'I didn't like to say anything about it, but it's that Major Porch. I didn't like the look of him. It all seems too easy to me.'

'Elizabeth, whatever it looks like now, try not to worry. You can't blame anyone wanting to make some easy money. After all, the Colonel is a man of the world. You'll see, everything will be all right.'

'I do hope so because we can't afford to lose that much money.'

Fred's serious tone now changed back to his easy-going voice. 'Well of course it's not doing well. You see, a euphorbia doesn't like draughts or extremes of temperature and you've got it by the window next to your cooker. I should move it if I were you.'

Without looking round Elizabeth knew that her husband had returned.

'Hello, squire. Just giving my opinion on your wife's euphorbia.'

'Afternoon, Root. Very good of you to take the trouble, I'm sure.' He paused and Elizabeth and Fred both wondered if he had heard anything of their conversation. 'By the way, if you are free next Tuesday, we should take a trip to town to meet Porch's MD.'

'Great. What time?'

'We have to be there at eleven hundred hours.'

'Right, then. We'll use my car.' He stood up. 'Well, that's my advice, Elizabeth. If you want to save that plant, I should move it if I were you.'

She nodded but looked so worried that Fred wanted to put his arms round her and bring back the sparkle to her eyes.

'Well, must be moving on. Cheerio for now.'

Strolling back to his garden he was in time to meet his son David coming out of the house.

'Hello, David. Going somewhere?'

'Hello, Dad. I'm just going back to work. I had to take a very late lunch break.'

'How are things in the office, then?'

David shrugged. He was a pleasant-looking young man but his face was clouded as he thought about his job in the office of the building firm for which he worked.

'About the same as any other office I expect. It's considered exciting to be the first to open the stationery parcel at the beginning of the month. And, last week, someone sent us a cheque without signing it. The excitement from that lasted two or three days.'

Fred smiled and looked at David. 'I get the message, old son. You sure I can't offer you something better?'

They had held a conversation like this for the past year or so. Fred wanted to try David as a manager in a fruit shop and was prepared to open one especially for him. But David had refused to take advantage of his dad's hard work by just moving in to be a ready-made manager.

'No thanks, Dad. I'll find something that suits me soon. This job is not exactly what I want, but it will have do for now. Hey, look at the time; if I don't hurry I won't even have a job to worry about. See you later.'

He hurried off down the drive, picked up his bicycle at the gate and pedalled furiously down the road.

Fred watched him go and slowly shook his head. You're a good lad, he thought. What a pity you had to inherit the pride of your mum and the stubbornness of your dad. Life could have been a lot easier for you. But he smiled to himself as he walked into his kitchen.

Tuesday dawned bright and clear, and the country's working population reacted to the promptings of the automatic tea-makers, alarm clocks, telephones, nudges in the back, bangs on the wall, clinking of milk bottles or the crowing of cockerels. They awoke, stretched themselves, and prepared to make their contribution to this new day.

Forsythia Avenue's buzzing symphony of tea-makers had not long been switched into sleepy silence before Fred Root was out of bed going quickly through a vigorous routine of morning exercises, then, just as quickly, showering, shaving and getting dressed. He wore a smart grey suit and he checked his appearance in the mirror, inspecting his individually tailored white shirt and grey tie with its diagonal yellow stripe and dragon motif.

'Not bad for a market trader,' he said.

'Did you say something, Fred?' asked a sleepy voice.

'Don't disturb yourself, Glad. I'll get you a nice cup of tea and then you can cook me some breakfast.'

Later, he sat down to his breakfast of fried egg, crisply fried bacon, button mushrooms lightly boiled in milk and, his favourite, looking uncomfortably out of place, a thick wedge of fried bread.

He sampled each item in turn. 'Glad, you're a marvel. If they ever make cooking an Olympic event, I've got you down to win a gold medal.'

'Oh, get on with you. Would you like some more bacon?'

'No thanks, love. I've just finished my morning exercise

routine which was designed to trim my waistline, and here you are trying to make it impossible for me to see my toes.' He pushed his cup forward. 'I could drink some more tea, though.'

Gladys busied herself round Fred in the way she had always done, ever since it had been necessary in his market days to stoke him up with food and get him out early.

Breakfast finished, Fred was getting ready to leave, when Gladys came into the hall carrying his briefcase. 'Do you need this, Fred?'

'I don't think so, love. Maybe on my next trip.'

'Mind how you go, won't you.'

'Of course I will and I won't be late. Bye, love.'

'Bye, Fred. Come back safe.'

'Always do.'

This last exchange was by way of being a sort of mantra they recited on parting and, although neither of them would have admitted to it, they secretly believed that if they said it, it would ensure that they would be safely reunited.

Fred walked next door and rapped on the back door which was opened by Hallett. 'Morning, Root. All set?'

'Ready when you are.'

There was no sign of Elizabeth, and Hallett called out a hearty good-bye that she echoed faintly from the dining room.

They climbed into Fred's car, backed slowly into the road and drove off smoothly down the Avenue with Hallett talking about advanced driving techniques and offering driving advice to Fred as made their way towards their meeting place.

About an hour and half later they pulled into the car park of a massive office block and, as they left the car, Hallett looked up at the mighty structure.

'You've got to hand it to Porch's company, Root. They certainly know how to look after themselves.'

Fred nodded. 'Looks very impressive.'

They walked towards the glass front doors to where a burly commissionaire stood as if on guard. By the look of the medal ribbons on his chest he must have travelled everywhere and fought with or against just about every nation in the civilised world. A man with a narrower chest would have had to decline the last few medals.

Hallett felt that he was the appropriate person to address this man who was so obviously an ex-soldier.

'Good morning. Colonel Hallett and Mr Frederick Root.'

The commissionaire stroked his chin thoughtfully. 'No. Never 'eard of 'em. You sure they work 'ere?'

'My good man, we are they. We have an appointment with a Major Porch at eleven hundred hours to negotiate a financial investment. Now will you please make an inquiry as to the location of our meeting.'

Commissionaire Harold Phitt stared at Hallett, obviously puzzled.

'Eh?'

Hallett was all set to explode into a 'get your heels together' type of reprimand when Fred intervened.

'Allow me, squire.' He smiled at Phitt. 'Look chummy, me and my old china 'ere 'ave gotta meet a geezer called Porch at eleven and we don't want to be tiddlers, do we? Y'see we don't know if the geezer is just rahnd the Johnny or up all them apples, but if you find aht where he is double quick, there's a Lady Godiva for ya.'

Phitt beamed and with a stubby forefinger tapped the side of his nose, the colour of which, clearly indicated where the Lady Godiva would be spent.

'You just foller me in 'ere and 'ang on while I find aht.'

They followed him into the building with Hallett looking quite baffled.

When the commissionaire had gone to inquire at an impressive leather fronted desk, Hallett turned to Fred. 'What on earth was all that about?'

'Just a question of 'when in Rome', squire.'

'How do you mean?'

'Well, I spoke his language, see?'

'No, I'm afraid I don't see. And what on earth did you say to him?'

'I told him that my old china, that's you – china plate, mate – wanted to see Porch and we didn't want to be tiddlers, – tiddler's bait, late, see? I said that we didn't know if he was just round the

71

Johnny, that's Johnny Horner – corner, or up the apples, – apples and pears, stairs.'

'What was that you offered him, then?'

'A Lady Godiva.'

'A fiver?'

Fred smiled. 'You're catching on, squire.'

Hallett still looked baffled as he shook his head.

A few minutes later Phitt returned from the desk and stood in front of Fred.

'Major Porch, Noo Look Investments Incorporated, fird floor, room firty ate.'

'Fanks, mate,' said Fred and offered a five pound note. 'Have this one on me.'

'Ta, guv, you're a sport and no mistake.'

The computer controlled lift carried them quickly and noiselessly to the third floor and they walked out into a wide, expensively carpeted corridor. They checked the door numbers.

'Here we are, squire, room thirty-eight.'

He knocked, they walked in and found themselves in a small, but expensively furnished office, with the wall to wall carpet carried on from the corridor. By the door marked "Managing Director" was a desk complete with trays, pen holders, note-pads and a huge white blotting pad. Behind the desk sat a smartly dressed man with thick black hair and a black drooping moustache. He peered at them through his large black-framed spectacles.

'Good morning, may I help you?'

'Good morning. My name is Simon Hallett and this is Frederick Root. We are here by arrangement with your Mr Porch.'

The man smiled. 'Of course, I remember it now. I have a note here.'

He consulted a leather bound book. 'Ah, yes, here it is. Colonel Hallett and colleague, to meet MD at eleven o'clock.'

He smiled again. 'My name is Rogers and I run the administration here. Please sit down; the Major will be out in a moment.'

Fred sat down in one of the very comfortable armchairs but

Hallett remained standing in front of the desk and was studying Rogers carefully.

'Have we met somewhere before? I have a feeling that I have made your acquaintance previously.'

Rogers looked up slowly and was about to reply when the Managing Director's door opened and Porch walked out talking over his shoulder. 'Very well, Sir Gerald, I understand. I will attend to that and it will be ready for you when you return from America.'

He closed the door, turned and saw his visitors.

'Colonel, how nice to see you again and it's Mr Root, isn't it?'

Fred nodded.

Hallett beamed and they shook hands warmly.

'My dear fellow,' said Hallett, 'allow me to thank you for arranging this meeting for Root and myself.' He nodded at the Managing Director's door. 'Is your MD free?'

Porch frowned. 'I'm sorry to have to tell you, but Sir Gerald has unexpectedly been tied up with a meeting of investors prior to his trip to America. He has to go there because of numerous enquiries from Americans about our restored buildings.'

Hallett looked disappointed. 'What time do you think he will be free, then?'

'Hard to say, really. There's quite a lot of talking going on.'

He waved his hand towards a far wall where, on a row of coat hooks, they could see about a dozen assorted raincoats, hats and umbrellas.

'Look, I'll see if I can have a quick word with him when I take the Kent figures for him to see.'

'Good man, Martin. Give him my compliments and ask if he could spare me a few minutes.'

'Right, Colonel, I'll do what I can.'

He picked up a manila folder from the desk and tapped on the door. He walked in, and as he did so, the murmur of many voices drifted through to Hallett and Fred.

They sat down and flicked without much interest through some building trade magazines. As Hallett was halfway through an article on how to transform your windows with wrought-ironwork, the door opened and Porch walked out smiling.

'Well,' he said, closing the door behind him. 'Good news. Sir Gerald has said that if I find you acceptable, then that's good enough for him. Quite a feather in my cap, really.'

He looked towards the desk and snapped his fingers impatiently at Rogers who was reading a document.

'Leave that, Rogers, and make a note of this.'

Rogers obediently picked up a pen, drew a pad towards him and sat waiting.

Porch cleared his throat pompously. 'I am happy to tell you that we can accept an investment from each of you of four thousand pounds. That is our limit. The project is a restoration just outside London which is really very fortunate because they give the best returns and usually, they give a quicker return.'

Rogers scribbled away in his note-pad then sat waiting.

Hallett smiled broadly. 'Well done, Martin. I knew you could do it.'

'Thank you. I will send you a copy of the letter I have just dictated.'

'Now, when would you like my cheque?'

Porch's voice became conspiratorial. 'I think I had better explain, Colonel. In the interest of speed and the chance for us all to avoid tiresome taxes, we process most of our investments in cash. In fact, I must confess that I have told my MD that you have already agreed to provide cash. I thought that it might help to sway him. I hope you don't mind. You will, of course, be fully safeguarded throughout the whole process. I will make myself personally responsible for keeping you informed of events as they progress and your receipt will be authenticated by a Chartered Accountant.'

'Well, that sounds fair enough to me. How about you, Root?'

'I'm with you, squire. Say where and when and I'll fix it.'

'Well that's that then. When would you like the cash, Martin? It may take a day or so to arrange.'

'Shall we say back here on Friday. Is that all right with you?'

'Friday it is then. We'll be here.'

'Good, I'll have all the papers ready for you.'

They turned to go and Hallett stared again at Rogers. 'I wish

I could remember where I have met you before.'

Porch snapped his fingers. 'But of course; you were in the Birnshires, weren't you, Rogers?'

'Yes, that's right, Major.'

Hallett nodded contentedly. 'That's it then. That's where I must have met you. Yes, I think it's coming back to me now. Well, well, what a strange coincidence.'

'We'll see you and Mr Root on Friday then, Colonel?'

'Right. Same time?'

'That will do fine. Good-bye for now.'

Having said their good-byes, they left the office with Hallett remarking to Fred how extraordinary it was to meet up with a member of one's own regiment in these circumstances. He was still trying to recall precisely where they had met, when the lift doors opened at the ground floor.

With a nod to Phitt that was acknowledged with a broad wink, they strode out of the glass front doors and over to the car park.

'Well,' said Hallett as they settled themselves into the car, 'I believe we are on our way to making a nice little profit. Very capable sort of chap, Porch, very self-assured, don't you agree?'

Fred nodded as he turned the ignition key to start the engine. 'Oh yes, squire. In fact, I think he's very capable.'

CHAPTER SIX

'More tea, Fred?'

'No thanks, Glad. I must be thinking about moving soon.'

'Have you put your briefcase in the car yet?'

'No, I've got it in my bureau. I'll get it now and check it over.'

Fred walked from the kitchen into the sitting room and crossed to his bureau-bookcase. He slid open the door at the bottom and pulled out his black, executive briefcase. Placing it on the coffee table he flicked the locks open. Inside he made a rapid check of the bundles of bank notes he had drawn the day before.

'That's it. Four thousand quid exactly. Wouldn't do to make a mistake at this stage. Lovely, sight, isn't it?'

'Oh, Fred, you will be careful, won't you.'

'You know me, Glad, I'm always careful.'

He closed the lid and snapped the locks shut. 'Time to go now. I'll see you later, love.'

'Bye, Fred. Come back safe.'

'Always do.'

Their mantra having been dealt with, Fred picked up his case and walked through the hall and out on to his drive where he saw Hallett walking towards his car carrying a battered briefcase.

'Morning, squire. Would you like me to put your case in the boot with mine?'

'Morning, Root. Yes, good idea. Can't be too careful, can we.'

Fred fitted a key and the sprung boot-lid yawned open. They stowed their cases inside and the lid was pressed shut.

Hallett looked anxiously at Fred. 'Root. We are doing the

right thing aren't we?' His normal, self-assured demeanour had left him. He seemed almost vulnerable.

Fred smiled and clapped him on the shoulder 'Yes, of course we are. You'll see; it'll all work out fine. Remember, fortune favours the brave.'

They set off in the car and after a few miles, Hallett seemed to have recovered his old confidence. He spent most of the journey telling Fred of his experiences in the Army, but Fred could detect, in his relating of the sometimes pointless reminiscences, that Hallett was disguising an uncharacteristic nervousness.

Eventually, Fred saw a direction sign. 'There's a big roundabout coming up, squire. I think we're almost there.'

A few minutes later they drove into the car park and parked between two opulent looking limousines. Fred went to the back of the car and recovered the two cases. Handing the much travelled case to Hallett, he locked the door of his car and they walked to the office block carrying their expensively loaded cases.

At the main entrance they met commissionaire Harold Phitt once more.

'Mornin', chummy, remember us?'

'Allo, guv. Course I remember you. You 'ere to see that geezer again?'

'That's right. Got the time on you?'

Phitt reached into his tunic and withdrew an ancient pocket watch. 'Nearly eleven I make it.'

'Time we was there, then. Tell me; anybody else asking for this Porch bloke?'

'Yer, quite a few. The last one was a big feller wiv ginger 'air and wearing a tweedy sort of titfer. Very serious lookin' boat-race, I noticed.'

Fred looked thoughtful and nodded. 'I see. Fanks, mate, you've been very 'elpful.' Phitt's eyes lit up as he took Fred's five-pound note.

'Your very good 'ealth, guv.'

Fred nodded and he and Hallett walked to the lift. Hallett pressed the button for the third floor then looked at Fred.

'Could you, perhaps, give me a brief interpretation of all that.'

'Easy, squire. Titfer is hat, tit for tat and boat-race is face, see?'

'Thank you, I think I'm beginning to get the idea.'

The lift stopped at the third floor and they were soon outside the offices of New Look Enterprises Incorporated. Fred tapped the door and they walked in.

Both Martin Porch and Rogers were there. Rogers was seated at the desk and Porch was standing by his side reading a legal-style document. Porch looked up.

'Oh, good morning, Colonel. Morning, Mr Root. Pleased to see you both again. Please excuse me, I have almost completed the check of your contract.'

He looked down at the contract again and read aloud.

'In the event that the stated financial return is not paid to the investor during a period not exceeding twelve calendar months from the date of signature of the said investor, the company will pay the said investor, an interim return of not less than twenty percent of the sum invested pending the payment of further moneys from the said investment.'

He straightened up. 'All right, Rogers, that's fine. Now just prepare them for signature.'

'Not too early are we, Martin?'

'Not at all, sir. The document I was just reading is your positive guarantee if, for instance, there was a delay in achieving a return within telve months. Please take a seat and we will soon be ready to sign the necessary documents.'

'We have the cash for the investments here, ready and waiting. Would you care to check it now?'

'To be honest, I always feel slightly embarrassed having to check instead of taking someone's word, but I am sure you will understand.'

'Yes, of course, my dear chap. Here's mine.'

'And mine.'

Porch accepted the two cases and was soon skimming expertly through the layered notes. After a short while he announced he was satisfied.

'Well now, shall we look at the contracts and see if the wording is acceptable to you.'

He snapped his finger at Rogers who handed a large document each to Fred and Hallett.

Fred looked at his contract and frowned. 'By the left, squire, this might as well be in Greek for all it means to me.'

Hallett did not reply but appeared to be absorbed in his reading of the contract.

There followed a long silence broken only by the rustle of paper as they turned the pages.

Hallett looked up, frowning. 'Martin, will you permit me a few questions of clarification on this?'

Porch darted a quick glance at Rogers then smiled.

'But of course, sir. Which part is giving you cause for concern?'

'Quite frankly, the whole of this document is giving me cause for concern,' said Hallett, in a solemn voice. The truth was, that so far, he had understood almost none of it. But he could hardly admit that and he now hoped that Porch might translate it for him.

'If you'll permit me, Colonel, I'll get my copy so that we can go through it together and I will try to answer your questions.'

He walked round the desk, opened a drawer, rummaged around for a while then drew out a document and flicked through the pages.

'Now, where shall we start?'

Before Hallett could reply, the door was thrown open and in strode a purposeful looking man wearing a long fawn raincoat and a black homburg.

'Just a moment!' he cried, dramatically.

They all turned to stare at him.

He walked towards Hallett and Fred and flashed a card.

'Sorry about this, gentlemen. I'm Detective Sergeant Fryer of the CID and I've had these men under observation for some time. You were about to be taken in by them.'

He turned to Porch and Rogers. 'You are both under arrest and I must ask you to accompany me to the Police Station. You do not have to say anything but it may harm your defence if you do not mention, when questioned, something which you later rely on in court. Anything you do say may be given in evidence.'

'You are making a big mistake,' said Porch, angrily. He turned to Hallett. 'I assure you that this is all some ridiculous mix-up. This fool of a policeman is going to regret this.'

'All right. That'll be enough from you. Let's go, both of you.'

He led the way to the door picking up the two packages of money as he did so. He paused at the door and spoke to Hallett.

'I will just hand these two villains over to my colleagues together with the evidence, then I will return and give you a receipt. After which, I will ask you both to make a statement.'

'I see,' said Hallett, but he looked baffled as he stared at Rogers and Porch.

Detective Sergeant Fryer opened the door and jerked his head towards it as an indication for his prisoners to get moving. The three men moved out of the office with Porch and Rogers loudly protesting their innocence.

The door closed and Fred quickly crossed the room and searched near the drawer from which Porch had taken the contract.

'Ah, just as I thought. A bell-push fitted just by the drawer and connected, no doubt, to another office.'

'What do you mean, a bell-push and another office?'

'This is how Porch managed to get his detective friend to come in at just the right moment.'

'Detective friend? Do you mean that detective was a friend of his?'

'He was no detective, squire. He's a crook like the phoney Major Porch and his little friend, Rogers, or whatever their real names are.'

Hallett slumped back into his chair. 'Root, please, I am getting confused. Do I understand you to mean that the three of them are felons?'

'They are what is commonly called con men or confidence tricksters. They invent a plausible story involving a lucrative investment, invite someone to put up some money, then make off with it.'

Hallett looked thoughtful. 'I must say I find that...' he

stopped and looked alarmed. 'But, if all three are in it they have just made off with our money.'

Fred smiled. 'No chance of that, squire. They'll be back, you'll see.'

A few seconds later the door opened and in walked Porch, Rogers and Fryer. Hallett strode forward and was about to deliver one of his military reprimands when he saw that there was a fourth man with them. He was tall, with startling ginger hair. He wore a raincoat and a tweed hat worn at a jaunty angle.

'You must be Colonel Hallett, sir.'

'I am he.' He turned to Fred. 'And this is Mr Root, my next door neighbour.'

'Hello, Fred.'

'Hello, Ginger.'

Hallett stared. 'You two know each other?'

'That's right, squire. This is Detective Inspector Arnold Bell, better known to all his colleagues as Ginger.'

Porch and his two companions had grouped themselves by the desk and were looking uncomfortable.

'Tell me, Inspector, how did you manage to apprehend these men so quickly?'

'I think I'll let Mr Root explain that to you, sir. First I will deal with these three.' He faced them. 'I am arresting you on suspicion of perpetrating a fraud and impersonating a police officer.' He completed the caution then turned to Fred. 'I'll get statements from both of you, then we'll get this money sorted out.' He indicated the two packages he was carrying.

'All right, Ginger. Neat piece of timing. Well done.'

'Thanks for your help, Fred. Bit like old times, wasn't it?'

Fred nodded.

They filed from the office, down the corridor and into the lift.

It was now about three in the afternoon. Root and Hallett had left the Police Station and were sitting in a small café attending to some very welcome tea and cakes.

'There,' said Fred, 'that's another three villains put away for a while.'

'Well, I can't say that I feel any regrets about what happens to them.'

'No need to, squire. Those three knew what they were doing; but they won't be conning anyone else for some time.'

Hallett set down his cup. 'You know, Root, this has all happened so fast, I feel that I haven't quite grasped the whole situation. Can you tell me how it all happened?'

Fred poured a measure of milk into his cup, added his customary half-spoon of sugar and poured his second cup of tea.

'Well, it was like this, squire. When I first saw Porch at your house I was just a bit suspicious of him as things began to happen.'

'Really? But he seemed genuine enough to me.'

'Yes, but take the telephone call he made to a local garage to fix his car.'

'That's right, he telephoned and a man came round to fix it.'

'So he did. But, if you remember Porch's conversation, he made no mention of your address, but the garage man found his way there all right.'

'I can't say that I recall the conversation with any sort of precision. But, in any case, he may have given the address at the start of the call. We were all talking together as I recollect.'

'Maybe he did,' admitted Fred. 'But do you remember, then, the businesslike way he went into your hall and made his call?'

'Yes, I remember at the time I was struck by his brisk, efficient manner.'

'Except that he was so brisk and efficient, that, although he came from the Midlands, he knew which local garage to call, and he knew their number because he went to the telephone and dialled straight away.'

Hallett looked thoughtful as he reached for a coconut macaroon which normally, he would tell Elizabeth not to even offer to him, because he hated the horrid, bitty little things. He thought deeply as he chewed his way through his first ever coconut macaroon. 'Do you know, that had quite escaped my attention. Was there anything else?'

'One or two things, squire. Do you remember when his car was repaired and the two of you came into the garden to meet the garage repairman?'

'Yes, but what was suspicious about that?'

'The garage man spoke to Porch and said he had fixed his car. But, how did he know which of you was Porch? It could have been you.'

Hallett had started on his second coconut macaroon. He thought for a moment. 'Ah, but if you remember, though, Porch was all dressed up and I was in my casual outfit of old corduroys and so on.'

'True,' said Fred, looking to see what cakes were left and rejecting a plain fairy cake with a cherry on top. 'But on the telephone, he didn't say he was a visitor, or that he had broken down in front of someone's house.'

'Yes, that is true. It was very careless of him.'

'I'm sure you recall that you thought you had met Rogers before.'

'Yes. I'm sorry that an ex-Birnshires man could get himself mixed up in something like this.' He looked hopefully at Fred. 'If he really was in the Birnshires, that is.'

Fred grinned. 'Well, if he was, he was wearing an RAF tie.'

Hallett's face clouded at having missed this clue.

'But it wasn't in the Army that you met him, squire. It was outside your house. He was the garage mechanic who pretended to fix Porch's car, but in the office he was wearing a wig and a false moustache.'

'You mean he was the same man? But how did you spot him?'

Fred shrugged. 'I took a chance there; but to me, it seemed that his hair didn't match his eyebrows.'

Hallett scowled and then he brightened.

'Well, at least he didn't serve in my old regiment.'

'I should be surprised if he served anywhere except Dartmoor and places like that.'

'Even so,' said Hallett, deciding that he might as well finish the last cake but was too late as Fred had just changed his mind about the little fairy cake. 'Even so, these are all minor points and I expect that you substantiated them in some way.'

'As a matter of fact, squire, there were quite a few more points they had overlooked.'

'Such as?'

'For example. Porch said he was in the Royal Hamlington Regiment, right?'

'Yes.'

'Well, the first time we visited his office I deliberately wore a Royal Hamlington Regimental tie that I bought for the occasion.'

'Yes, I can just recall that. It had a dragon on it.'

'That's right. I saw Porch look at it but he never flickered. In other words he didn't recognise the tie of the regiment he was supposed to have served in.'

'I see. Anything else?'

'Yes, the office we visited. I found through a telephone call I made from home that it was rented for just two weeks.'

'But why two weeks when it could have been done in a few days?'

'Because, I suspect we weren't the only mugs they had lined up, and, through a tight programme, they were interviewing others and preparing them for fleecing.'

'And that clinched it, eh? Good work on your part, Root.'

Hallett picked up his cup and finished his tea. Suddenly, he banged down his cup with such vigour that he received many admonishing stares from his fellow diners enjoying their tea and cakes. But he would have ignored their stares even if he had noticed them.

'Root, there is something we have overlooked. Do you recall when we visited Porch's office for the first time, there were about a dozen hats and coats hanging in the outer office. And, from the Managing Director's office we could hear the sound of a number of people speaking. Should we contact your friend, Bell?'

Fred shook his head. 'Just another prop, squire. All those hats, coats and brollies belong to Porch and his mates. They just keep them for this sort of deception. But they let themselves down, though. You see, all of the building we saw was decorated to a very high standard. In their office it was all good class stuff. But the coats were hung up on cheap, stick-on plastic hooks and they didn't seem to go with the general decor. It was important, though, for them to display the coats and I daresay they had to buy those in a hurry.'

'But what about the voices we heard.'

'Tape recorder switched on, no doubt, by their fake detective.'

'Maybe. But there were more than three voices we heard and, if you say there were only three of them, how did that work?'

'Simple. You use two recorders. First you record the three of you mumbling and murmuring, then you set the other recorder to record and, while you play back the first recording, you do some more mumbling and murmuring. You can keep on repeating this until you have the effect you want.'

'That's very ingenious. One more thing, though. How could you know that the first detective was a fake? He could have been sent by your colleague, Bell, couldn't he?' finished Hallett triumphantly.

Fred shook his head. 'No chance, squire. And there were two good reasons why I knew he was a fake. One, he arrested them without telling them the charge, and two, he didn't wait for the fraud to be committed. Up to then, no-one had stolen anything and an arrest at that point could have been a waste of time.'

'I see.'

'But, any doubts I might have had about this project being crooked, vanished when you challenged the contract. That really threw Porch into a spin and he was forced to fall back on his emergency plan. That is, if anything goes wrong, press the buzzer, in comes his mate, arrests them and they make off with the evidence and leave us sitting there. Good job you spotted the flaws in the contract.'

'Eh? Oh well, you know, one does what one thinks is best in the circumstances. Of course, you had already arranged for your friend Bell to be there?'

'Yes, I told him the plot and he warned me what might happen. I was content to leave the rest to him. He's a very experienced copper is Ginger Bell.'

'Tell me, Root,' his voice was softer that usual, 'did it never occur to you to back out of this altogether? After all, it was just my lack of thought that had landed me in that situation and there was really no need for you to take a risk.'

'Well, the way I saw it, squire, if we didn't stop Porch and his mates, they would get someone else who wasn't, perhaps, as wise to them as we were.'

'Very useful your knowing a detective like that. Known him long?'

'Ever since my market days. We got acquainted because the market was on his beat. And, from time to time I was able to tell him of my suspicions about various activities. We became quite good friends.'

Now visibly more relaxed, Hallett, leaned back in his chair. 'From what you have said I think you would have made a good policeman yourself. You're very observant.'

'Well, when you stand behind a stall all day, squire, you find that you take an interest in people and what's going on around you.'

'Yes, I see. Well, I think we had better start for home, it's been quite a day.'

Fred reached for the bill but Hallett beat him to it. 'Please allow me to pay that.'

'Just as you like, squire. Thanks for the treat.'

When they pulled into the drive of Fred's house, he could see Gladys peering anxiously out of the window. In a few seconds she was out of the door to welcome him.

'Everything all right, Fred?'

'Yes. Of course, Glad. It was as I suspected, one big con trick, but we got all three of them and they are all in the nick now.'

He looked across and saw Elizabeth hurrying towards them. 'Oh, there you are, Simon. I've been so worried. Is everything all right?'

Before Hallett could reply, Fred spoke.

'Yes, it's all right now, Elizabeth. You see, me and the Colonel knew we were dealing with villains but we couldn't tell you ladies because you might have given it away if someone had telephoned. So, we had to play it for real and that way we caught them. There were three of them in it and they're now in the hands of the police.'

She looked so relieved that Fred felt that the whole operation had been worthwhile.

'Look, squire, why don't you and Elizabeth come in for a celebration drink. I'm sure I could do with one. How about it?'

'Splendid idea, lead the way.'

The two ladies went ahead, chattering in a very animated way now that the tension had been relieved.

Hallett hung back. He looked at Fred. 'You know, Root, you really are a most extraordinary chap.' He paused. 'And, thank you.'

'Don't mention it, squire. You know, you're not so bad yourself.'

They smiled as they joined the ladies.

CHAPTER SEVEN

'I don't know about you, Root, but I found that interview to be a worse ordeal than actually dealing with those confidence tricksters.'

Hallett and Root had just left the offices of a local newspaper after giving an interview on their experience with Porch and his 'partners in crime' as Hallett now called them.

'I think I'm with you there, squire. I don't think I've ever had to answer so many questions before. Anyway, let's hope that's the end of it. Are you going back home now?'

'Not straight away, no. Elizabeth has asked me to get a few items of shopping for her. That reminds me, where did I put that list?'

He searched through his pockets and brought out a folded piece of paper. 'Ah, this is it.' He unfolded the paper then unfolded it again then again. 'A few items?' His voice was almost falsetto. 'A few items? There must be enough supplies on here to keep us for a month. A few items indeed.' He snorted.

Fred smiled. 'Better leave you you to it, then; but I should hurry if I were you. It looks like rain coming on. See you later.'

'Yes, see you later when I have completed this restocking exercise that Elizabeth has organised.' He looked again at the list then started the task of shopping. This was a task which, unquestionably, rated a fairly high position on his mental list of 'Jobs I Dislike Doing'.

As he arrived at the first shop he looked up and frowned at the ominous looking sky. It was heavy, and with the chance, in fact, almost the guarantee, of rain soon. Hallett had neglected, against Elizabeth's advice, to take his raincoat with him. His confident forecast to her that rain was hours away, had now come home to roost. He sighed and started his shopping. He had just finished his shopping when the rain started. He bundled the plastic shopping bags onto the back seat and climbed quickly into the car. The rain started in earnest as he headed for Forsythia Avenue.

In Forsythia Avenue, the rain poured down in a steady, seemingly never-ending torrent. It was not a day to venture out without raincoat, hat, wellingtons and, for the over cautious, an umbrella.

Parked on the road outside his house, Hallett sat in his car gloomily surveying the sodden scene. He was not in the best of moods, what with the enforced shopping marathon, the rain and because he had again, bumped over that pothole just a few yards from his house. He was well aware that it was there, in fact, it seemed to him that it had always been there. Unfortunately, Hallett never remembered to steer round it and, as if all that was not enough, now this near-tropical downpour.

He had stopped outside the house because he had originally intended to take in the shopping, and then, after collecting his library books, drive down to the Public Library to see if "Great Tacticians of Our Time" had yet been returned. Now he regretted the lack of his usual foresight and planning. Stopping outside the house was a mistake. By the time he scampered up the drive, he and the shopping in its two bulging plastic carrier bags would be soaked. Well, *he* would, anyway. He should have driven straight up the drive, but no, instead of that, here he was, parked outside on the right-hand side of the road. Well, nothing else for it but to reverse up the drive to his kitchen door. No sooner had he decided on this plan of action, than it was rejected. Firstly, his visibility was limited, secondly, he was not very good at reversing at the best of times, and these were most certainly not the best of times. What he must do now is to reverse and steer towards the middle of the road to allow enough room for him to drive the front of the car through the gate. He reversed a short distance, then steered the car through his gateway and slowly up the drive until he was almost opposite the kitchen door.

He switched off the engine, unbuckled his seat belt, turned to the back seat and set about returning his shopping to the two carrier bags in which they had started their journey. He cursed silently as a few tomatoes proved difficult to round up. Turning further he lunged at the wayward items and at last managed to propel them into a paper bag which he then placed in one of the carrier bags. Carefully, he lifted the two bags over and rested them on the passenger seat. As he had no raincoat with him he would have to make a brisk dash to the door. Suddenly, it came to him. Elizabeth had bought him an umbrella last Christmas, but he had put it in the car because it was one of the retractable models and he secretly disapproved of them. He wanted an umbrella that looked and acted like an umbrella. But, whether he liked or disliked retractable umbrellas was of no consequence when he realised that to get out the car with two carrier bags, would not permit him the luxury of an umbrella. The answer was, of course, never mind the umbrella, just grab the two bags, get out and round the car as quickly as possible.

He lifted the two bags and, by briefly supporting both bags with one arm, managed to push open the car door and swing his legs out. The prevailing wind ensured that its direction was such, that the moment the car door was opened, a substantial shower of rain was blown into the interior. This was greeted by a barked curse from Hallett who had taken most of it in the face. Struggling with the difficulty of having to get out of the car with both arms full he at last managed to stand upright and shut the door with his knee. He hurried round to the kitchen door and, again clutching both bags with one arm, seized the door handle. To his surprise and annoyance he found that it wouldn't open. There was no question about it, he was locked out of his own house.

'Who the blazes has done this?' he asked the door, fiercely.

His only move now, he decided, was to use the front door and he trotted through the rain round to the front of the house.

Built onto the front was a porch, the lower half of which was constructed of white bricks and the top half of dark reddish wood fitted with panes of lightly tinted glass. Hallett had never really liked it, but Elizabeth had found it an ideal place in which to display and develop her pot plants. Hallett once more clasped the two bags to his chest with one arm and wrenched at the door handle. Not only did this, too, refuse to budge, but the combination of rain and repeated huggings of the sacks had caused the bag of tomatoes to be partly pulped and the resultant mess was making its appearance through a slit in the carrier bag and onto his jacket.

'Damn and blast it,' he shouted, and risked further pulping of the tomatoes by letting go with one hand once more and using his free hand to pound on the door. At that moment he heard his wife's voice from the kitchen door.

'Simon, is that you?'

He snorted and squelched round the house again ready to blast Elizabeth or anyone else in his line of fire for this ridiculous over-zealousness in the simple matter of securing the house. As he rounded the corner he heard the kitchen door close and the click told him that the night lock once more barred his way into his own kitchen. He trotted forward, the shopping preventing a full-blooded run, and, releasing one arm, banged on the glass panel of the kitchen door. The tomatoes were, by now, almost pulp and the stain on his jacket had spread into a dark mess which had formed itself into a blob, roughly the shape of the continent of Africa. Both of the carrier bags were feeling the unexpected strain of tomato pulp, rain and repeated clutchings and both were near to the point of collapse.

Hallett realised that as well as getting soaked to the skin, he risked having two bags of assorted groceries soon cascading down his front and into one of the many puddles round his house.

Angrily, he walked round the car and once more subjected the bags to a one-armed bear hug while his free hand attempted to open the car door. He had just managed to swing it open when the first of the groceries found its way out of the bag and a tin of peach halves thudded perilously close to his foot then rolled under the car.

'Damn and blast it,' he said, for the second time that morning.

He scrambled on his knees into the driver's seat and carefully lowered the sodden packages onto the passenger's seat. Seizing his umbrella from the floor he started to back out into the rain once more.

How it happened he could not say, but he must have touched the release button on the handle of the umbrella. There was a whooshing sound and the car seemed to be full of erected umbrella. He glared at it and tried unsuccessfully to refold it but the button controlling the release mechanism remained obstinate and unco-operative. Reluctantly, he decided to abandon it, but then found that he could not close the car door because the umbrella handle was stuck in the air. He rapidly decided that he did not like automatic umbrellas, he had never liked automatic umbrellas. In fact, he was quite sure that he had made this plain on more than one occasion, but still his family had once more disregarded his wishes and presented him with an umbrella, the opening of which, was gimmicky, unpredictable, dangerous and downright un-British. He snorted his way round the car and marched resolutely through the pouring rain to his kitchen door where, with both hands free, he was able to pound vigorously on the door.

He waited and, hearing nothing, stepped to the window and peered in just in time to see Elizabeth come into the kitchen and stare at the door. Seeing no-one through the reeded glass panel of the door she turned to go. Frantically Hallett rapped on the window and saw her stop and hurry across. Flinging open the window she stared at him as he stood there. His hair was plastered down on all sides and rivulets of rain ran down his face; his clothes were soaked and on his jacket was a large, ominous stain.

'Simon, where on earth have you been?'

'Will you please close that window and open this blasted door.'

Quickly, she closed the window and a few seconds later the door swung open. He stepped inside, closed the door and stood there, a sorry, soaking figure with rain dripping from him onto the mat.

He breathed heavily a few times as he stared at Elizabeth.

She frowned. 'Didn't you take the car?'

Hallett was surprised at his own composure. 'Yes,' he said calmly, 'I did take the car.' The volume increased and he gestured at his sodden clothing. 'I achieved this state merely by getting out of the car and trying to get into my own house.'

'But, why didn't you use your key?'

'How could I use my key when both of my arms were full of shopping?' he exploded.

Elizabeth looked at him wondering what had become of the shopping but was not sure whether she wanted to ask.

He looked down at his now empty arms. 'I mean, of course, that my arms were full of shopping when I arrived but I was forced to return the bags to the car.'

He hoped that she would not pursue the subject of his key because he knew that it was in the pocket of the raincoat that he had neglected to take with him. He was never tired of telling his family to pay some regard to crime prevention and ensure that they always had their keys with them whenever they went out.

'But you had your umbrella.'

Eagerly, he seized the one subject on which he could justifiably, and safely, hold forth. 'That umbrella is at this moment in the car having opened of its own accord and refuses to close again. I have often said that it would happen one day.'

Elizabeth couldn't remember any occasion when he had made this prediction but was wise enough not to continue with the subject. She picked up a towel.

'Well, first, we must get you dry.'

He waved her aside. 'No. Before that I must get the shopping from the car and somehow force that blasted umbrella to close.' He turned. 'And please leave this door open.'

He hurried out through the still driving rain. Crouching in the car he tried to refold the stubborn umbrella and, after a few moments of coaxing, it relented. But still, it would not admit complete defeat, and remained half-open. He pulled it from the car but failed to notice that it had, in his absence, accumulated a small pool of rainwater through the open car door. As he jerked the umbrella forward this spurted out onto his trousers. Even though he was already soaking wet, a stream of cold rainwater down the front of his trousers was most unwelcome and he retaliated with a stream of abuse.

Casting the treacherous umbrella to one side he climbed into the car and recovered his two bags of shopping. With some apprehension for their fragile state he backed slowly out of the car and kneed the door shut. As he did so, he levelled one more charge against the malevolent umbrella. If it had not been so unreliable as to get stuck inside the car, he could have retrieved the shopping from the passengers side quite easily and saved himself the discomfort of having ice-cold water thrown onto his person. Quite clearly, he had not bothered to think this through in detail.

Back in the kitchen he carefully unloaded his cargo onto an adjacent worktop and then stood back on the kitchen mat. Elizabeth busied herself unpacking the bags and, to her credit, made no comment on the tomato pulp she found in one bag.

Hallett, meanwhile, had removed his wet shoes and was drying himself vigorously on a towel. He stopped suddenly.

'Elizabeth; could you please explain to me why our house is barricaded like Fort Knox?'

She smiled. 'Well, as you know, Simon, the porch door is usually locked ever since that time when that awful double-glazing salesman refused to leave and you said that no-one was to be allowed into the porch until we had identified them.'

'Yes, all right. But what about the kitchen door?'

'Well, that was because I was working in another room and you always ask for doors to be locked if we are in a different room. And anyway…'

'Yes, yes. But it took you long enough to answer the door.'

'I know; but it seemed to me, that, as soon as I started to go to one door, someone knocked at the other one.'

Hallett felt that this line of defence was going to be difficult to attack and, in any case, further discussion might lead to the question of the whereabouts of his key. He resumed his vigorous towelling.

When he had dried himself sufficiently he looked up from the towel and his normally tidy grey hair stuck out in spikes giving him a sort of wild, electric look.

'It seems to me,' he said, as he stood with Elizabeth staring out at the relentlessly pouring rain, 'that there must be an answer to getting out of the car in the rain in one's own drive, without getting soaked to the skin in the process.'

94

Elizabeth turned from the window to answer him but her reply was delayed as she gazed at his wild appearance.

'Well, what about...' she paused, then pointed to his hair, 'don't you think you had better comb your hair, Simon?'

'Never mind my hair, what were you going to say?'

'What about a carport?'

He hesitated. The answer was so obvious that he now wished he had never posed the question.

'Er, yes, certainly that is one solution,' he said, his tone giving Elizabeth a mental pat on the back. 'But I'm not sure that the expenditure would be justified.'

'Are they expensive, then?'

He had no real idea of the cost of a carport, never having considered whether or not one was really necessary. He decided to go for the middle ground.

'Well, they're not cheap but I wouldn't think that they could cost too much. After all, there's not much in a carport, is there?'

'No, I suppose not. Do you think we could afford to get a builder in to build one for us?'

'Oh, I hardly think there's any need to call in a man to do a simple job like erecting a carport.'

Hallett always referred to 'calling in a man' whether it was a plumber, electrician or gardener.

To Elizabeth, his words struck a chill. Unless she was mistaken, they meant that he intended to do it himself. This, she knew from experience, would mean a minor disaster where in the end they would have to get someone in to put things right. Also, it was probable that they would eventually pay more than if they had employed a builder in the first place. But, she also knew that there was no point in trying to talk him out of it. 'Well, you know best, dear. I just hope it doesn't start your back trouble again. By the way, are you going to change out of those wet clothes, Simon? We don't want you going down with double pneumonia, do we?'

Deep in thought he walked across the kitchen, his wet socks leaving a clear trail across the tiles.

By the time he returned to the kitchen looking more or less his old self, he had made three important decisions about the carport. It would be a distinct asset, it was very necessary and he would design and build it.

'Elizabeth, I am just going down to the library.'

'Would you wait for just a moment, Simon, I have some books to go back.'

He scowled. He knew that as Elizabeth handed him the books she would ask him to look out for any books he thought suitable for her. Not only did he dislike trying to guess what she would like, he detested having to take books to the librarian bearing titles like "At Last it's Spring", "Her Cavalier Lover" and "The Gypsy's Return". He always took great care to explain to the librarian that they were for his wife, but that young girl with those large, horn-rimmed spectacles always grinned knowingly at him.

Elizabeth came into the kitchen carrying a small pile of books. 'There we are, dear. There are no fines on any of these this time.'

Hallett nodded an acknowledgement. He knew that Elizabeth did not share his unalterable practice of ensuring that books were invariably returned on or before their due date. He would have regarded it as a personal failure if he neglected to return any of his books to the library on time. Elizabeth treated it far more lightly and, over the years, had happily paid a number of small fines. But she knew now that it was a rule of Simon's to refuse to take back overdue books. He was quite firm that he would not be a party to this sort of sloppy behaviour. It had been a great source of embarrassment to him on one visit to the library when he was told that "The Gondolier and The Lady" was two weeks overdue and a fine was imposed. He hastily explained that his wife had borrowed the book. Then, in his confusion, decided that this might be interpreted to mean that she had borrowed it from him after he had finished it. So, he went on to explain that he meant that his wife had borrowed it from the library. The Chief Librarian, Mrs Ellis, had naturally assumed that anyway and began to get confused. She wondered if another Branch was involved. But it was all sorted out eventually and Hallett was asked to pay the fine.

He had reached into his pocket and found that he was

wearing his gardening trousers where, not only was there no money, there was hardly any pocket lining. He blurted out that he had no money with him but that he would return with the fine just as quickly as he could. At this point Mrs Ellis insisted on calling to her young, bespectacled assistant and explaining that there was a fine to pay on "The Gondolier and The Lady" and this gentleman would be bringing in the fine later on. The assistant looked up, recognised him, then shook her head slowly giving him a knowing grin.

Simon Hallett scowled at the memory as he picked up the books.

'Are you certain that none of these is overdue?'

Elizabeth smiled and nodded. 'I checked them all personally.'

'Good. I will return these and if, by chance, I happen to stumble across any books you might like, I will bring them for you.'

'Oh, thank you, Simon. The last few you chose were really good. You are a darling.'

While Hallett did not appear to notice this endearment it did in fact give him a warm glow of pleasure. He would sometimes reflect on his home life and had formed the contented conclusion many years ago that, although it may not show to the rest of the world, he considered that he was a very fortunate man. However, he would find it difficult if he had to put any of this into words.

Elizabeth watched him as he buttoned his car coat. He refused to wear these ridiculous, padded, fur-collared, zip-up garments. He insisted on a car coat that looked like a car coat and not a garment that looked like the first stage of a space-suit. He let himself out of the door and, as she watched, he climbed into the car, started the engine, switched on the windscreen wipers and reversed slowly down the drive. He had not gone far when he bumped over something, stopped and climbed out. He picked it up and marched back to the kitchen door. He walked in holding a squashy, yellowish mess between finger and thumb and dropped it into the waste bin.

'Blasted peach halves.' He said. Then he was on his way to the library.

Behind the reception desk in the library, Lorna Goodbody

made her regular but unknowing adjustment of her large horn-rimmed spectacles and gloomily resumed her contemplation of the scene before her. At the reference section a pale-faced young man in a faded tweed suit and deer-stalker cap was busily making notes from an encyclopaedia. Presumably, because he was vague about the exact nature of the information he required, he had spread round him the whole set of thirty-five volumes built into rather precarious columns. For quite a long time now he had been writing at the same steady pace and Lorna idly wondered if he was trying to save himself the price of a set of encyclopaedias by copying out the entire volumes. No, perhaps not. Next to him was an old, professorial looking man who was checking some yellowed sheets of paper against the pages of an imposing looking book that seemed to be at least four inches thick. Other readers and browsers were dotted around the room and an air of studious quiet was observed.

Lorna gave a sigh, adjusted her spectacles again and was about to turn away when she saw a regular library user enter through the double glass doors. What was his name? It was something to do with stars, wasn't it? No. It was something about a comet. Halley? No, it was Hallett, that was it.

Hallett walked to the reception desk and put down the stack of books that had been his and Elizabeth's reading matter for the past two weeks.

Lorna flicked expertly through them. 'All clear, Mr Hallett,' she announced with a smile.

Hallett nodded. He had never become accustomed to being addressed by the title of 'Mister'.

'Thank you. Tell me, has "Great Tacticians of Our Time" been returned yet?'

"Great Tacticians of Our Time"? Oh yes, it came in yesterday afternoon. Do you know,' she continued, with a twinkle in her eye, 'when I first heard the title I thought it was all about those men who do the signalling of odds at race meetings.'

This was by way of a little joke to while away the time, but Lorna Goodbody was disappointed to see that he just looked puzzled.

'Really, how interesting.' He paused, thought about it again, then gave a brief nod and wandered off to the Fiction Section to choose something for Elizabeth and wondering how it was possible for anyone to confuse military expertise with horse racing.

He made his search round and round the fiction shelves reading countless descriptions of books from the publishers' blurb. He rejected many books for describing stories that were, in his opinion, so banal that he refused to subject his wife's intellect to the tedium of ploughing through what amounted to mindless drivel. Some he rejected because of lewd sounding titles and others because of outrageously suggestive illustrations on the cover. He was instantly disgusted by one colourful cover showing a girl in ragged clothes apparently begging this man not to beat her. The man was an evil looking swine with a thin, black moustache and a cruel mouth set in a pitiless sneer. The girl was crouched in front of him, her arms outstretched in supplication, while he stood over her brandishing a riding crop. Not only was the whole atmosphere most distasteful, but, in addition, the victim's skirt had been artfully torn to reveal her long, shapely legs and her blouse ripped open just enough to show a glimpse of her ample breasts. But, worse than that; the evil coward was dressed in the uniform of a British Officer! That particular volume was thrust back onto the shelf with vigour.

Eventually he completed his selection for Elizabeth and started on the Do-It-Yourself Section.

In this section it seemed that there were books on every aspect of doing it yourself and it was necessary now for Hallett to seek and locate the type of book he required. A book giving step-by-step instructions on how to design and build a carport.

He worked his way patiently past books on Electricity, Plumbing, Tiling, How to Convert to Coloured Windows, Bricklaying, Greenhouse Design and Construction, Crazy Paving and Patio Design, but nothing yet on carports. He saw a book that indicated that it would tell its reader everything needed to be known about carpentry. This seemed a promising start and he carried the book eagerly to the tables in the Reference Section. He settled himself comfortably and opened the book to see if a complete knowledge of carpentry included the skill needed in erecting a carport. The first glance was not promising but he continued his examination of the book.

The first three chapters he skimmed through were long, plodding and irritatingly detailed instructions on the selection, sharpening and general care of tools. He had never realised what a variety of saws were available and the care in choosing a hammer was made to sound akin to choosing your lifelong companion. The author had pleaded with his readers to be sure, really sure, that this hammer is for you. Does it feel that it is yours even before you buy it? Do you think that the both of you can work happily together? It was at this point, Hallett decided to skip that chapter altogether. The following two chapters concerned themselves with choosing the right wood for the job and gave rapturous descriptions of the colour, texture, strength and characteristics of the various woods available. The enthusiastic writer had again waxed lyrical and made it sound like the appraisal of an expensive menu. 'Look at the long, straight grain with its warm, almost sensuous glow', he enthused. Hallett sighed heavily and was obviously nearing the end of his patience. Next followed general chapters on building a shed to work in, a bench on which to work, and instructions on how to construct a tool rack to hold all of your so carefully chosen tools. Finally, there was a chapter on how to put all of this knowledge and skill to a practical test. Eagerly, Hallett turned the page and read the chapter heading: "How to Build a Sturdy Bird House for Your Garden".

He gave an impatient snort and slammed the book shut which caused several raised heads among the browsers, some of whom gave a few quiet 'shushes'. He seized the book, marched back to the Do-It-Yourself Section and returned "Carpentry For The Householder" to the shelf. As he pushed it into a vacant slot his eye was caught by a colourful book entitled, rather pompously, "Improve Your House – My Way". He took it from the shelf.

The cover showed two coloured drawings. One was an ancient cottage and the other showed the cottage after the author had, presumably, improved it his way. He had miraculously turned the ugly looking cottage with its tiny windows into an attractive house with large picture windows. Somehow, though, the building seemed to have increased its length by about ten feet and it looked a good deal higher than before. In addition, it had acquired a further half acre of immaculately cultivated garden. But, and most important of all, it now boasted a smart carport holding a dark blue, executive looking limousine.

Hurriedly, he turned the pages to the list of contents and read his way through titles of chapters dealing with rejuvenating kitchens, uplifting lounges, adding patios, designing fishponds and eventually he arrived at a chapter entitled, "A Carport – Why Not?" Eagerly he turned to that chapter and after a brief scrutiny decided that it would suit his purpose admirably.

Back at the desk he offered his choices to Miss Goodbody, who flipped through them stamping them with great speed and enthusiasm. When she had finished she looked at the titles again.

'Didn't you find "Great Tic-Tac Men Of Our Time"?' she asked.

'Great Tic-Tac Men...' it dawned on him that she had attempted earlier to be humorous and he had not noticed. He smiled, 'Oh, I see, yes, quite amusing. I'm sorry I didn't see it the first time. In fact, I have quite forgotten to look for the book and thank you for reminding me.'

She favoured him with her big, friendly smile as he turned to go to the Non-Fiction, Military Biographies and Autobiographies, etc., Section, to find the book that had been recommended to him at various points in his military career.

Lorna sighed. Why is it, she thought, that I can flash big smiles at middle-aged men who hardly notice me, but when it comes to my own generation I always keep my face deadly serious. Is it because it might encourage them to be friendly and then get chatting? I suppose it's because I know it could all go wrong so easily and I don't think I want to go through all that again. Not just yet, anyway. She sighed again. Her reluctance to be friendly with her own generation was a pity, really, because Lorna Goodbody was a very apt name for her. But, as she had found, real life was seldom in keeping with the idyllic life found in the romantic novels that her library held in such profusion.

Back home, the rain had now stopped and Hallett took the

books from the car and carried them into the kitchen.

'Elizabeth,' he called.

'Coming, dear.'

In a few moments she hurried into the kitchen where her first task was to glance quickly at her library books to see if she recognised any favourite authors.

'Oh, thank you, Simon, what a good selection.'

He nodded and set about removing his coat and changing into his slippers so that he could settle down comfortably with the book which had promised to teach him how to construct a carport. By now, designing and constructing a carport had assumed the importance of a major military operation and he anticipated the forthcoming activities with some pleasure.

Calling out that he would be in his study if required, he mounted the stairs and settled himself down at his desk in the spare bedroom. He first arranged a pad of paper, two pens – one red, one blue and a ruler. He then carefully adjusted his spectacles and opened the book.

He was now ready to be initiated into the world of carport design and construction.

CHAPTER EIGHT

The first thing Hallett read was the list of chapter headings and it caused him some irritation to find that they were wordy, flippant and hardly an indication of a serious writer applying himself to the important task of imparting his knowledge and skill to his untrained readers. He tutted and sighed his way through such titles as, "Why a Carport and Not a Garage, or Better Still, Why Not Both?", "Getting Our Thoughts on Paper Before We Start" and "Buying Our Wood and Other Essentials Without Going Bankrupt in the Process". The others that followed showed the same chatty approach and he wondered if this frivolous style extended to the body of the text itself. He was annoyed to find that, not only was the style used throughout the book, but that it bordered on the insolent. He frowned on finding such phrases as "otherwise we shall end up making a horse's backside of the whole thing" and "whatever you do, don't take risks when lifting things into position, and, if it looks like you could bust a gut, get your better half to give you a lift".

This is really not good enough, he told himself. If one has had the decency to buy your book, then one is surely entitled to a little courtesy and a little less of this back-slapping familiarity. He had evidently decided to overlook the fact that he had not bought the book but had borrowed it from the library. But even if he had been forced to concede this point, he would still have argued about the uncalled for mateyness of the author, Mr Arnold Beaumont Geesely. However, it was too late to consider anything else now and the sooner one made a start, the sooner the carport would begin to take shape.

He turned the early pages on which were printed details of other books by the discourteous Mr Geesely. These included, in between, "An Idiot's Guide to Home Heating" and "The A to Z of Concreting", the unlikely title, "A Collector's Guide to Seventeenth Century China and Glass". Arnold Beaumont Geesely, it seemed, was not quite the uncultured oaf that Hallett had first assumed. There then followed a short tribute to those who had assisted him in the "My Way" series. Hallett was getting impatient by now and briskly turned one more page to find himself looking at "Chapter One, Getting Our Thoughts on Paper Before We Start."

Eagerly, he started to read. "Right then, where shall we start?" asked Mr Geesely in his breezy style, and immediately provided the answer himself. "At the beginning; what better place?" The author then described at length the desirability of making a detailed plan including a list of required materials, then a list of the various jobs to be done and in what order. He then returned to his one-sided quiz technique. "Do we yet know what we want? How many foot-run of timber or how many foot-super of translucent corrugated plastic? Have I lost you already? Right! Let's get down to an explanation of trade terms and jargon".

Then followed a jocular but useful explanation of the various terms to be used and at the end of this, Hallett felt quite well informed and able to talk business with any DIY dealer. Slowly, he was beginning to warm towards Mr Geesely for taking the trouble to explain in detail and not to take it for granted that we all understood terms like transverse timbers and flashing and so on. This slight easing of their relationship was quickly spoiled when Geesely suddenly launched into a string of rapid questions concerned with whether or not we had considered our screen walls and would they have brick pillars with infill panels? This last question was lost on Hallett who had no idea what a brick pillar with infill panel was, and thus, was, despite his recent tuition in trade terms and jargon, in no position to give an opinion on the selection of an appropriate infill panel. After all, he thought, how can one give an opinion when one has not been given a clear explanation of the rudiments of brick pillaring and infill panelling. Damn and blast the man, he thought; now what am I to do? But all was not lost. Even though the author appeared to assume that the reader understood all his terms so far, his step by step explanation of how to proceed, gradually made it quite clear again. Once more, Hallett began to feel enthusiastic and keen to start.

Not surprisingly, just as he felt that he was making progress and beginning to understand, he suddenly saw Geesely revealed as an uncaring and incompetent instructor by his referring exclusively to metric measurements. To Hallett, this was quite unacceptable and he recalled that he had made the point several times that no good would come of adopting this suspect, continental system of millis, decis and so on. After all, what had it ever done for the French or the Italians or any other continentals? They are just afraid to tackle the complexities of our system, he had maintained firmly over the years. And so, he complained, we are landed with a method that does not even sound British. With this firm opinion, he had over the years paid scant attention to this unfamiliar style of measuring and weighing with the result that the mere mention of metres or kilos threw him into a mild panic that he rapidly disguised as his disgust with the whole system.

Despite his disapproval of his tutor's choice of a measurement system, Hallett read on with determination, pausing now and then to make notes which he occasionally highlighted with his red or blue pen.

After about two hours of study he removed his spectacles, leaned back in his chair and stretched. He felt that even if he could not actually build his carport at the moment, he could take some measurements and design it. And, if that were possible, why not estimate the amount of materials needed, then go to a builder's merchant to order them? At the idea of this positive move Hallett felt that he had earned a break.

He went downstairs and found Elizabeth in the kitchen busily engaged in a session of cake baking and noted with some satisfaction a large batch of tea-cakes arranged on a cooling tray.

'Hello, dear, how's the carport coming along?'

'Quite well, really. I can see some parts that might be, well, just a bit tricky, but generally it looks all fairly straightforward.'

Somewhere in that statement, Elizabeth, with her long experience of listening to and analysing her husband's comments, could detect a distinct note of apprehension.

'You are sure you can manage?' she asked, trying to sound casual.

Her fears about his apprehension were confirmed by his tell-tale pause of two seconds before replying.

'Yes, yes, of course I can. My first job is to assess the materials I require, then I shall go down to Brimleys; you know, that builder's yard on the corner just before High Street.'

Elizabeth had felt slightly uneasy about this whole operation from the beginning, and now, the act of actually ordering materials based solely on Simon's calculations caused her uncertainty to start up again. It wasn't that she thought little of him – quite the reverse. But she knew him well and this sort of venture was not really his forte. She would do anything, though, rather than let him suspect that her confidence in him was anything less than complete.

She smiled. 'Can I get you anything, Simon?'

'Well yes, I was rather hoping for some tea, please, if you're sure you are not too busy,' he said with a quick, sideways glance at the tea-cakes.

'Yes, of course. Would you like a tea-cake?

'A cake? Oh, you've been baking. Yes, please, I'd love one.'

After two cups of tea and as many tea-cakes Hallett felt refreshed and ready to get to grips with "Getting Our Thoughts Down on Paper Before We Start".

'Well, must get back to it,' he announced.

Back in his study he rummaged around and found a few large sheets of white paper and a ruler. He sat down and after a few minutes of consulting his notes he realised that he could not begin until he had taken measurements of the width of the drive, the length of one side of the house and estimated the required size of his carport.

Now faced with the first practical step in the creation of his car port, he paused, looked again at his notes, not realising that his expression suggested doubt and a faint lack of self-confidence. Nevertheless, he told himself, let's get started. He took a deep breath and marched off downstairs to search for a suitable measure for his preliminary survey of the carport site. All that his search revealed was a tape measure from Elizabeth's workbox and he strode out to his drive clutching the measure.

He stood for a few seconds unsure of where to start. He quickly made up his mind that the width of his drive was an important dimension to include and was a nice easy measurement to start with.

He crouched by the house, laid the end of the tape against the wall and started to edge backwards paying out the tape as he went. He had almost come to the end of the tape measure when a gust of wind blew the end away from the wall and it would have fluttered away down the drive had not Hallett been holding firmly onto the other end. He cursed silently and pulled in the wayward end. Searching around he found a couple of small, flat stones and laid the tape in position once more but with a stone holding it in place. Paying out the tape he managed to measure the width of the drive in stages with the aid of the flat stones.

He straightened up and realised that although he now knew the width of his drive, he had brought nothing with him to record the details. He sighed and went back into the house to find writing materials.

When he returned, he first jotted down the drive width then began the more tedious job of measuring the length that he envisaged his carport should be. As to height, he had a few guesses at what it should be then decided to compare the height of his garage and make one or two adjustments. He had just made his fourth, and, fortunately for his temper, his most successful attempt at measuring the height of his garage when, next door, Fred Root strolled into the garden.

'Afternoon, squire,' he called, in his friendly way.

'Oh, hello, Root,' said Hallett, while carefully rerolling Elizabeth's tape measure then scribbling a brief note on his scrap of paper. He felt that he should explain to Root why he had found it necessary to spend his time holding a dressmaker's tape measure against the side of his garage.

'I'm just taking a few measurements before I get down to planning it on paper.' He paused for slight effect. 'I'm going to design and build a car port, you see.'

'Really? Well, I take my hat off to you there, squire. That really is ambitious. Design and build, eh? It's a very good idea and I've often thought about something like a canopy to cover the kitchen door when it rains, but I've never had the confidence to think of anything as ambitious as designing and building my own car port.'

This complimentary speech had the odd effect of bringing back Hallett's feeling of apprehension.

'Well, it's not that difficult, surely. I mean, lots of people do it, don't they?' he finished hopefully.

'Yes, I expect they do. When do you expect to start?'

'Well, the first thing to do, of course, is to get our thoughts down on paper, that is, get my thoughts down on paper. So, I thought first a few measurements then put pen to paper to see how it shapes up. Then off to the builder's yard to order the necessary timbers and other essentials and, after that, make a start.'

'Well, you certainly seem to know what you're doing, so best of luck. If you need any help like lifting something, just give me a call.'

'Thank you. I may need some help that way.'

He went back to his study and for the next thirty minutes or so he drew and redrew the now eagerly awaited Carport Plan. When it was completed, he consulted his notes to check on the part that instructed him how to convert his drawing into lengths of timber, panels of translucent plastic and even nails, screws and other essential items.

There was a delay while Hallett studied his notes again and set himself the task that had been troubling him ever since Arnold Beaumont Geesely had first made mention of metric measurements – the conversion of the so familiar feet and inches into metres or millimetres or whatever it was. This involved much scribbling and referring to the back pages of his big dictionary. Finally, he jotted down the last quantity and checked his list. It was very impressive and looked quite professional. Now all that was left was the trip to the builder's yard. That, and of course, the actual building of the car port, he added, soberly.

The drive to the yard was only about two miles and on the journey he bolstered up his flagging spirits by going over the details of his plan. He had just reached the part which dealt with the fitting of the translucent panels when he saw that he was approaching the builder's yard. He signalled, steered cautiously into the open gateway and parked just inside.

There was a notice on the wall proclaiming the owner of the yard. It was a heavy, wooden notice, well weathered and in an elaborately carved frame, mitred at the corners with microscopic precision. It read "Jeremiah Brimley, Building Materials Supplied to the Trade". The letters were in gold with a shadow effect in black on each letter. The late Jeremiah Brimley had been the original owner who had started the business many years ago. It was well known that he held strong convictions on religion, morals, business ethics and hard work. His son, Joe Brimley, (christened Josiah) was made in a different mould. He had been heard to say on many occasions 'make your pile when you can, as quick as you can and sod everybody'.

In order to cope with the growing number of house-owners attempting their own repairs, Joe Brimley had added to the bottom of his father's notice board, "DIY Supplies a Speciality".

Hallett walked slowly into the yard and looked around him at the stacks of supplies for the Trade and the DIY enthusiast. There was timber, corrugated sheets, roof tiles, chimney pots, wrought iron gates and paving slabs. As his eyes roved over this unfamiliar scene, he freely admitted that he was in an alien world of which he had no experience, and he made a rare resolve that this was no time for bluff or pretence of experienced knowledge.

He saw a small notice which read "Office and Enquiries" and featured a black fist extending one pointing finger.

He walked to the office indicated by the black finger, opened the door and walked in. Seated behind the desk was the present owner of the yard, Mr Joe Brimley.

Josiah Brimley was a large, slow-moving man, who, like his father, held strong convictions. But his were not on religion, morals, business ethics or hard work. His concerned an unshakeable belief in the total uselessness of DIY enthusiasts, for all of whom he held a deep contempt. In addition, he believed fervently in the necessity to watch for any chance to make some extra money fast – even if it meant that someone else went short. He would state boldly to anyone prepared to listen, that he despised what he called 'short-cut gimmicks'. He would talk sneeringly of 'electric playthings' which claimed to allow an unskilled man to gouge out 'perfect joints' or those mamby pamby paint pads that fool people into thinking they can do their own decorating. His scorn and contempt, though, did not prevent his offering a wide variety of DIY gadgets for sale. Gadgets that he would recommend to his customers with an enthusiasm and warmth which were a good deal less than sincere.

He sat behind his desk in his customary outfit of an ancient, dark-blue, double-breasted pinstripe jacket that was always open, revealing his matching waistcoat; the stains on which, showed clear evidence of the odd careless cup of tea or clumsily eaten meal. On his head was a brown trilby which he never removed at work and, in between the trilby and his head, was tucked a flat carpenters' pencil. With this he did most of his calculations on any convenient surface. His office walls and the stacks of materials in his yard bore much evidence of his scribbling. His trousers were in great contrast to his jacket and were a dark brown with just a hint of herring-bone pattern. His boots were black, unpolished and turned up slightly at the toes. In his mouth he clenched tightly on a short, black pipe that, for some reason, needed frequent relighting with the result that many of his sentences were punctuated by puffs.

As was his usual practice he waited for his visitor to speak first.

'Good afternoon. Mr Brimley?'

'Aye. What can I do for you?'

'I am doing a building extension and I need some materials. Shall I look round the yard or can I just give you a list?'

'Got a list, 'ave you?'

'Yes, can I leave it with you?'

'Is that all you want, then?'

Neither party seemed aware that so far, all of their exchanges had been questions and that each question had been answered with another question.

Hallett fumbled in his pocket for his much toiled over list and meanwhile, Brimley was sizing him up and assessing him. Ex-Army I shouldn't wonder, and with that voice probably ex-officer. Not short of a bob or two, I'll bet. Never done any real grafting by the look of him and looks as if he could make a real foul-up of any job he tackled. Still, business is business.

He took the proffered list, glanced at it and looked up at Hallett.

'You building a sun-house, then?'

'No, a car port, actually. I thought it would add value to my property and give good protection from the rain.'

Joe was searching for his lighter as he ran his eyes over the list once more. 'These screws you got here (puff, puff) what sort do you need (puff puff) countersunk, roundhead, (puff) Phillips, Pozidriv (puff, puff) clutch head or what?'

'Er, what do you suggest?'

Joe blew forth a cloud of not very pleasant smelling pipe smoke.

'Well, it depends what sort of a job you're going to make of it. Leave it to me if you like. I'll fix it.'

This brief exchange had the effect of confirming for Joe that he was dealing with that most pathetic of creatures, an inexperienced DIY man. This, for Joe, had the same effect as on a spider watching a plump fly about to entangle himself in his web.

'Do you want me to deliver this lot, then? It'll cost extra of course.'

'Yes, perhaps that would be best. When can you manage it?'

'Late Monday afternoon suit you?'

'Certainly, that will do well. Now, let me write down my address for you.'

This having been done he nodded good afternoon to Mr Brimley and walked from the office.

Brimley watched him go and for some time continued to stare at the closed door with a very thoughtful expression on his face.

Slowly he shook his head. 'Never even asked for the prices,' he murmured, with a world of meaning.

He picked up the list, withdrew his flat pencil from its customary storage place and swivelled his chair to face the wall. He studied the already numerous figures and notes that covered the cream painted wall until he found a small unused area on which he might scrawl his latest calculations. He scribbled away with frequent glances at the list. He sat back searching for his lighter as he looked at the results.

'That'll do, (puff, puff) better not try for more than that.'

He swivelled back to the table and wrote a list of his latest customer's requirements and with a final comparison of his list against the customer's list, he heaved himself out of the chair and ambled out into the yard.

What he needed now was Amos, the man he referred to as his Yard Foreman. Amos Kittridge had started as lad in the days of Jeremiah Brimley and who was, it seemed, content to continue in the employ of the junior Brimley. Just how content he really felt may never be known because Amos was not the most communicative of people and there were many who had met him who felt that one of his ambitions must surely be to go through a whole day without saying one word.

Summoning Amos, who might be anywhere in the yard, was one of the few tasks for which Joe Brimley found it necessary to remove his pipe. He withdrew the pipe, took a deep breath and bellowed at top of his voice.

'Aaay… moss. Come 'ere a minute!'

He replaced his pipe, turned to go back into his office and found himself face to face with Amos, who had appeared, genie-like, behind him. Amos had come from the back of the office on his way to see Mr Brimley. Joe just stared at him then took a pace back.

'Where the hell have you been?'

Amos jerked his head in the direction of the sand and gravel bays by the by the fence at the back of the office.

'Working.'

'Well, come in, I've got a job for you.'

They went into the office and a few minutes later Amos emerged holding the list of items for delivery next Monday afternoon.

On the afternoon of the following Monday, Hallett spent some time peering out of his bedroom window to see if Brimley's lorry was in sight and, after several fruitless trips to the window, he pretended that it was not so important anyway and he retired to his study.

After about half an hour Elizabeth called to him that he was wanted at the door and he descended the stairs briskly to find Mr Brimley waiting at the front door. He was holding a clip-board on which were secured a number of pink copies and yellow copies of delivery notes.

'Brought your materials, Mister. Where do you want them put?'

'Come with me, Mr Brimley and let me show you.' He guided him to the side of the house and waved his arm over the general area. 'Stack it about here, please.'

Brimley looked dubiously at the chosen site, half turned as if to say something then turned away. He shrugged, sniffed and walked slowly down the drive and out to his lorry. Sitting in the back of the lorry was half of Mr Brimley's entire work force, namely, Amos Kittridge and young 'Chatty' Harris, so called because of his almost constant flow of talk. This flow more than made up for the lack of conversation from Amos. It seemed that 'Chatty' found it necessary to gabble his way through the day because of the absence of any communication from his companion. The fact that almost all of his questions were not answered and that his observations created no response did not worry young Harris at all.

'Right, lads, come on, let's get this lot inside, I'll show you where.'

Both men climbed off a lorry and started to remove the pins holding the hinged side.

Soon 'Chatty' was in full flood and gabbling eagerly. 'I think we should take the wood in first, Amos, then the plastic sheets and after that we can take the small bits and pieces like screws and things. Remember when we delivered to that block of flats when that bloke was renovating his kitchen and we had to carry all the things up to the fifth floor because the lift wasn't working. In fact, I sometimes wonder if the lift really breaks down or...'

On and on he went but even as he chatted away they were both busy lifting off planks of wood and leaning them against the side of the lorry ready to carry down the drive. From time to time

Amos nodded and occasionally gave a little sigh hoping it indicated to 'Chatty' that he was not interested in the conversation. 'Chatty', though, was not so much interested in having a conversation, as having an audience, however inattentive.

If pressed, Amos might have admitted a sort of fatherly affection for his garrulous workmate, but not surprisingly, his feelings were not discernible to the casual onlooker.

It took some time to off-load the lorry, carry the materials up the drive and stack them neatly in the space allocated by Hallett. When it was at last completed, the two men went back to the lorry and stood there waiting for Mr Brimley to complete the proceedings by presenting his bill. They knew that he liked payment on the spot and had his own methods of presenting his account to ensure that this was forthcoming.

Joe Brimley cast his eyes over the neatly assembled building materials, gripped his pipe even tighter in his mouth, removed the clip-board from under his arm then made a show of seeming to check the materials and tick them off a list. This completed, he nodded a few times and removed a sales invoice from his board. He approached Hallett, removed his pipe and offered him the bill.

'I think you'll find that that's all in order, sir,' (a little civility he reserved for the occasions when he presented his bill). 'If you'll just check it, I'll get you a receipt.'

The implication of this last sentence was lost on Hallett for only a few seconds. 'What? Oh, right then. I'll get my cheque book.'

A few minutes later he emerged from the house holding his cheque book and struggling with the top of his fountain pen.

Joe Brimley, seeing the resistance being put up by the fountain pen top, valiantly came to the rescue with a cheap ball-point pen, the end of which had been well chewed. Hallett had always disliked ball-point pens and considered this one particularly repellent. 'Thank you, but I think I would rather use this one,' he said, holding out his fountain pen.

The pen top was eventually removed and Hallett stood, pen poised, ready to make out the cheque.

'To whom shall I make this payable?'

'J. Brimley, please, sir.'

Hallett scratched away then looked baffled. He scratched again. 'Blast, it's run out of ink.'

He was turning away to enter the house to refill his ancient pen when he saw Fred Root wearing a set of paint-spattered overalls, standing on the other side of their low hedge. He was looking at the assembled stacks of building materials.

'Afternoon, squire.'

'Oh, hello, Root. Been decorating, have you?'

'Just the landing and stairs.'

'What do you think of this, then. Pretty impressive, eh?'

'Very nice. Can I come over?'

'Of course, come and have a look.'

Fred stepped over the hedge and strolled over. He nodded at Joe.

'Afternoon.'

Joe Brimley nodded a response and, for some reason he could not yet fathom, he felt slightly uneasy in Fred's presence.

Fred looked over the stacks of timber, bricks and other materials. 'I've been thinking, squire. If I wanted to build a car port you might just have saved me some work. I don't need to measure up, I can just copy from you.'

He glanced at Joe and with one swift, smooth movement he removed the clip-board from under Joe's arm.

'Mind if I have quick squint just to see what I'm letting myself in for?' he asked, giving Joe a big smile.

Joe nodded. 'Aye, that'll be all right,' he said, but the uneasy feeling was beginning to gnaw at him.

Checking through the contents of the delivery note, Fred paused several times and stared at the building materials. Once, as he paused, he swivelled his eyes up to Joe without moving his head, and stared for some seconds. Joe tried to return the stare but he soon began to fidget.

'Something wrong, is there?' he said suddenly, in a strained voice.

'Depends really, old son. Might be. On the other hand it might just be a bit of carelessness on somebody's part.'

He continued his scrutiny of the delivery note and by now, Hallett had taken an interest in the proceedings. Although he was not sure quite what was wrong, he decided to put his cheque book away until whatever it was had been sorted out

At this point, and noticing the disappearance of the cheque book, Joe felt compelled to say something.

'Look, what seems to be the trouble?'

'Well, let's see. This figure here refers to the overall length of timber, right?' Joe nodded.

'And WRC, that's, let me think, Western Red Cedar?'

Again, Joe nodded, but the uneasy, gnawing feeling was increasing in intensity.

Fred looked down at the timber and then at Joe Brimley. Fred grinned. 'Looks more like Parana Pine to me.'

Without waiting for confirmation or denial, he walked over where the timber lay. He gave the top piece a sideways tap with his foot then followed this with a deft flick with the toe of his paint-spattered shoe and the end of the plank of timber was flipped into the air where it was caught quite casually by Fred.

For some time he examined the wood, twisting it and squinting along its length. Joe watched with growing concern.

'Nothing wrong with that,' he said, rather unconvincingly.

Again, Fred gave him a big, friendly smile. 'Nothing except that it's not Western Red Cedar, it's waney edged, it shows a slight tendency to cupping, it's over-knotted, it's PBS and you've charged for PAR.'

By this time they had been joined by Elizabeth and she and Hallett now stood watching with great interest.

'Fred, what's PBS and PAR, then?'

'Hello, Elizabeth. Well, PBS, as the Colonel will tell you, is planed both sides and PAR is planed all round. PAR costs more, and that's what you've been charged. But your timber is only PBS – planed both sides.'

Hallett nodded agreement as he strove to recall the technical details of timber as explained by Mr Geesely.

By now, Joe had come to the conclusion that here, in full view of the buying public, was a colleague in the building supplies trade, stabbing him in the back.

'You in the trade, then, are you?'

'Not in your trade, old son. I'm in fruit and veg. But, when I first started out, I didn't do too well so I worked weekends. I worked for my dad's brother, Uncle Bob, in his Timber Yard making up orders like this.' He looked down at the piles of timber. 'I can tell you that if I ever made up an order like this, Uncle Bob would have broken one them planks over my head.'

Josiah Brimley looked thoughtful and he played for time by relighting his pipe. When he had finished he looked over his shoulder at his two men standing by the lorry. When he spoke his voice was low and confidential. He inclined his head towards his two employees. 'It's always the same. If you want a job done properly, do it yourself. Those two men there are all right but no real pride in their job, do you know what I mean? They still have trouble even sorting out the difference between the different woods.'

Fred turned as if to leave. 'Well, the difference between Parana Pine and Western Red Cedar is fairly easy to see. I'll just go and explain it to them so they don't make that mistake again. That'll save you a bit of trouble, won't it?'

Quickly, Joe seized his arm. 'No no. that's all right. I'll have word with them later. You leave them to me,' he finished with a sickly smile.

He looked towards them. 'I'll just get them to put this stuff back onto the lorry.'

'While you're at it, I should load some of the plastic corrugated sheets. The first few have got a fair number of scratches and scuffs on them. As for the rest of the stuff, well, under the circumstances, you wouldn't mind a use or return deal, would you?'

Joe stared tight-lipped at Fred. 'No, that'll be all right,' he said, without much enthusiasm. 'I'll be back tomorrow with the Western Red Cedar. Is that OK with you?' he said, turning to Hallett.

'Tomorrow? Yes, that is quite acceptable.'

Brimley beckoned his two men and they started the task of removing the rejected items.

Elizabeth, Hallett and Fred turned and walked towards the

kitchen door. Elizabeth paused.

'Fred, we can see you're very busy,' she said, glancing at his overalls with spatterings of paint. 'But, do you have time for a quiet cup of tea?'

'Thanks, Elizabeth, I'd love a cup of tea.'

'Good. You two men go in and get started and I'll get Gladys.'

Inside the kitchen Hallett busied himself with the unfamiliar task of filling the kettle, searching for and setting out cups and saucers.

He paused and turned to Fred. 'I must say that I was more than pleased to have your help out there this afternoon. I thought that I understood a little of the technicalities but I never expected that this sort of thing could happen.'

'You're very welcome, squire. I've seen his sort before in the building trade and out of it. No harm done, though.'

Elizabeth and Gladys came in and Hallett was relieved to hand over the tea making duties to them.

Fred chuckled. 'It's a good job that he didn't enquire too closely into my technical knowledge, though. I'm more than a bit rusty and well out of date by now.'

'Even so, it and sounded most impressive to me,' said Hallett, 'and to that man Brimley judging by his furtive expression.'

'I think it might have been enough just to make him cautious, but I don't think we'll get any more bother from him.'

Back in his office Joe Brimley lowered himself into his chair and sat swivelling gently from side to side. He looked to be deep in serious thought. The door opened suddenly and in came Amos. He had never once knocked on that door since the day Jeremiah Brimley had walked slowly out of the yard for the last time having just handed the business to his son Josiah. This practice of just barging in, irritated Joe and he would always sneer sarcastically that he hadn't heard anyone knock, but Amos would carry on as if Joe had not spoken. It now remained as an irritating habit that annoyed Joe more on some days than others.

It was predictable that today was a day on which the

irritation graph could be measured as a fairly steep rise.

'Why don't you come in?' he said, the irony in his voice sounding loud and clear.

Amos gazed steadily at him for a few seconds then turned his head and looked over his shoulder as if to see the person to whom Joe had spoken.

'Well, what do you want?' Joe snapped.

Amos turned back and stared once more at him.

'Come on, come on, I haven't got all day.'

After a few more seconds of steady gazing, Amos spoke in his quiet voice and made one of his longest statements for weeks.

'That were a bad mistake were that, and it wouldn't have 'appened in 'is day,' he said, with a curt nod in the direction of a large sepia photograph of the late Jeremiah Brimley. He had been photographed in his best going-to-chapel outfit complete with cotton gloves and carrying a Malacca cane. It was easy to see just by looking at the picture that Amos was right. Brimley Senior's abhorrence of any sort of devious business practice was clearly written on what could be seen of his face staring through his impressive set of whiskers.

'He often used to say,' continued Amos, 'give value for money and you'll sleep easy in your bed.'

Joe had many times been forced to listen to his late father expound on the subject of honesty and its rewards, and he was certainly in no mood now to receive a potted version of one of Jeremiah's lectures, and particularly from a member of his own staff.

'You've quite finished, 'ave you?'

Amos Kittridge stared steadily at him. 'Aye. It'll do for now.'

'Good. Now you can sod off back to work.'

It occurred to Amos as he turned to go that bad language was also against his old employer's beliefs, but he felt that a further correction would not be well received. He shook his head, this time in sorrow, and walked out of the office, deliberately leaving the door wide open. He was secretly pleased when, after he had walked a few steps from the office, the door crashed shut with a noise like a contribution to the 1812

Overture.

Back in the office and having vented his anger on the open door, Joe sat once more in his chair. He was not swivelling now and he leaned both elbows on the desk cupping his chin in his hands. Taking place inside him was a battle that surged this way and that as he tried to fight back a small but insistent voice that told him Amos and his father might well have been right.

But, right or wrong, he had better get busy and sort out some Western Red Cedar and the other bits and pieces then send them round to that blasted DIY amateur with his nosey, trouble-making neighbour in Forsythia Avenue. Also, he'd better revise a few prices. He sighed. Sometimes, he wondered if it was all worth it.

On the following Saturday morning it was clear and sunny and Hallett felt that now was the time to make a start on the carport and he sat in his study looking at his master plan, now completed in colourful detail. From time to time he consulted his notes and then went back to his plan. After about ten minutes he realised that he was just putting off the moment when he had to start. Picking up his plans he started off downstairs.

He walked out of the kitchen and onto the drive, then, as he looked at the mass of building materials stacked by the side of the house, he slowly realised why, when he had told Brimley to stack them there, he had looked doubtful. Of course, all the materials were in the area destined to be covered by the carport and it now meant moving everything to a new location. Resignedly, he made a start with some of the timber but after about twenty minutes he found he was in a fair muddle and his back was hurting. Perhaps I should ask for some help, he decided, after a little thought.

Crossing over to Fred's drive he tapped on the door which, after a few seconds, was opened by Fred.

'Oh, er, morning, Root. I'm sorry to bother you if you're busy, but the fact is, I'm trying to organise my timber and stuff and I'm having a bit of back trouble.' He paused. 'I wondered if you could find time to give me a hand to move it.'

'Course I will, squire. Be with you in a couple of shakes.'

In about half an hour with both men working steadily but with no-one giving orders or directions, they had organised the materials into a convenient and tidy lay out.

Hallett straightened up and looked at the orderly piles of building materials. The carport area was now clear.

'Well, that's that. Thank you for your help; perhaps I can be of assistance to you sometime.'

Fred did not reply at once but stood looking thoughtfully at his drive and then at Hallett's drive.

'Look, squire, I don't know how you're going to set about this and it's all uncharted waters as far as I'm concerned. But, you seem to have some idea of what to do, so, if I let you lend a hand now, we can sort it out together and then some other time we could both have a go at building a carport on my drive.'

Hallett's face brightened. 'Splendid idea. In fact, I would welcome your help.'

'Only one thing, though. I'm not fooling when I say that this building lark is all new to me. I just hope I don't foul things up for you.'

'I expect that you and I will be able to sort it out and learn as we go along, don't you?'

'Right, squire, you're on. What's the first move?'

Hallett glanced at his notes. 'Well, as I understand it, we have first to examine the drive for soundness and it must be at least 100 millimetres thick.' He looked down at his drive. 'I rather think I've left that just a little late seeing that I've already bought the materials, don't you?' This had the effect of starting off the task with a smile from both men and they carried out a not very serious examination of the drive.

'Seems all right to me, squire.'

'Very well, let's make a start?'

Hallett explained that they needed to start with the screen walls and piers. He then explained these in detail to Fred from the notes he had taken after reading Mr Geesely's book. They worked carefully and rather slowly through the morning and each took his turn in mixing mortar and laying bricks. When they had completed three courses between the first and second piers Hallett laid down his trowel.

121

'You want me to have go now, squire?'

'Not just yet, no. According to the book we must only go three courses high then allow the mortar to go off. Otherwise, the wall may bulge and go out of shape.'

Fred nodded. 'That makes sense.'

By the end of the day they had made fair progress and agreed to continue the next day. Over the next few days they worked away at the carport getting more and more enthusiastic as it took shape. It was many days later when they put the finishing touches and they then stood back and together looked at their carport.

Hallett was about to say that perhaps they ought to celebrate it in some way when he noticed that it had begun to rain.

'Just look at that,' he said, 'we finished just in time.'

He and Fred walked forward under the carport and gradually the rain increased until it was lashing down with some force. They looked up a little apprehensively at the translucent corrugated panels as the rain beat out its steady rhythm, but the roof was sound and under the protective shelter of the carport, all was dry. Hallett looked at the rain bouncing on the drive and thought back to that day, now seeming so long ago, when he made his squelchy, sodden trip from his car to the kitchen door.

He smiled broadly. 'Well, that's that. A good job well done, eh?'

'Very well worth it. You'll have no more problems with the rain now.'

'Not for me, no. But we must arrange a date to start on yours as soon as possible. Preferably while we both remember what to do. After all, although summer will soon be upon us, we could still get some storms.'

Fred nodded. 'Right, squire, you're on.'

There they both stood, under the carport, quietly watching the rain.

CHAPTER NINE

The early May sunshine shone brightly across the gardens of Forsythia Avenue warming the backs of the Saturday morning gardeners and providing them with the excuse to slip inside the house occasionally for a refrigerator-cooled can of lager. The sun also shone on the newly unfolded awnings over swinging garden seats, drawing from the multi-coloured floral upholstery the slightly musty smell of winter storage.

The warming rays lured some reluctant gardeners into a deckchair for a half-hour's rest before tackling their neglected gardens. A half-hour that frequently stretched into a couple of hours of deep, noisy, open-mouthed breathing punctuated by grunts and hand waving around the face to discourage unsporting mosquitoes. If the brief nap could be made to stretch until almost lunch-time, then the excuse of not wishing to work on an empty stomach could be made, only to reverse it after lunch into not wishing to work so soon after a meal. Yes, with a little imagination this gardening business need not leave one totally exhausted nor place a strain on the heart that was surely not good for one.

In the garden of number twenty-three, Colonel Hallett had started the morning by pushing his ancient mower up and down his lawn a few times and had spent a good part of that time picking up the grass-box. This, with monotonous regularity, would unhook itself from the front of the mower with the result that the Colonel would crash into the grass-box and push it along for a few feet until he could bring the mower to a standstill. He would replace the grass cuttings in the grass-box, then the grass-box onto the lawnmower. This practice almost always caused him to address the mower using some choice military terms, but, whenever Elizabeth suggested scrapping the mower and buying a more up-to-date model, he would fly to its defence like a mother hen to her chicks. He would pour out his usual words of scorn about anything manufactured in the last twenty years. To this he would add his lament about the passing of craftsmanship and how one could not now buy goods approaching the quality of this mower. It was a genuine Barlow mower, he would say, it was just not possible to obtain one like it today. In this surmise, Elizabeth longed to tell him, he was undoubtedly right.

After a few skirmishes with his Barlow mower, the Colonel decided to relax and prepare himself for the encounter to come by resting for a few minutes in his deck chair. He eased himself into the deck chair with his usual fear that the whole structure was about to collapse and deposit him on the ground. It creaked, the canvas grew taut with his weight, but it held, and he slowly relaxed and closed his eyes. Soon, the gentle warmth of the sun, the droning buzz of insects and his general lack of enthusiasm for lively combat with the lawn, combined to lull him to sleep.

About ten minutes later Elizabeth walked into the garden looking lost in deep thought. She saw her husband in his deck chair and walked over to where he lay, mouth open, dozing peacefully.

'Simon.'

Hallett slumbered on.

'Simon.'

This slightly louder call caused him to snap his mouth shut then noisily smack his lips.

'Simon.'

'What was that? Who is there?' He opened his eyes and looked up. 'Elizabeth? What is happening?'

'Nothing, dear. I'm sorry to have woken you up, but I wondered if you had seen the cheque-book?'

'The cheque-book? Why, is there some special need for it?'

'No, not really. Only I just thought that I might have lost it.'

'Well, if you have lost it, then surely it's unlikely that I could have seen it.'

'I know, but I wondered if you had seen it before I lost it, and perhaps you could remember where you saw it, if you saw it at all, that is.'

Her voice tailed off as she became aware of the verbal entanglement she was creating.

'Well, I have not seen the cheque-book and I can't think why it's suddenly a matter of such great concern.'

'I'm not really concerned, it's just that I would like to find it, that's all. Anyway, I expect it will turn up somewhere. No need for you to worry, you just go back to sleep.'

'I think I can guarantee that I shall not worry about it in the slightest. Now, I really would like the chance to relax before I tackle the lawn once more.'

Elizabeth did not reply but appeared to be staring at the top of a tall tree several gardens away. Hallett grunted and tried to make himself comfortable, but he found that he could not ignore the fact that his wife was still there standing silently by his side.

'Was there something else?'

She stopped her contemplation of the tree and turned to him. 'Have you seen Richard lately?'

'Look, until a few minutes ago I was fast asleep and that would prevent me from seeing anything, including Richard or the cheque-book.'

'Well, it's just that I haven't seen him since breakfast and I wondered where he might be. Still, I expect he'll turn up soon. Why don't you go back to sleep, dear.'

He looked as if he was about to reply then changed his mind and made a big show of settling back in his deck chair. He closed his eyes, grunted a few times, then slowly relaxed.

At that moment, Valerie came out of the front door and, seeing her mother, walked across to join her. 'Mother, have you seen my address book anywhere? I used it only last night and now I can't find it.'

'No, I can't say that I have noticed it anywhere.'

'I'll just ask father if he's seen it.'

Elizabeth could quickly see that it would be most unwise to tax him with the whereabouts of anything else at the moment. Hurriedly she restrained Valerie. 'I don't think I should bother your father just now, Valerie. He has had enough questions for one day.'

'Oh, I see. A bit crabby is he?'

This was really too much and Hallett leaned forward.

'No! I am not in the least bit crabby as you call it. All I am trying to do is merely to get a few minute's peace. Something that seems to get more and more difficult by the minute.'

'Well, dear, you've had so many interruptions this morning, no-one could blame you if you were a bit crabby.'

Hallett failed to see the faint smile on Elizabeth's face and his expression took on a slightly deeper hue.

'For the last time, I am not in the least bit crabby!'

She laughed. 'If you say so, dear.'

He now suspected that he was the victim of a little gentle fun but he gave an impatient snort and tried once more to make himself comfortable.

He was just settling down again when Richard walked up the drive. He gave his family a friendly wave, came across and sat himself on the grass by the garden seat where Elizabeth and Valerie had seated themselves.

'Have you been to the shops, Richard?'

'No, mother, I've been to the library to see if "Journey to Isonicus" was in yet. I'm told it's a great book. All about these four space travellers who find their way to Isonicus, which is about a hundred light years from Earth, and they find that the Isonicusians have reproduced conditions on their planet exactly the same as on Earth. It leads to all sorts of confusion.'

A keen observer might, at this point, have noticed the Colonel's mouth tighten slightly.

'Did you manage to get it from the library, then?'

'No. Christopher Philips had just beaten me to it.'

'Oh, what a shame. Perhaps next time.'

'Yes, he said he'll let me know when he takes it back.'

'Christopher Philips. Is he that boy with those enormous spectacles?'

'Yes, that's him. And, guess what? He told me that his father is taking them all on holiday to the Bahamas this year.'

Up until now, Valerie had not taken much interest in the conversation, but her face lit up at the very thought of spending a holiday in the Bahamas. She leaned back and imagined herself lying on the warm sand, her smooth, lightly tanned skin contrasting perfectly with the white of her bikini. Valerie felt that a white bikini must surely be the thing to be seen in when in the Bahamas. She imagined a group of young men surrounding her as she lay there in the sand. They would all be bronzed and good-looking and all pleading with her to come for a swim. She sighed and wriggled her toes in the soft, white sand.

'Is that a spider on your shoulder, Valerie?'

She returned to Forsythia Avenue with a supersonic burst.

'Where?' she shrieked, twisting her head into impossible positions.

'Oh, sorry,' said Richard, fighting back a smile, 'must have been the shadow of a twig or something.'

'Richard, you are a wretch! The next time you run out of money in mid-week, don't come to me for a loan.'

'It was only a joke.'

'Silly sort of joke if you ask me.'

Elizabeth's calm acceptance of this minor squabble indicated that is was not altogether an unusual event. However, she thought she might as well divert their attention onto something else.

'Did you say the Bahamas, Richard?'

'Yes, Mother, they're going for three weeks.'

'I wish we could go there,' said Valerie, looking meaningfully in the direction of her father as he lay asleep in his deck chair.

Richard beamed. 'Why don't we ask father.'

Elizabeth immediately recognised the ingredients of a potentially explosive situation. 'I don't think we should bother your father just at this moment, Richard.'

'Why? Is he a bit…'

'Yes,' said Elizabeth hastily, 'he is a bit tired and he is trying to get a little rest.'

'Anyway, I don't suppose he would agree to a holiday in the Bahamas this year,' said Richard gloomily.

At this point the Colonel 'awoke' once more. 'In that supposition, Richard, you are perfectly correct. We are not spending our holidays in the Bahamas this year.'

'Oh, why not Father?'

'There are many reasons, young man, why we cannot embark on a holiday in the Bahamas, but the main reason is finance.'

'In what way?'

'Your father means that we can't afford it, Richard.'

'That is not exactly what I meant. What I meant was, although we could afford to spend a holiday there, I believe it to be a not very good investment. After all, there is still a good deal of this country we have not yet visited.'

Richard and Valerie shared the thought that, in terms of holidays, most of the country had yet to be visited since they always went to the same place each year.

'Have you thought about holidays this year, Simon?'

'Yes, as a matter of fact, I have. I thought that it would not do any harm to return to Weppleton Bay, do you?'

Glancing at Richard and Valerie, it was clear to Elizabeth that this news had been received with little noticeable enthusiasm.

'What a splendid idea. I wonder if our little hotel, the Bay View is still owned by that charming ex-infantry officer, Captain Webster?'

'I don't see why not. Why do you think it might not be?'

'Well, it's just that the last time we were there, I heard Captain Webster talking to some of his guests. It was on that rainy morning when we couldn't go out and you refused to have that pot of tea because it was made with tea-bags. Do you remember?'

'Unlike most people, I do not clutter my mind with trivia and I have no recollection at all of refusing pots of tea or anything else. So, would you please tell me the rest of this story about Sheridan Webster.'

'As I said, I heard Sheridan talking to some guests, and he mentioned that he had been approached by a London Company who wanted to buy the hotel. He said that they wanted to modernise it and introduce juke-boxes, fruit machines and that sort of thing.'

'Modernise Bay View? Never.'

'Nevertheless, Captain Webster said that he was most

impressed with their letter.'

'Did he indeed? Well, as far as I am concerned, they will get the sort of guests they deserve in future. Damned impertinence, expecting us to put up with their blaring machines. We will go elsewhere this year.'

'Whatever you think best, dear.'

In relating the incident of Bay View, Elizabeth had thought it unnecessary to mention that Captain Webster had made it quite clear to his listeners that he was not in the least interested in selling the hotel, but that he had thought that the embossed letter heading was very impressive.

'The problem now remains, where to go. Any suggestions?'

'Well, Simon, I have been thinking and this will surely be the last year that we will all go on holiday together, so, why not leave the choice to Valerie and Richard?'

'Very well. I expect that you would both like to think about it so please let me know later. But, no Bahamas, mind.'

They nodded and hurried off quite excited by the prospect of going somewhere other than dreary old Weppleton Bay.

Hallett turned to Elizabeth. 'I just hope that they come up with some sensible suggestions. Any idea where you would like to go?'

Elizabeth seemed deep in thought, then her face brightened. 'Of course, in the dining room, behind the clock.'

'What?'

'The cheque-book, I remember where I put it now,' and off she went happily back to the house leaving Hallett wearing a look of disbelief.

He decided that he might as well try again to get a few minutes in the deck chair and, as he settled back comfortably, he closed his eyes and was soon in that pleasant state of hovering between sleep and full consciousness. If only people would leave me alone, he thought, as he started to drift into a peaceful sleep.

'Mornin' squire.'

Oh, really. He had just got rid his family only to be pestered by neighbours. Must act in a civilised manner, though. He opened his eyes.

'Good morning, Root. Nice morning.'

'Beautiful, squire, beautiful. Having a kip are you?'

'Well, I was trying to get a bit of a rest, yes.'

'Very nice too. I expect you feel better for it.'

Hallett considered this for a moment, but decided that to tell of his unfortunate attempts to get some peace and quiet would be tedious.

'Apart from the odd intrusion, yes. Among other things we have been discussing possible places to spend our holiday this year.'

'That's funny, so have we.'

'Were you discussing where to go?'

'No, we settled that a few weeks ago. What we were talking about this morning was whether or not the two boys still wanted to come on the family holiday.'

'Yes, Elizabeth was saying much the same thing about our two. Personally, I would like to see us going as a family. Wouldn't you?'

'In some ways, yes. But we have to see that they are growing up and might like to try a holiday away from us for a change.'

'Are the two boys going with you after all your discussions?'

'Yes, they are, but David is still a bit reluctant to be still going on holiday with Mum and Dad. He wouldn't go, I think, if it wasn't for the fact we're going camping.'

'Camping, eh? Have you very much experience of camping?'

'Not much. Only a brief go at it when we first bought the gear. I managed to get the whole package at a bargain price. How about you?'

'Naturally as a military man I can say that I have had my fair share of sleeping under canvas. Can be tricky, though. You say that you have bought the necessary equipment? One of these modern tents, I expect. Rather like a big orange and blue bungalow with all modern conveniences.'

'Well, it's two tents actually, squire. Like I said I picked up the whole package at a knock-down price. Look, I've got an idea. Why don't you and your family come with us in our tent, there'll be plenty of room.'

Hallett hesitated. He wasn't too keen on the idea of spending a holiday with his neighbours and he was even less keen on sharing a tent with them, but he didn't like to refuse straight away.

'That's most kind of you but I have already told Valerie and Richard that they can make suggestions for a venue for this year's holiday.'

'Well, if you decide to come, you might like to use the spare tent.'

'Thank you, but as it happens I already have a tent large enough for all of us.'

'Great. You'll let me know then if you decide to come along.'

'Yes, of course.'

As the Colonel walked back to the house he was assuming that neither Valerie nor Richard would be very keen on a camping holiday and he didn't think that he was very enthusiastic either. He reflected on the times in the Army that he had lived under canvas, then a thought struck him. With his experience in camping and Fred Root's lack of experience, he could show what a little training and living in the open could prove. Yes, perhaps this would be his opportunity to shine. All he had to do now was to steer everyone round to the idea of a camping holiday. A case for a little subtlety and use of tactics, he thought. He made his way to the house, deciding as he went what was to be his approach about this holiday.

'I thought that you would still be asleep, dear.'

The Colonel almost started to explain that, thanks to continuous interruptions, he had virtually no sleep at all, but he decided that it might not be wise at the moment.

'I have been chatting with our next door neighbour about holidays. I explained that we are asking Valerie and Richard for suggestions this year.' He looked towards where Valerie was sitting. 'Any ideas, yet?'

'Not at the moment, Father.'

'Well, apparently, the Roots' are, for the first time, going on a camping holiday.'

To Valerie, the idea of a camping holiday sounded only a

miniscule improvement on Weppleton Bay. She thought carefully. 'Are they all going on this holiday, then?'

'As I understand it, this is probably the last time they will have a holiday together. Next year, they will make other plans.'

Valerie appeared deep in thought. 'Well, as it's probably our last holiday as a family, I think a camping holiday might be a good idea.'

'I'm sure you are right. How about you, Richard?'

There was a long silence. 'Richard!' Hallett tried unsuccessfully to keep the sharpness out of his voice.

'Sorry, Father, I was engrossed in my book. What did you want?'

The normal remonstrations about his son's choice of literature and general lack of awareness were, with some difficulty, held back.

'We are discussing holidays, Richard. You and Valerie were going to think about it and give us some suggestions. Valerie has already agreed that a camping holiday might be a nice change for us. What do you think?'

'Sounds all right to me.'

'Good, that's all settled then.' He stopped. 'But how do you feel about all this, Elizabeth?'

She had been sitting listening to all this with some amusement as she witnessed Simon trying, for some reason or another and without much subtlety, to get everyone to agree to a camping holiday. She smiled. 'It sounds very nice to me. Does anyone know anything about camping?'

The Colonel smiled what he believed to be a modest smile. 'I think you can safely leave all that to me.'

There followed one of those long silences where all except one are thinking much the same thing. Elizabeth broke the silence.

'Just as you say, dear,' she said.

'Well, that's that settled. It just remains for me to tell Root that we can join him and his family on this camping holiday.'

'Just one point, Simon. What about tents?'

'It's odd you should say that because Root offered to let us share their tent or even to lend us a tent but I explained that we already have one.'

'You don't mean that old green thing in the attic, do you, Father?'

'Yes, Richard, I do. And, since we only have one tent, I don't see the reason for your question.'

'Well, I suppose I just never thought of anyone using it again, not to live in anyway.'

'Then you may well find this camping expedition a memorable experience.'

Both Richard and Valerie had the slightly chilling thought that in that statement was surely a grain of truth.

Hallett rubbed his hands together vigorously. 'You know, this might do us the world of good. I wish we had thought of it years ago.'

'Father, didn't you say that Mr Root offered to let us stay in their tent?'

'That is quite right, Valerie, I did. But I am confident that we can all be accommodated in comfort without troubling the Roots.'

'Your father's quite right dear. I'm sure that there will be more than enough room for all of us. Just think, it will be a bit like that year at Bay View when we were double-booked and we all had to spend one night in the same room. Don't you remember, Simon?'

The Colonel's face took on a puzzled expression. 'Yes, I do seem to recall that.'

'First there was Richard who spent most of the night shouting in his sleep. Then, of course, there was Valerie who thought that an earwig was crawling over her. Do you remember the scream she gave?'

'Yes, quite distinctly.'

'Yes,' said Elizabeth, smiling, 'I can almost hear that scream now and all over an earwig that didn't exist.'

By now the Colonel's puzzled expression had changed to one of worry. 'Yes, I do remember it.' He gave short, dry laugh. 'Look, if any of you wish to accept Mr Root's very kind offer, I think, perhaps, we ought not to appear ungrateful.'

Richard beamed and Valerie looked equally pleased. 'You

mean we can ask to stay in Mr Root's tent, Father?'

'Yes, Richard, of course you can. After all, it was very kind of him to offer.'

'Great. When are we going?'

'I think we can safely leave your father to sort out the details, Richard.'

'Quite right, Elizabeth. I will as usual make the decisions for all of us.'

'Well, that's settled, then. What next, Simon?'

'I think that I had better go and see Root and start making arrangements.'

Within a few minutes Hallett had spotted Fred in his garden and told him that they would be coming with them on holiday and he arranged with Fred for Valerie and Richard to stay with them.

'I'm really pleased you're coming with us, squire, I'm looking forward to it now.'

'I think we all are.'

Fred went to his house to let the family know the new arrangements and the Colonel stood for a few moments thinking about the forthcoming holiday. Well, at last we come to a subject where my experience is of some importance. I think I can soon show everyone what a little training and experience will do when we all try our hand at camping. Yes, this is my chance to show what Army life has done for me.

What the Colonel had forgotten, or maybe not even realised, was that his experience of camping was limited to riding in the front of the lorry, ordering the tents to be unloaded, then telling the sergeant to carry on and make camp. The next time he would see the tents they would all be erected and he would inspect each one in turn even though all he could do was twang a few guy-ropes and point out any litter left lying around. The siting and erection of the tents was the province of his sergeant. At night he would find his camp-bed assembled and made up. All of the cooking arrangements were taken care of by his corporal and Hallett's only contribution to the culinary operations was to emerge from his tent after poring over maps and exercise battle plans, stretch himself and say. 'About time for a brew-up, Sergeant?'

But all these details were vague in the Colonel's mind and he relished the thought of demonstrating the skill and experience that he fondly believed to be his.

He decided that now he was in the proper frame of mind, he may as well continue with mowing the lawn. He strode across to his Barlow mower, took a firm grip of the handles and gave it a vigorous push. The grass-box kicked up and distributed its few lawn snippings onto the uncut grass. As usual, he was unable to stop and rammed the grass-box amidships. He cursed silently and stooped to refit the box. Hooking it firmly on the bar, he decided to pull the mower back a few feet in order to get a good surge forward. He pulled backwards on the handle only to find that, in some inexplicable way, the grass-box had already unhooked itself and was now lying on the grass awaiting a re-union with the Barlow mower. With commendable restraint, Hallett managed to keep himself from rushing forward and wreaking his vengeance on the treacherous little grass-box. He glared at it and wondered whether to start again. He walked away. 'Damn and blast the lawn,' he said, as he strode towards the house.

Inside the Root household Fred was telling his family about the addition to their holiday plans.

'So, although they won't be sharing our tent, they will be coming along.'

David looked up from his magazine. 'Are they all coming along then, Dad?'

'Oh, yes, she'll be there.'

'Who will? Oh you mean, wotsername, Valerie.'

Fred gave a big smile. 'Yes, that's right, old wotsername, Valerie.'

David's face deepened slightly in colour as he apparently continued to read his magazine. Inwardly, he was excited. Just think, to be on holiday together and camping too. There would be plenty of occasions to get to know each other. After all, the only things he had said to her so far were 'good morning' and things like that. Yes, this could turn out to be a very happy holiday.

'Have they got a tent then, Fred?'

'Yes, it's one he used in his Army days.'

Gary, who was very keen on the Army and hoped one day to join, was more than usually attentive as he listened to this and he was fascinated to hear that an ex-soldier would be coming on holiday with them and bringing an Army tent.

'An Army tent, Dad. I bet that's a good one.'

'Yes, very likely. Well, Glad we'll start making the arrangements soon. I'll just need to clear the date with the Colonel and we'll be on our way.'

'Right, Fred. I'll start sorting out what we need. And we'd better take lots of warm clothes with us, you never know what the weather will be like. '

This meant that they would probably take about three thick jumpers each plus plastic raincoats, thick socks, woolly hats and any other item of clothing that Gladys decided they should take 'just in case'. The fact that most of these extra items would not be used or even unpacked would not worry Gladys. She felt that it was her duty to protect her tribe, as she called them.

Fred sat thinking about where to go camping and carefully considered all the places that had been recommended to him. He opened his thick brochure on British Camping Holidays and began to narrow his selection. David was still reading his magazine but a close observer would have seen that he was still on the same page that he was reading when his father had told them about their new companions on holiday. For Gary, the thought of actually camping with an ex-soldier and seeing what coping with the outdoor life was like; that was a really exciting prospect, Gladys was halfway through her mental inventory of things to take on a camping holiday. Lost in their separate thoughts, they whiled away the Saturday morning in pleasant contemplation.

'I wonder how I can find out about recommended camp sites?'

The Colonel had started on his Camping Plan that included an impressive inventory of Required Items and a smaller inventory of Items To Take If We Have Room.

'Why don't you get one of those books from the newsagent that show camping sites.'

Again, the Colonel found that Elizabeth had arrived at an answer that he could have found if he had only thought about it for a moment.

'I'm not sure how reliable they would be. What I really need is someone who has actually been camping and can advise me of the sort of site to go for.' He paused and thought for a moment. 'Even so, it wouldn't hurt to get one of those books to get a sort of rough starting point.'

Elizabeth smiled. 'Yes, that's a good idea.'

'Well, that's settled, then. I think I'll just go up to the attic and inspect that tent.'

'Mind how you go, Simon.'

A few minutes later, after a rather puffing climb of the attic steps and scrambling with accompanying grunts through the trap-door, Hallett switched on the light and gazed round at the variety of items consigned to that part of the house rarely visited. Old toys, a play-pen, a cricket bat, a hockey stick, school photographs and souvenirs of countries they had visited. It was a sort of melancholy family album.

After a little searching he found his tent, covered in old newspapers and odd packages. He glanced inside one of the cardboard boxes. Slowly, he pulled out a creased photograph showing himself wearing what were obviously new insignia of a Lieutenant Colonel. In the picture he was shaking hands with a tubby little Brigadier.

'Well, well, old 'Piggy' Styelow. Time really does fly. It all seems only a short time ago, though. There I was, just promoted to Lieutenant Colonel.' He shook his head. 'Ah, it all comes back so clearly.'

He sat down on one of the bundles and sighed as those years came flooding back to him.

CHAPTER TEN

'Congratulations, Simon. I always knew you would make it.'

'Thank you, sir. I must say I am very pleased with my promotion, of course.'

Brigadier 'Piggy' Styelow's normally ruddy complexion positively glowed as he beamed at Lieutenant Colonel Simon Hallett.

'Yes, of course you are; so am I. But we must give this a proper christening in the Mess sometime.' He leaned forward.' You know what I mean, don't you?'

The newly promoted Colonel knew only too well what his Brigadier meant. He meant that Hallett would soon be facing one horrendous Mess bill. This would cover the cost of the considerable quantity of drinks that his well-wishers would assuredly manage to consume on his behalf. Some of his well-wishers might even manage to force down a double to reinforce their congratulations.

'Well, of course, sir, I would be honoured.'

'Good man, Simon. See you at lunch, then, if not before.'

He returned Hallett's salute and ambled off in the direction of the Headquarters; his portly figure a familiar sight in the unit.

'Excuse me, Colonel?'

It was some seconds before Hallett remembered that he was a Colonel and that this remark was addressed to him. He turned to face a rather pale looking young Captain who had evidently forgotten that he should salute. He wore horn-rimmed spectacles, which he would, from time to time, remove, polish and place them in his pocket only to recover them seconds later, polish them once more and replace them on his rather prominent nose. Hallett recognised him as Captain Evans, the Education Officer.

'Yes, er Ivor, what is it?'

'Well, sir. It's to do with the Current Affairs classes that I am running. Lately, I've been covering the subject of statistics and how they are arrived at which has lead, quite naturally, to such things as Gallup polls and how they affect Council decisions and such like, now isn't it?'

Hallett, by now was mystified. What on earth can the man be asking for? Nothing straightforward, I'll be bound.

'So you see, sir, I hoped to take the men into town and let them conduct a Gallup poll of our own.'

'A Gallup poll? What on earth for?'

'Well, I thought that it would give the men some practical experience so that they could understand more clearly how decisions in their own home towns are made, based on such statistics.'

Hallett frowned. 'Is that how Local Government makes decisions, then?'

Captain Evans looked uncomfortable. 'Well, in theory it is, sir, yes.'

Hallett's mind was made up. 'I think that I prefer the men to learn facts. Much more useful.'

'If you will just allow me to conduct this one poll, sir, I will bring you the summary of results. I guarantee that the results will surprise you.'

'Oh, very well. But I want this closely controlled, mind.'

'It will be that, sir, I can promise you.' He walked off, again neglecting to salute.

On the afternoon chosen by Captain Evans as Gallup Polling Day, his class drove into the town and parked their military coach in a side street. His students received their instructions from Captain Evans and appeared to be listening intently. One or two were considering a trip to the local cinema because they reasoned that, although the Current Affairs classes were compulsory, this compulsion did not extend to Gallup polls and they were not in the slightest bit interested in Gallup polls. This was a view, it seemed, held by many in the class.

The question to be put the inhabitants of the town was – "How Do You Feel About Having a Large Military Camp So Near to Your Town?"

So, armed with bundles of questionnaires, the so-called students were unleashed on the town.

It took about twenty minutes for the trouble to start.

One of the soldiers put the question to one man who promptly replied that he would like to see the whole bloody lot of the idle buggers told to sod off. The soldier putting the question was not quite sure how he should record that sort of reply nor even how to answer it. His colleague, Lance Corporal Bright, standing within hearing of this outburst, had no such uncertainties.

'Tell that thick, civvy bastard that he'd better bugger off and be quick about it.' His voice rang out loud and clear and could be heard all over the market square.

That was just the beginning.

A building worker, named Claude, was standing right behind Bright, and tapped him on the shoulder. As he turned round, Claude's rock-hard right fist landed with some force on Bright's nose. His head snapped back and for a few seconds, he must have thought that somehow, someone had managed to shunt a goods train onto his nose. Then he reacted. 'You bastard,' he shouted.

One of Bright's close friends, Private 'Thicky' McGraw, saw the incident and slouched across to where Claude was still grinning at Lance Corporal Bright's efforts to stem the flow of blood. 'Thicky' tapped him on the shoulder with the intention of flattening his nose when he turned round. Instead, Claude took one step forward and turned. While 'Thicky' was still trying to sort out this change of tactics, the rock hard fist was in action once more and landed with force and accuracy on 'Thicky's' nose, causing an immediate flow of blood. Claude's fists had been hardened by the numerous occasions on which he had been forced defend the choice of his name. This second letting of Army blood then triggered off a series of scuffles with a good many blows being exchanged. Occasionally, a sheaf of the survey papers would be flung into the air and scatter themselves over the struggling mass of bodies.

At intervals, Captain Evans' voice could be heard shrieking at his men to 'Stop this at once, I am giving you an order.' But it had no effect.

Evans' gaze swept round the battle area noting, among other things, that his men were getting the worst of it. He knew that there was no point in shouting at them from where he stood, so he must get to a vantage point. He spotted a concrete litter bin and he managed to scramble up onto it. He braced himself to give what he intended to be a thundering call to cease hostilities at once and it would have a distinct ring of authority.

Before he could call out one word, a local garage hand climbed onto the bin with him and tried to push him off. Evans clutched his opponent and for a while they swayed backwards and forwards. Suddenly, the garage hand, known to his associates as 'Knocker', lifted a booted foot and brought it down on Captain Evans' instep. His cry of pain was heart-rending and he released his hold. He leaned forward towards his throbbing foot and 'Knocker' Dorman bellowed with laughter then seized Evans' nose tightly in his oil-stained fist which brought his head up again. For a few seconds 'Knocker' was helpless with laughter at Evans' screwed up face and he tightened his grip still more. Finally, he gave the nose a savage tweak then pushed Captain Evans backwards where he landed heavily on the back of a newly arrived policeman who was just in the act of blowing his whistle.

Later, when all the scuffling had finished, Captain Evans coaxed his men back onto the coach for their return to camp.

As they pulled up at the guardroom, the men climbed off a coach in varying states of distress. The coach, too, had not escaped the fury of the local populace. It had one headlamp kicked in, both windscreen wipers bent back at an unusable angle, a heel dent on the back and three obscene words spray-painted on the side.

The injuries to the men included black eyes, cut faces, puffy lips and swollen noses. One man, Private Carper, had an egg-sized lump on his head. He had gained this during the fighting when he saw an elderly lady getting too close to the action. Fearful for her safety, he took her by the elbow and tried to lead her away from the action. She gave one shriek of 'Help, I'm being assaulted' then swung at him with her shopping bag. It contained

141

one small tin of Heinz baked beans. Lastly, Captain Evans emerged from the coach. His uniform was torn, his nose was inflamed and the peak of his cap had been half ripped off so that it now bobbed up and down as he walked.

The following morning Evans reported to Colonel Hallett and described the afternoon in detail. Hallett stared at Evans whose nose was still glowing. When he at last managed to speak, his voice was hoarse with disbelief. 'I can hardly dare believe what I have just been told. Are you telling me, Captain Evans, that your men managed to inflame the local inhabitants to the point where they retaliated with violence?'

'Not exactly, sir. It was the locals who started it and my men were caught in the middle.'

'Then why did you not order your men back to the coach?'

'Well I did try, sir, but what with all the goings on and so forth I couldn't make myself heard.'

'Well, I hope you realise that this will mean a Board of Inquiry.'

Evans nodded took off his spectacles, polished them vigorously then put them into his pocket. 'Yes, I thought as much.'

'You may go, Captain Evans.'

Evans turned, forgetting as usual to salute, and walked from the office.

As Hallett had predicted, there was a Board of Inquiry and it was chaired by Major-General Neville-Saunders. He listened with barely disguised impatience to the sorry tales told by the various witnesses and at the conclusion he spoke bitterly about incompetent officers who allow such idiotic activities to take place when the meanest intelligence could spot a potential disaster. Lieutenant Colonel Simon Hallett was mentioned in the final report and not in very complimentary terms.

Shortly after the Board, Hallett sent for Captain Evans. 'Captain Evans, I appreciate your zeal in trying to broaden the outlook of the men but I insist that your future activities must be of a more controllable nature.'

Evans looked uncomfortable for a moment. Then he spoke. 'Well, sir, as it happens, I have got something in mind which I think might help the men and I don't see really how it could go wrong.'

'Good. I hope you can manage to keep them occupied and out of trouble this time. What are you proposing as your next enterprise?'

'Well, sir, I thought that I would keep up their interest in current affairs.'

Hallett's stomach gave a distinct lurch at this.

'So I hoped to get permission for them to sit in at a Town Council Meeting so that they can see how...'

'No, I'm sorry, but no. It won't do.' Already he could visualise the uproar and turmoil inside the Council Chambers. 'There must be something else, surely?'

'What do you suggest then, sir?'

'I don't know. How about stamp collecting?'

Evans' face showed no enthusiasm for this.

'Or a male-voice choir.'

'Thank you, sir. I'll give it some thought.' He turned and wandered off.

Meanwhile, Hallett decided that life must go on. His hand hovered over the buzzer and he hesitated only because he did not relish a visit by his Chief Clerk, Warrant Officer Horace McKindle.

McKindle was a human dynamo. From time to time he would rush into the Colonel's office, deliver a tray full of files. Each letter or circular was complete with a note so that the Colonel could make a decision based on all known circumstances. This, though, only made the situation more complicated because every move had its advantages and disadvantages clearly listed in each file by the tireless Chief Clerk. In almost every case, though, the advantages and disadvantages were about equal and showing the Colonel no clear answer. He sometimes thought he might as well toss a coin.

He sighed. Such was the price of promotion. More responsibility, more work and more things to keep track of. He decided that he needed some fresh air; he picked up his hat and headed for the door. He looked into the main office. Good, no sign of McKindle. He walked out and had gone but a few strides when he stopped and swore softly to himself. His Chief Clerk was striding towards him at a rate more suited to jogging. He stopped in front of his Colonel and offered a salute that was so rapid that Hallett was unsure whether to return it.

'Can I, with respect, sir, ask when I can expect you back in the office?'

Warrant Officer Horace McKindle was a Scot and he had a clipped, almost metallic voice. He always spoke quickly, not always waiting for answers to questions he posed.

'You see, sir, we will soon be having our Admin Inspection and I am keen that we are ready for that, as I am sure you are. After all, we have always had a good report and I expect you would like that to continue. So, can I expect you back in about ten minutes, sir? I have many things ready for your decision so I'll wait for you in the office and go through them with you.'

He flicked up another salute and marched away before Hallett could even frame a reply.

He thought bitterly, 'I do wish that man would slow down a bit. I find his rapid approach to everything a little bewildering.'

A few minutes later, though, he found himself heading back towards his office and was soon settled once more behind his desk. The rest of the morning was punctuated by darting visits from the inexhaustible McKindle, who would rush in with a file, explain the purpose of the letter, point out the kind of decision needed, give the alternative courses of action and wait for a reply. Mentally, Hallett would toss a coin and then settle for a decision, but they all seemed to him to be fraught with the same grim disadvantages and the eventual risk of explanations being demanded. However, he reasoned that he had given his decision and that, after all, was what he was paid for.

He was more than a little pleased when the time came for lunch, but, just as he stood up, there was a sharp rap at the door and McKindle hurried in and placed two files in the tray.

'Before you go, sir, could you please scribble your comments on these two files. One is about the preparation for the Admin Inspection and the other concerns office accommodation. If you would indicate what your replies might be I can have them typed and away in this afternoon's post.'

All this had been chattered out with the consistent delivery of a computer printer.

'Really, Mr McKindle, could they not wait?'

There was a brief silence while McKindle reacted as if his Colonel had uttered a foul and blasphemous remark. His voice was shocked and carried a hint of reproof as he replied. 'Wait, sir,' he said, forcing out the hated word, 'wait for what?'

'It's just that I thought that the world wouldn't come to an end if I went to lunch.'

'Lunch *now*, sir?'

Hallett glanced at the clock. In his former post he would have gone for lunch at least ten minutes before this.

'Look, Mr McKindle, whatever the urgency of those letters I insist they can await my return from lunch and I will then deal with them promptly. Now, take them away and let me have them this afternoon. If you would, please,' he finished, rather lamely.

Warrant Officer McKindle rapidly picked up the two offending files and, without another word, strode quickly back to his office.

Hallett felt exasperated that a Warrant Officer could have the effect of making him feel guilty merely because he wanted to go to lunch. After all, his stomach was rumbling and therefore, clearly in need of sustenance. Damn it all, we are not all human dynamos and there are those of us who know how to get our priorities right. So, lunch it shall be, and a pox on Mr McKindle's files. So, with this rather spirited thought, he set out for the Officers' Mess.

Once inside the Mess the Colonel automatically doffed his cap and took it into the cloakroom. As he turned to go out he almost bumped into a florid faced Lieutenant Colonel with grey, wavy hair and wearing the insignia of the Royal Army Medical Corps.

'Hello, Simon,' he said, in a rich, booming voice.

'Hello, Alastair, didn't see you. How are you?'

The rich voice boomed again. 'How am I? Well, as the medical man I should be asking you that, shouldn't I?'

With that he gave a loud, guffawing sort of laugh that echoed round the cloakroom.

'Anyway, Simon, I'm pleased to know that congratulations are due. Well done.'

Hallett nodded modestly. Truthfully, he would rather not continue this conversation, because his colleague, Lieutenant Colonel Alastair Disley always spoke with enough volume to fill a large room.

'Thank you, Alastair. Coming to lunch?'

'Not right now, Simon. Going to have a double gin first. Sure you won't join me?'

'No, thank you. See you later perhaps.'

'Right. Must go and get started, got a lot of pressing cases to see this afternoon.'

Simon paled a little. Disley had a habit of relating all the lurid details of his latest cases, but always taking care not to identify his patient. The medical detail, though, was such as to make all but the strongest stomach squirm. Hallett sometimes felt that the nickname given to him of Grisly Disley was well chosen.

'Yes, of course. Well, I must get into the dining room for lunch. My regards to Annabel.'

They parted and Hallett walked into the dining room, took his table napkin from the rack and sat in his favourite seat by the window. A rather elderly waitress shuffled over to him as he studied the menu.

Where most of us give a polite cough to announce our unnoticed presence, Mrs Pratt was less delicate. She sniffed.

'Made up your mind, 'ave you?'

He looked up. 'No, Mrs Pratt, I have not.'

She sighed a noisy sigh. Mrs Pratt was known to suffer with her feet and, particularly on wet days could be quite irascible. Her favourite targets were young subalterns arriving late for a meal.

Hallett continued to study the menu closely. 'I think I'll have the beef bourguignon with creamed potatoes, broccoli and vichy carrots.'

Taking out a note-pad, Mrs Pratt prepared to write. As always, she stubbornly insisted on calling out each item as she wrote it down and pronouncing it as it was spelt.

'Right, then. That's beef bore gooignon, creamed potatoes,

broccoli and vye chye carrots.'

She shuffled off and left the Colonel to occupy the wait by helping himself to the water-jug.

He enjoyed his meal when it at last arrived and he reflected as he left the dining room on how much better he felt. Certainly the lunch had been most satisfying. After the main course he had selected compote of pears with honey and ginger and all this lay comfortably within giving him this feeling of well-being. In the ante-room he helped himself to coffee, sank into an armchair, then with a long, contented sigh, he lay back.

'Hello, Simon,' cried the rich, booming voice, 'finished already?'

He looked up, slightly startled. His unease was returning. 'Hello, Alastair, Yes, must get back you see. Got a stack of things to do.'

'Think I'll just join you while I finish my gin and you get that coffee down you.'

He flopped into the armchair next to Hallett and lay back sipping at his gin.

All was quiet and the Colonel hoped it would stay that way. He had almost finished his coffee and hoped to slip away before Disley started his medical reminiscences.

'Had an interesting case in this morning,' the voice boomed.

A few of the more experienced Mess members looked up from their newspapers, quickly drained the remains of their coffee and struggled out of their chairs.

His voice was well known to the whole unit. When anyone attended sick parade it was embarrassing for them to know that, while they were in his surgery, all of his questions and comments could be clearly overheard by patients in the adjacent Waiting Room. Questions like 'Have you opened your bowels today?' and 'Do you ever have any trouble in going?' were regularly heard through the thin partition wall. Any soldier waiting to report a quite personal complaint was well aware that all of the personnel in the waiting room would soon be as familiar with his condition as the Medical Officer. A crowded Waiting Room had once heard the Colonel ask a Lance Corporal, quite clearly. 'Don't you find that a very inconvenient place to have a wart?' It was admitted, though, that waiting outside Grisly Disley's door was more interesting than a visit to your average GP.

Hallett stirred uneasily in his chair. His beef bourguignon was mingling happily with the compote of pears and he did not wish to hear anything now that might tend to upset that relationship.

He made a desperate try. 'An interesting case, eh? That reminds me, would you and Annabel care to dine with us on Saturday. You see, I have just received an interesting case of wines from my supplier in London.'

'That's jolly nice of you, Simon. We'd love to. Anyway, as I was saying. This interesting case this morning. A Lance Corporal had his ear badly bitten by his dog. An Airedale, I think, or was it an Alsatian? Anyway, whatever it was; when they brought him in to me I had quite a task in persuading him to take his hand away. When at last he did, it was a ghastly sight. Quite clearly a job for the old darning needle, but quite honestly, it was a bit difficult to see what was what. Awful mess with lots of blood and saliva and so on. Poor chap, he was quite upset. To tell you the truth I had to restrain myself from saying 'What's all this ear?'

The loud, guffawing laugh rolled round the ante-room causing several pairs of eyes to be lifted from newspapers and followed by a few tut-tuts. All unheeded by Colonel Disley.

'By the way, Simon, I had your Sergeant Penbridge in just before lunch.'

'Penbridge? The last I heard of him he was at football practice preparing for that big match.'

'That's right. He stopped a kick from one of the full-backs.'

'Well, that's damned inconvenient. I've got a job for him this afternoon. Will he be fit, do you think?'

'Not a chance I'm afraid.'

'Is it serious, then? Where was he kicked?'

'Had the bad luck to catch it right in the family jewels. Still, from what I hear he's a randy little sod. At least the local girls can get a bit of peace for a while. Even so, he was luckier than that poor wretch who got his fingers jammed in that chip-cutting machine last week. I had to get him out myself, you know. It was ghastly. Blood all over the place and his fingers cut and broken and all flopping about everywhere. Dreadful business.'

The beef bourguignon was now disputing territorial rights with the compote of pears and the rest were adding their grumbles and protests. Hallett made a last desperate attempt to steer his companion away from medical matters.

'Are you going in for lunch yet, Alastair?' he said, then instantly regretted his choice of subject.

'In a moment, I expect. Anything good on the menu?'

'Well, there's beef bourguignon.'

'Can't stand it. Personally, I don't think that fatty stuff like bacon belongs with great jollops of stewing beef and I'm not wild about mushrooms. Can't get over them being a fungus, you know.'

Hallett's stomach evidently resented this slight against its choice of main course and it fluttered uneasily.

'Anything else?'

'Oh, usual things, you know. Chops, kidneys, curry, ham in spiced orange sauce...' Hallett stopped there with an instruction from his stomach to continue at his peril.

'Hmm, might have a couple of chops if they're not too greasy. Don't like kidneys; they're filters, you know, doesn't do to forget that. Never did like curry; over-spiced muck. And as for ham in spiced orange sauce, it sounds like a most unholy alliance if you ask me.' He stared at Hallett. 'I say, Simon, perhaps you had better call in and see me in my surgery some time, you don't look too well.'

Hallett eased himself out the chair and straightened up. 'Nothing serious. I think I'll just get a little air.'

'Good idea. See you later perhaps,' and he swilled back his gin in one gulp.

On his slightly unsteady way to the door, Hallett consoled himself with the knowledge that Disley would certainly forget about their dining arrangements for Saturday and spare him further medical recollections.

Once back in his office he felt slightly better and settled himself behind his desk to deal with the afternoon's work.

He was in the middle of reading a sheaf of new administrative instructions when Warrant Officer McKindle swept in. He swooped on the desk and began to empty the in-tray with all the enthusiasm of a young terrier unearthing a bone. He snatched up a file, flicked it open, riffled through the letters and slammed the file onto the desk. Swiftly, he made a few notes in his note-pad and smartly returned the file to the tray.

'Thank you, sir,' he said, even as he was turning to go out.

It was difficult not to feel inadequate when one watched Mr McKindle at work. He always worked at the same driving pace, reading and writing at the same rapid rate and only losing patience when he considered someone intolerably ponderous. That was not an infrequent occurrence.

No sooner had the door closed than it opened once more and McKindle hurried in, crossing the room in a few strides.

'Sir, message for you from the Brigadier. There is a newly promoted Captain who has been posted in and he arrived this afternoon. But, because the Brigadier can't be available to interview him, he sends his compliments and asks if you would see the Captain and give him the usual talk. The Brigadier says he will see him personally later in the week.'

'Yes, very well. When he arrives, show him in.'

'He is in my office now, sir.'

'In that case, show him in at once.'

'Sir.'

He whisked out of the office and almost instantly re-appeared.

'This way, sir,' said McKindle then returned to his office.

In walked a tall, gangling figure with a languid expression and protruding teeth. He waved a limp salute.

Hallett tried to stop his expression from showing the surprise and regret he felt at seeing Captain Jeremy Butterworth beaming at him across the desk.

'Hello, Medger. Sorry, I forgot; it's Colonel now.'

'Good afternoon, Jeremy. Please come in and sit down.'

'Thank you, sir. Rather lake old times, what?'

'Yes, quite. What I have to do now, is just chat to you about general matters because the Brigadier is not available this afternoon. He will see you personally later this week. Have you reported to the Mess yet?'

'Yes, Colonel and I'm quite impressed with my room.'

'Good, good. Well, I won't discuss your new post. Instead I will just talk generally and see if I can help you with anything. I can't say that I remember any of your hobbies or interests but if we can talk about them now I can tell you of any clubs or societies you might find helpful. Do you play bridge for instance?'

'Eckchewly, Colonel, one is not very keen on plain cods.'

Hallett tried not to show his irritation at Butterworth's nasal mangling of the English language.

'Any sporting interests of any sort?'

'Well, I have played cricket a few times,' he gave a horsey sort of laugh that grated on his Colonel's nerves, 'but I don't think I was awfully good at it.'

'I see. I think we'll talk about it some other time. In the meantime I'll show you round the unit to familiarise you with the layout.'

'Thenk you, sir, terribly caned of you.'

'I'll just tell Mr McKindle that I will be leaving the office for a while.'

They walked round the unit and Hallett pointed out various items of interest and interpreted Butterworth's rather insipid replies. Normally, he would have handed over to a junior officer, the task of conducting a new officer around the unit, especially one such as Jeremy St John Butterworth. However, he was relieved to get any opportunity to escape from the office vortex created by the activities of the energetic McKindle.

They made their way to the Quartermasters Stores and went inside.

'In your new post you will have quite a few dealings in this establishment and so you had better have a preliminary reconnaissance.'

'Erse, of course, sir,' said Butterworth, and weaved his way round the wooden racks containing boots, blankets, pickaxes, shovels and all the rest of the usual equipment jealously guarded by Quartermasters throughout the British Army.

In his recollections, Hallett had forgotten that Butterworth had a natural gift for clumsiness in a measure rarely found in one man. He turned by the end of one of the racks and displaced a pyramid of metal pots. The noise of their clatter was almost unbelievable and was enough to make the head vibrate.

'Sorry,' he called out, 'didn't notice those pots there.' But even as he spoke his elbow dislodged a long-handled, wooden grass rake which fell sideways and cleared a pile of papers from a small shelf. 'Sorry.'

'Mr Butterworth, would you please be good enough to join me here at the counter,' said Hallett, anxious to continue their tour before Butterworth could reduce the Quartermasters Stores to a muddled, broken heap of assorted military kit.

'Erse, Colonel.'

The Colonel hardly dared to look in the direction of Sergeant Bowe, the man responsible for the store. He had been watching Butterworth with the sort of sullen, resigned air of a man who has seen his fair share of what he called 'jumped-up twits'. Bowe, a man devoid of any sort of humour, looked on impassively as Butterworth lumbered towards the counter.

'Sorry about all that, Sergeant. Made a bit of a mess, I think.'

'Just leave it to me, sir, I'll see to it.'

'Would you like to me to lend a hand?'

'It's time we were leaving, Mr Butterworth,' said Hallett, sharply, thereby saving Sergeant Bowe the task of thinking of a reasonably acceptable way of declining the Captain's offer.

He looked at the Sergeant and nodded. 'Er, carry on, Sergeant.'

The Sergeant just looked.

They walked towards the door and Hallett was determined to get Butterworth out of the place as quickly as possible. At the doorway, in some extraordinary mix-up, Butterworth tried to open the door and stand to one side to allow his Colonel to precede him. In doing so he managed to dislodge a framed chart showing details of some rather obscure statistics. This thudded to the floor but, miraculously, the glass front remained intact. Butterworth tried to turn and see what damage he had now inflicted on Sergeant Bowe's stores, and crunched heavily with his highly polished black boot onto Hallett's left foot. He gave a gasp of pain and pushed Butterworth forward to ease the pressure off his foot, which felt as if it had been gripped in a vice then thrust into a furnace. Butterworth lurched forward and there was a nasty crunch as the glass front of the statistics chart succumbed to the pressure of a size eleven Army issue right boot.

Butterworth looked down and there was a long, awkward silence.

'Oh, I'm afraid it's broken.'

Sergeant Bowe raised his eyes heavenwards.

Hallett snorted with impatience. Why, he asked himself, why do I seem to get every misfit, every inept and clumsy oaf for my staff? Why can't I have normal, efficient soldiers like other officers do? He looked at his new Captain who seemed about to speak...

'Simon, have you found the tent yet?'

He came out of his reverie, looked round and sighed. He started removing old newspapers and packages from his tent. Sometimes it was not a good idea to dwell on the past.

'Yes, Elizabeth, I'm uncovering it now.'

CHAPTER ELEVEN

The Saturday morning nominated by Hallett as Departure Day was bright and clear and without a cloud in the sky. The Roots were up first and busied themselves with preparing a fortifying breakfast. The camping equipment had been loaded onto the car the previous evening and it remained just to pack a few personal items and they would be ready. Gladys was doing her usual check on her husband and children, quite convinced that, whatever their age, they could hardly be expected to pack all the necessities for a camping holiday without some help from her.

'Fred, have you packed your spare razor, just in case?'

'Yes, Glad.'

'And your razor blades?'

'Yes, Glad. Everything is taken care of.'

'It's all very well to say that, but who do you turn to when you've forgotten something?'

Fred smiled as he nodded his reply. Gladys was quite right. On previous holidays any items forgotten by them, she had somehow remembered or could produce a reasonable substitute. She really did worry about them and, from time to time would organise them. They all loved her for it but any mention of this affection for her would bring the response of 'Oh, get on with you, don't be soft.' They all knew, though, that this in itself was an expression of her love for them.

Inside the Halletts' house, preparations were well under way, and, despite Hallett trying unsuccessfully to keep everyone to a rigid timetable, things were going smoothly. The feeling of excitement that precedes a holiday was beginning to make itself felt in all of them.

It was not long before the two families were moving quietly outside and making their way down their respective drives. The two cars had been first backed into the roadway in preparation to receive the passengers and the trailer that Fred had decided to tow was hauled out and fixed to his car.

The two families stood chatting on the pavement while the two men made their final check of the house doors and windows. Then Fred and Hallett walked out talking about the forthcoming journey.

'I think, Root, that you had better follow me. I believe I have been this way before, and, in any event, Elizabeth will be map-reading for me, so we should be all right.'

'Just as you like, squire. In fact, I shan't take my eyes off your rear.'

'What? Oh, yes, quite. One other thing. Are you sure your load is securely lashed in position? After all, we don't want any delays on the way whilst we have to rope it on again, do we?'

'No worries there, squire. It's on as tight as it'll go.'

'Would you like me to check it for you? It's the sort of thing I would do before starting out on an Army expedition.'

'Help yourself.'

Hallett walked past Fred's car and peered at the well-loaded trailer. He pushed it then tugged on a loose strap. The whole load was held firmly in place.

'Good, good, well done.'

He walked to his own car and was about to open the door when he noticed the end of a rope hanging down from the roof rack. He lifted it, tried to see what it was tied to then gave it a quick tug. There was a snapping sound then about a dozen tent pegs clattered down onto the pavement.

He looked uncomfortably at Fred. 'Well, at least you can see what I meant by the delay this could cause.'

'Not to worry, squire. I'll give you a hand to tidy it up and then we'll be on our way.'

It took the two men only a few minutes to pick up the tent pegs and stow them securely on the roof rack and they were ready to set off.

The families were then sorted out and made themselves comfortable in their respective cars. The two drivers were the last to enter and, having made a final check of the houses, declared themselves ready to go.

A few minutes later they were cruising down Forsythia Avenue with the Halletts in the lead. They had almost reached the end of the road when the leading car stopped, Hallett climbed out and walked back to Fred who had pulled up a few yards behind.

'Trouble?' asked Fred, noting that Hallett was again looking uncomfortable.

'Not really, it's just that we have forgotten; that is, I have forgotten to bring the necessary map.'

'Nothing to worry about, squire. Are you going back or would you like to borrow one?'

'I think that, under the circumstances, I will accept your kind offer and borrow a map.'

Hallett was eager to borrow a map because he knew that if he returned to his house, Elizabeth would wish to accompany him. Then, in accordance with one of her few superstitions, she would insist that, before he left home for the second time, he must sit down facing the door from which he was about to leave. Having done that, he must, while holding out at arm's length the object he had returned to get, count slowly to twenty out loud. He would have agreed to this only because he knew that she would be terribly worried if he didn't. He watched as Fred rummaged about and produced several maps, riffled through them then presented one to him.

'Thank you, I'm much obliged and I will return this to you later.'

He returned to his car and climbed in. He exchanged a few words with Elizabeth who unfolded the map and tried to examine it as the convoy moved off once more.

For some miles they sped along gradually leaving familiar suburban landmarks and getting into quieter country surroundings.

Inside the leading car Elizabeth was frowning at the map. 'Shouldn't you have turned left there, Simon?'

'Left? Nonsense, this is a straight run for some miles yet.'

'Not according to the map is isn't.'

'That is probably because you are not used to map-reading. I go by the feel of it and I can tell you that we are heading in the right direction.'

'But it's a bit quiet. Are you sure that this is the right road?'

He smiled a tolerant smile. 'Elizabeth, I think that with my experience on manoeuvres I could be expected to follow a simple route like this.'

'Yes, I know, but it's just that we haven't seen a signpost for some time.'

He smiled a slightly less tolerant smile. 'The presence or absence of signposts has no significance at all. It is merely a question of knowing that we are heading in the right direction. Trust me.'

'If you say so, dear.'

In the back of the car Richard and Valerie looked out at the rural scenery and sighed. They seemed to have been travelling for hours and they wished they could stop somewhere for a drink and a chance to stretch their legs.

'Where are we now, Father?' said Richard, looking out at the quiet fields dotted with grazing sheep and the occasional group of mournful-looking cows.

There followed that sort of pause which indicates that someone is not quite willing to reply.

'Our precise location is not of the utmost importance, Richard. What matters is that we are heading in the right direction and we are well on the way to our camping site. I deliberately chose not to calculate an ETA and so time is of no significance.'

'What's an ETA?'

'Estimated time of arrival,' said Elizabeth, drawing on her officer's wife experience.

'Oh,' said Richard, sounding a little depressed.

They travelled for some miles in silence until Elizabeth, noting the fidgeting of their two passengers, asked her husband if he was still certain that he was on the right road because, if anything, the road seemed to be getting narrower and narrower.

He looked around with a faint air of desperation but when he spoke, it was with seeming confidence. 'Just because we are on a quiet road and missing the multitude of less prudent drivers is no reason to suppose that we are lost.'

'Do you know exactly where we are then?' said Elizabeth, poring over the now crumpled map.

Hallett thought for a moment and then he looked with interest at a sort of monument at the side of the road. It was made of rough stone and set in a small plot of earth. Square at the base, it tapered gracefully to a chiselled point at the top.

'Look at that, Elizabeth,' he said, in tones of admiration. 'This may be just a quiet corner of England but it does one's pride good to see that even here, they have made a humble effort to honour their war heroes with this simple monument. Quite touching, really.'

By this time had he had slowed his car to a stop and for a few moments they all stared at the simple obelisk. In Fred Root's car the occupants were puzzled as to the reason for the unexpected stop.

'What's he doing, Fred?'

'Search me, gal.'

'Are we lost then, Dad?'

'I hope not, Gary, but I'll be interested to know just where we are.'

'Shall I nip out and ask Mr Hallett?'

'No thanks, son. You sit tight, we'll get there soon.'

The leading car then moved off with the driver giving a short lecture on the sterling spirit that still exists even in the remote areas of this country. The sort of spirit that forged a nation destined to earn the respect and admiration of the world. The sort of spirit that produced people capable of shaping the destiny of the civilised world. It was no fault of Hallett's but the dramatic tone of his delivery was severely diluted when Richard accused Valerie of having borrowed his binoculars and not returning them. She answered that she had returned them and that she had seen Richard with them before the trip started. This prompted Richard into a squirming search under the front seat and behind cushions where he eventually found them. This excitement having subsided they settled back both aware that the lecture on The British Sterling Spirit had now faded away.

They had travelled a few miles when Richard gave a shout.

'Hey, look, Father. It's that monument again.'

Hallett looked out of his window and scowled. 'Rubbish. Of course it's not the same one, how could it be? It's nothing like the other one.'

'Well, it looks like it to me.'

The Colonel pulled into the side of the road.

'Look, Richard, I know what I am doing and in any case, it is virtually impossible for it to be the same one, unless you are inferring that we are travelling in circles.'

'Well, we have been doing a lot of turning.'

This was true and it was caused by Hallett's frantic efforts to get off the rural track and back to more familiar ground.

'The turning to which you refer is based on my knowledge of the general direction of our destination,' he said, then added, in a voice lacking in real confidence, 'I am in full control of the situation so you can all relax and we will soon be there.'

Richard glanced at the monument again. 'Look, it's got a litter-bin by it just like the other one.'

Hallett stared at the monument and decided that there was little point in arguing about whether or not it was the same monument and he decided on a new approach. He unbuckled his seat-belt. 'I think that if the people of this area have seen fit to erect these tributes to their war heroes, the least I can do is pay my respect by reading the inscription on at least one of them.'

'Oh, must you Simon? It's getting late and I'm sure we don't know exactly where we are, do we?'

'As I said, I am confident that we are truly on the way to our destination. And now, if you will excuse me.'

Once out of the car he walked back to Root's car and Fred wound down the window to enquire the reason for the hold-up.

'Trouble, squire?'

'Not at all. I merely wish to inspect that monument then we shall move off.'

'Right, ready when you are.'

Hallett walked over to the obelisk and stopped a few feet short. He gave a slight bow then stepped forward to read whatever moving inscription had been engraved on this tribute to fallen warriors.

He read: "Norwich 27 miles".

He snorted his well-practised snort, turned and walked away.

Back inside the car he struggled into his seat-belt.

'What did it say, dear?'

'It is of no great importance, Elizabeth, let us get on our way.'

'I just wish I knew where we are,' said Elizabeth, returning to the map.

'I estimate that we are about twenty odd miles from Norwich and we can expect to arrive at our destination in about half an hour.'

Once more they moved off and, after a few twists and turns, they found themselves on a main road where a signpost announced that Norwich was twenty-five miles distant. Hallett accepted the compliments on his navigational skill with a strange modesty.

Briskly they travelled onwards and after a little under thirty minutes they saw the signs indicating that their camping site was near. They slowed down and soon saw a large open gateway giving access to their site. A local farmer who allowed a limited number of campers to stay there, owned the field. They had all agreed when choosing a site that this field sounded a bit more rugged than the average camping site, although there were toilets and water available at the adjacent farm.

They steered the cars through the gateway then stopped and allowed the passengers to stretch their limbs. They looked around at the field which would be their home for the next two weeks. It was a good-sized field with clumps of trees and bushes dotted around and it gave an easy view of the surrounding countryside.

Fred walked over to the Halletts rubbing his hands together with enthusiasm. 'First job is to get the tents up. Right, squire?'

'Quite correct. We should make camp at once.'

Glancing round the field Fred pointed to a corner. 'That looks like a good spot over there.'

'Yes,' said Hallett, giving his tolerant smile, 'but there's more to choosing a site than making a random stab like that.'

Fred grinned. 'Maybe, but I think that will do us for a start.'

'As you wish, but don't say I didn't warn you.'

'Thanks, squire. Come on folks, let's get started.'

The Root family scrambled back into their car and, with much shouting and laughing, they trundled across the field to the corner Fred had selected and Hallett watched them go with an air of amused tolerance, then he turned to his family.

'Right, now to select a site for ourselves.'

He walked away from the car looking round the field and up at the sky. He peered in the direction of a clump of trees perched on top of a mound in another corner of the field. He kicked at the ground with his heel then stooped and picked up a few wisps of grass which he then threw lightly into the air watching as the gentle breeze wafted them along. If asked to explain the significance of his actions he would have found it difficult to answer, but, as he had made it look very confident and authoritative, no-one questioned his actions.

He gave a satisfied smile as he made another panoramic inspection of the field. He looked down at the ground as he rubbed a patch of soil with the toe of his canvas shoe, which he regarded as the ideal camping footwear. Suddenly, he looked up at the mound with the clump of trees as if in the hope of catching it off guard. Having, it seemed, made his decision he turned and strode back to his family.

'All right, Elizabeth, let's get back into the car, I have chosen our site.' He looked at Valerie and Richard. 'In the meantime perhaps you two had better offer Mr Root your assistance since he has been kind enough to invite you both to stay in their tent.'

Richard looked genuinely concerned. 'But, won't you need our help, Father?'

Again the tolerant smile. 'Thank you, Richard, it's kind of you to offer, but I think I can be relied upon to erect one tent on my own.'

'Well, if you need any help just give us a shout.'

'Thank you both. Now off you go.'

They made their way to the Roots' site where everyone seemed to be engaged in unloading the car and sorting out the equipment.

At the same time the Halletts were driving to their chosen site under the trees at the base of the mound.

They stopped and climbed out of the car.

'Right, Elizabeth. This is our site let us get this car off-loaded.'

'Why did you choose this spot, Simon?'

He beamed. 'It's really very simple. The trees provide shade when it's hot and the mound will protect us from the wind.'

'But doesn't that depend on which way the wind is blowing?'

Hallett looked just a little flustered. 'Do you think we might leave this discussion until later? I really think that unloading the car comes first.'

Elizabeth shrugged and moved towards the car to start unloading but she was not happy about his explanation of the principles of selecting a camping site. She felt that something was not quite right.

They turned their attention to the car and were soon surrounded by bundles, boxes and items of camping equipment in disorderly heaps. The task of unloading was now complete and Elizabeth looked to Hallett for an indication as to their next move. He seemed to be busy with some sheets of paper.

'Shall we start, Simon?'

'Yes, of course.' He held up the sheets of paper. 'Let us first check the inventory to see if it all tallies and then we can erect the tent.'

'Do you mean you want to check all this stuff?' There was more than a trace of impatience in Elizabeth's voice.

'But of course. How else shall we know that we have everything? We don't want to start to erect the tent only to find that some essential component is missing, do we?'

'Of course not. But even after you check this lot,' she waved an arm over the mass of equipment that they had brought, 'if you *do* discover that something is missing, you won't be any better off, will you?'

Hallett disliked feminine logic. It was cold, calculating and irritatingly accurate. Further, it had thwarted many of his grand schemes in the past.

Before he could reply Elizabeth added 'But in any case, I think that we had better get started right away.'

'Very well, we will. I'll start at this page and read out the names and you see if you can find the item.'

She gave a long sigh to show that she was, despite her misgivings, ready to start.

'Very well then, what's first?'

He cleared his throat, pompously. 'Bodies, tent, one.'

Elizabeth wandered through the chaos looking for anything that could possibly be a 'bodies, tent, one'. She held up a bundle that looked a giant version of an exploded cigar.

'Could this possibly be it?'

'No, no, it's a much larger bundle than that.'

'Is it as big as the one you have your foot on?'

'What?' He looked down. 'Oh, I see what you mean. Yes, this seems to be the one I'm looking for.' He ticked his list. 'Next, pegs, tent, twenty.'

'Got them; next.'

'Good, now we're getting somewhere. Next, pegs, brailing, thirty.'

Elizabeth searched through the bundles and identified the brailing pegs more by their quantity than knowing what they looked like.

'Right, here they are.'

'Good, good. Next, bedrolls, two.'

Elizabeth looked bewildered. 'That seems an odd thing to have on your list, isn't it?'

'Odd things to have on my list, bedrolls?'

'Bedrolls? I thought you said bread-rolls.'

'Oh, really, Elizabeth. We are getting nowhere. Please try and concentrate.'

'It's not my fault. How was I to know you called them bedrolls? I thought we called them sleeping bags.' Before he could reply to this she added. 'Look Simon, it is getting overcast and I think that we ought to start putting up the tent.'

The Officer in Charge of Camping was now looking petulant. 'Oh, very well. Let me first assemble the components.'

There was a lot more rummaging as Hallett started to

collect together the various bits and pieces that made up his ancient tent. He struggled with ropes and pegs and staggered to and fro tripping over trailing ropes and complaining loudly. At last he announced that all was present and correct and that he was about to pitch the tent.

'Can I be of any help, Simon?'

'Thank you, Elizabeth. Yes you can. If you would just wait there and when I want you to pass me something I will let you know.'

He looked down at the scattered components and searched his memory for a clue on how to begin. It had all seemed so simple at home. He thought that it would all come back to him but now he was only too aware that his experience was, in the main, as a spectator. The task of erecting tents had interested him only as a means of having his accommodation prepared and it was slowly dawning on him that he had taken on a task with barely a theoretical knowledge. He recalled one of his sergeants giving instruction to a group of soldiers on the art of pitching a tent. He remembered his admiration of the sergeant's style of instruction and how he had approved of the crisp, efficient delivery of the instruction. Because he had been so interested at the time he found that he could now remember most of what the sergeant had said. Now, how did he start?

'Nah, listen you lot. This is 'ow you puts up a tent, right. Are you paying attention, lad? Well, wake up, then. First you lays the ridge-pole on the grahnd and you marks it with two pegs, got it? Right. Next, you removes the ridge-pole and then you spreads the tent aht on its side keepin' the lower edges in line with the two markin' pegs. 'Ere, what are you doin' lad? Well, don't blow your nose when I'm talkin' to you. I don't care what it's doin', let it run! You just pay attention to me. Now, where was I? You, lad, what was the last thing I said? No, not about 'is nose you dozey man. The tent in line with the markin' pegs. Wake up! Right, then. Next you inserts the uprights and the ridge-pole makin' sure you don't stick nothin' through the canvas. Take four small but smart paces away from the markin' pegs and put in two pegs for the main guy ropes.' It went on until the sergeant's voice had become a hysterical scream as his class failed to carry out his instructions with the necessary smartness, skill and precision.

Hallett nodded as he recalled the instructions. He thought that he could remember enough now to make a good effort at putting up his tent.

He picked up the ridge-pole and placed it on the grass. He stood back and surveyed it then moved it forward a little and was apparently satisfied that this new position, which was about nine inches from the old position, offered something that the other places lacked. He rummaged through his equipment and produced two tent pegs. He placed a peg at each end of the ridge-pole and then looked about him as if in search of something.

'Have you lost something, dear?'

'The maul, Elizabeth, the maul. Where is it?'

She searched through the bundles lifting each one in turn. After a few minutes she straightened up.

'What do you want it for?'

'I need it to knock in these tent pins. Is it there?'

'Well, there's this big mallet.'

'Oh, for goodness sake, Elizabeth, that *is* the maul. Now, please hand it to me.'

She steered her way through their scattered possessions and offered the maul to Hallett who was still crouched by the ridge-pole. Realising the difficulty of manipulating it from his hunched up position, he straightened up and took the maul from Elizabeth. He decided that he would explain to her his plan of how to erect the tent and he stood holding the maul by the small portion sticking out of the head. He had failed to notice that the handle was tapered and that the head was held on merely by being forced along the tapered handle until it wedged itself into position. Hallett went on about his intentions regarding the tent, then, to emphasise a point, he lifted the maul a few inches and thumped it firmly on the ground. This caused the maul head to become dislodged and it slid rapidly to the bottom of the handle and onto his foot. His canvas shoe offered little protection from the heavy maul head and he gave an agonised gasp as a searing pain shot through his toes. He flung the offending object to one side and limped away a few paces biting his lip to stem the flow of ripe military curses that hovered on the tip of his tongue.

'Are you all right, Simon?'

'No, I am not. My foot feels as if it's been crushed by that blasted thing. You'd think they would feel obliged to at least put on some sort of warning about that. Why on earth people cannot manufacture a simple thing like that without building in all sorts of hazards I do not know. I could have been crippled by it.'

Elizabeth tutted sympathetically. Hallett had never been one to suffer in silence.

He straightened up and hobbled bravely back to his chosen tent site and picked up the discarded maul. He slid the head back into position and thumped it vigorously on the ground to wedge it firmly in place.

'Isn't that mallet a bit big for that small tent peg, Simon? Couldn't you use something smaller?'

'Look, please let's get this tent put up. This maul is designed to drive tent pegs into the ground and that is precisely what I intend to do with it. Now, please stand clear.'

He bent forward, pushed a peg into the ground then straightened up, grasping the handle of the maul. He glared at the tent peg with a sort of cold hatred and then prepared to lift the heavy mallet over his head.

'Be careful, dear.'

'Thank you, I have already learned how treacherous this thing can be. Just leave this to me.'

With one heave he swung the maul high over his head where it thudded against the low branch of one of the adjacent trees. There was a brief pause and the maul head, now dislodged by its contact with the branch, slid quickly down the handle and crashed onto Hallett's right thumb. The maul was again flung to one side as he gave another agonised gasp and cupped his injured thumb in his other hand. Elizabeth had been looking in the direction of the Roots' site at the moment of impact and so was baffled to see that her husband had injured his thumb whilst using both hands on the handle of a big mallet. However, she knew better than to ask probing questions at a time like this.

It was some minutes before the thumb stopped its painful throbbing and settled down to a dull ache.

'Are you sure you couldn't use something else, Simon?'

This had become a 'It's The Peg or Me' situation. 'No. The maul is the instrument provided to drive pegs into the ground and that is what I shall use.'

Elizabeth was beginning to despair. 'But, perhaps it's too big for those tent pegs.'

'Nonsense. I can't be expected to take different items of equipment to match every variation in camping gear. In camping we have to make do with what we've got. Now, where is that maul?'

Once more the maul was fitted together and this time, Hallett made sure that the head was firmly in place and that the way overhead was clear. He looked down at the tent peg still standing where he had pushed it into the ground. He rubbed his hands together, grasped the handle of the maul and, with one final glance at the branches of the tree, swung it high in the air. His face, framed by his upstretched arms, wore the same expression of grim determination that we would expect on the face of an official executioner before he brought down his blade onto the neck of his helpless victim. After a second or so the maul whooshed through the air and landed squarely on the peg. There was a sharp, cracking sound and the peg lay splintered into a sort of exotic wooden flower. He glared at it with an expression of baffled fury.

'Damn and blast the thing! What on earth is the good of a tent peg if all it will do is to break into pieces as soon as one tries to drive it into the ground,' he said, despairingly. 'But I suppose, that as we have been provided with sub-standard pegs, I had better find something smaller.'

He rooted round and discovered a small mallet with which he quickly tapped the two pegs into the ground and the position of the ridge-pole was marked.

Hallett stood up and considered his aching toes and thumb.

'I wonder if Root is finding all this more difficult than he anticipated?' he said, thoughtfully.

CHAPTER TWELVE

'Pass me that mallet, David.'

In the Root camping site the frame tent had been erected, and Fred had merely to put on the finishing touches.

'Here you are Dad.'

'Thanks.' Fred took the mallet, finished tapping in a tent peg, straightened up and unzipped the outer tent.

'There, that's that. All we have to do now is just set up the sleeping quarters, fix the awning and we're ready. Not bad for a first effort.'

Gladys looked up from her activities at the portable cooker and looked approvingly at their living quarters. 'It looks nice, Fred. Will it be all right if it rains?'

'Course it will. That'll stand a typhoon, that will. How's the cooker performing?'

'Well. I think I've got the hang of it. I'll soon be ready to start getting the tea.'

'Great. First thing we must do is to get everyone fixed up with a job of some sort.' He looked around. 'Gary, you and Richard take those containers to the farm and get some water. It's only on the other side of those trees.'

'Right, Dad, here we go.'

The boys picked up the two water containers and set out for the farm.

'David, put this mallet back in the tool bag, please.'

The tool bag lay on the ground near David's feet and as his father spoke he was looking across at Valerie as she helped Gladys with the adjustments to the cooker.

'David, the mallet.'

'Yes, Dad,' he said, picking up the tool bag. He rummaged inside for a few moments. 'It's not in here.'

'I know it's not, I've got it. I was just asking you to put it away for me.'

'Oh, sorry, I didn't hear you.'

Fred smiled as he realised the cause of David's distraction. 'That's OK. Give me a hand to clear up, will you?'

They busied themselves for a while then Fred spoke quietly to David. 'Nice girl that.'

'Who? Oh, Valerie. Yes, she is quite nice.'

He looked at her as she stood there, her light brown hair occasionally blown across her face by the light breeze, whereupon she would return it with a toss of her head that he found simply fascinating. He could still not get over the fact that this girl, who had attracted him from the day they had first moved in next door to her, was actually with them on their camping holiday. He couldn't understand why he had not spoken to her very much. He knew that whenever the opportunity presented itself, his confidence evaporated. This now was surely his big chance, and he knew that if he was to get to know her, it was to be during this holiday or not at all. It was a pity that she had never shown the slightest interest in him, but then, why should she? A beautiful girl like that probably had a whole string of boy-friends. He needed desperately to know whether he stood a chance with her. Well, there was only one way to find out. There was a town quite near so perhaps he could ask her out for a meal or maybe a trip to the cinema.

They finished tidying up and Fred started opening packages looking for some of the supplies they had brought with them. They had packed enough for a few meals and intended then to shop at the nearby town. Fred sorted out the makings of an evening meal and passed them across to Gladys who was unpacking the cooking utensils.

'Would you like me to help you?' said Valerie, as Gladys set about preparing their first camping meal.

'Oh, thanks, love, that would be nice. Would you like to open a tin of peas while I start the cooker going.'

Valerie picked up the tin-opener as she reached out for a tin of peas. She glanced across to where David was crouched packing odds and ends into a plastic sack. Not for the first time she found herself wondering why he had never shown any interest in her. She had often seen him at home as he cycled down the Avenue, or as he played a game of badminton in the garden with his father. She liked the smooth, athletic way he moved and, as she had often observed to herself, he was rather good-looking. I suppose he must have a regular girl-friend, she thought, although I have never seen one at his house. She sighed and occupied herself with opening the tin of peas.

'Have you finished opening the peas, Val?' said Gladys, still busy with the cooker.

'Yes, Mrs Root, here they are.'

'Please, not Mrs Root. Why don't you call me Gladys or Glad, if you like.'

'All right, I will,' said Valerie, 'and here are the peas.' She tipped them into a non-stick saucepan which she then handed to Gladys.

There was a pause as they both gazed into a saucepan of pineapple cubes.

'Oh, I'm sorry, Gladys.'

'Never mind, love, they'll go a treat with the chips.'

They both laughed as Gladys tipped them into a basin and put the saucepan to one side to be washed up later.

'Shall I help to set the table? I don't think I can go far wrong there.'

'Yes, please, that would help, and just think, now we can have pineapples cubes for afters.'

There was a warm and friendly atmosphere about the camp as everyone busied themselves with their various jobs and it produced an air of relaxed efficiency.

On the other side of the trees Richard and Gary were on their way back from the farmhouse with the water.

'I wonder how your dad is getting on. He's got a real tent, hasn't he?'

'No he hasn't. He's got a rotten old tent and he wanted us to sleep in it. It's a mouldy old dark green thing and I shouldn't be surprised if it's crawling with things.'

'But it is an Army tent, isn't it?'

'Yes, but it must be years old.'

170

'Gosh, I'd like to see it. Can we go over there?'

'Well, yes if you like, but it pongs a bit.'

They struggled on with the water containers, chatting about soldiers, camping, space travel, parents, computers, pocket money and teachers all in the short space of time it took to walk from the farm to the camping site.

'The boys are back with water, Glad, now we can get cracking.'

'Right. Bring it over here, please, boys. The sooner we get started the sooner we shall have tea.'

Inspired by this promise the ever-hungry water carriers struggled to hurry the last few yards.

'David, why don't you walk across to Mr Hallett and invite him and Elizabeth over here for tea. We can soon put on some extra.'

'All right, Dad, I'll go now.' He paused, then, with a mammoth effort at sounding casual, he turned to Valerie. 'Would you like to stroll over with me?'

There was a clatter as Valerie dropped two knives onto the camp table. She paused for a few moments, apparently considering whether or not to accept this invitation. She shrugged.

'Yes, all right. I suppose I had better see how they are getting on with their tent.'

They walked away from the camp site and headed for the trees on the mound where they could see signs of activity on the Hallett site.

For a while there was an awkward silence, then Valerie spoke. 'I think this camping holiday was a good idea, don't you.'

'Yes, camping can be good fun.'

'Have you been before, then? I thought that this was new to all of us.'

'Well, it was a long time ago,' he looked slightly uncomfortable. 'I was in the Boy Scouts.'

She glanced at him, her eyes twinkling. 'I can't imagine you as a Boy Scout. Did you like it?'

'It wasn't bad. I was patrol leader of the Peewits.' He smiled. 'You see, you didn't know you were in the company of a man who once wielded enormous power and authority, did you?'

They laughed together and a keen observer might have seen that they now walked a fraction closer to each other. Together they strolled towards Hallett's site now chatting in the easy manner of old friends. As they arrived, they found Elizabeth standing in front of an untidy bundle of canvas, pulling on a rope that seemed to be caught up in the middle of the heap.

'Hello, Mother. Here, let me give you a hand with that.' She looked around. 'Where's Father?'

Elizabeth fought back a smile and pointed to the canvas. 'He's in there.'

Valerie spluttered. 'Why, has he hibernated or something?'

There was a ripple of laughter from the three of them and from the canvas muddle came Hallett's muffled but unmistakable tones. 'Who is out there? Elizabeth, did you say something?'

'It's Valerie, dear.'

'What? What did you say?'

'It's Valerie, dear.'

'I can't hear what you're saying. Just help me get out of this muddle before someone comes. Now hurry, please.'

The canvas bulged at various places as the captive tried to find a way out and Elizabeth joined in the effort by grasping handfuls of canvas and trying to pull the enveloping shroud from her husband. There was a sudden muffled yell from within.

'Aaah, stop, you're pulling my hair.'

She stopped and began to probe the canvas seeking another entrance. It was not long before there came another shout.

'Elizabeth! What are you trying to do? You have just poked me in the eye.'

'Sorry, dear. I'm just trying to get you out.'

'Speak up, Elizabeth, I can't hear a word you're saying.'

Valerie and David looked at each other in amused amazement.

'How did he get in there, Mother?'

'Well, you see, he had just got the tent erected to the point where it actually started to look like a tent. But, there was a rope entangled inside and he crawled in to free it. Before I knew what was happening, the whole thing collapsed and then in his efforts to get out, he just got more and more wrapped up.'

'Elizabeth, will you please stop mumbling. I can't hear a word you're saying.'

In an effort to tell him what was happening, she put her face close to the canvas and shouted. 'Simon, I'm trying to get you out.'

'Well, hurry up about it, this is quite ridiculous. Find an edge somewhere and lift it.'

After some searching David found an edge of the canvas and eased it up to reveal Hallett's left leg. A few seconds later and all but the head was revealed. Hallett fumbled round his neck and lifted the canvas from his face. The effect on the three rescuers was to make them struggle to keep a serious, concerned expression on their faces, while inwardly quaking with laughter.

Hallett's hair was standing on end like a character in a child's comic who has seen a ghost. His face was a deep red and his blue and white spotted cravat, which he had that morning tied in a large, loose knot under his chin, was now in a small, tight knot under his ear. His trousers had worked themselves up over his knees and on his shoulder two earwigs wandered about aimlessly. He sat there blinking and gasping.

'Are you all right, Simon?'

He was about to launch into a heated description of his incarceration in his collapsed tent when he noticed Valerie and David standing watching. He struggled to his feet. 'Hello, Valerie, hello, young man. Have you been here long?'

'We've been trying to get you out of the tent, Father.'

'Oh that.' He gave a hollow laugh. 'Silly thing to happen, really. Must have pulled on the wrong rope. Still, no harm done.'

Elizabeth waved a hand at the canvas bundle. 'Except that your tent has collapsed.'

Again the hollow laugh. 'I can soon put it up again.'

David stepped forward. 'Can I be of any help?'

'That's very good of you to offer. Have you any experience of tents?'

'David's an expert, Father.'

'An expert, eh?'

'Well, I wouldn't say expert but I would like to help.'

'Good man. Perhaps you would have a preliminary look at it while I tidy myself up a little. Then I must try and find some things my wife has apparently mislaid.'

Before Elizabeth could defend herself against this allegation he walked away with her past the numerous boxes and bundles still strewn about.

David looked at the tent and, with Valerie's help, began to sort it out. About twenty minutes later, when Hallett had recovered from his ordeal, he returned to find a serviceable-looking fully erected tent. He strode round nodding approvingly but could not resist twanging at the guy-ropes.

'Well done, a very good effort.'

'Thank you. Look, I don't wish to question your choice of a site, but are you sure that you wish to be under these trees and at the bottom of this slope?'

'You may rely on my experience, young man. I have, during my service career, spent many long weeks under canvas and I am very much aware of the necessity of choosing a satisfactory site.'

'Yes, of course. I didn't mean to imply anything. It's just that camping under trees means that the trees drip on you after rain and at the bottom of a slope you may get slight flooding problems.'

'Well, thank you for your concern.'

'You're very welcome. By the way, it looks a bit like rain and if it gets any worse any tight guy-ropes should be slackened.'

'You need have no fears there. I am well acquainted with the inclement weather procedures.'

Elizabeth had inspected the tent and looked anxiously up at the sky. 'Shouldn't you be getting back to your camp, David?'

'Oh, I almost forgot what we came for. Dad says would you both like to join us for tea? It won't be much but it would be nice to have our first meal together.'

'Has your father managed to get his fire going already then?'

'Actually it's all cooked on a portable cooker.'

'Ah, I see. Not quite like camp cooking in the old style. But, we accept your father's kind invitation and we will return to your camp with you.'

They all helped in tidying up the remaining equipment and

174

storing it in the tent or the car. They then set out for the Roots' site.

As they arrived Fred walked forward to greet them. 'Hello, squire, how's it all going?'

Hallett looked swiftly at Elizabeth before replying. 'Oh, we're making fair progress, you know, after one or two snags initially. We are very grateful to you for this invitation.'

'You're both very welcome and if you will all be seated, Glad will serve the first course which is mushroom soup.'

'Mushroom soup, eh? That's an ambitious effort under these conditions.'

'Dead right, squire. Combination of my tin-opener and some help from Mr Heinz.'

They tucked in to a hearty meal of tinned mushroom soup, chips, peas and luncheon fritters – a speciality prepared by Fred. This was followed by pineapple cubes inadvertently selected earlier by Valerie. When they had finished, Hallett remarked that it was an excellent meal and a good start to their camping holiday. While the washing-up was being done, the two men sat at the table and chatted about general matters.

Soon it was time to be seeing to the sleeping arrangements and Hallett and Elizabeth bade everyone goodnight then made their way back to their camp. When they arrived they lit the hurricane lamp in the tent then Hallett stood back, stretched and yawned.

'I must say I think this country air has made me feel quite tired. We may as well turn in.'

They prepared for bed and he stowed their clothes in two plastic carrier bags.

'Can't be too careful, insects and all that, you know.'

Elizabeth was sitting up in her sleeping bag on her folding camp bed and Hallett was about to climb into his sleeping bag when there was an ominous roll of distant thunder. He looked across at Elizabeth, saw her expression of concern and he ducked through the tent flap to look up at the sky. For a few moments he stood looking at the ominous black clouds as they rolled menacingly across the sky.

'Now let me see,' he murmured to himself, 'what was that he

said about the rain, tighten the guy-ropes was it? Yes, that was it. I'll do it now.'

He walked round the tent tightening each guy-rope as he came to it. When he had finished he entered the tent again.

'Well, that's that. The rain can do its worst now.'

'Have you slackened all the guy-ropes, then?'

He gave snorting laugh. 'Elizabeth, you do not slacken guy-ropes when it rains, you tighten them.'

'But, why would you do that?'

He cleared his throat as he thought for moment. 'Well, you see, you tighten them so that the canvas cannot bulge inwards and so hold water.'

'Are you absolutely sure, Simon? I thought that David said to slacken them.'

He shook his head. 'Positively not. Worst thing you could do.'

Humming happily to himself, he got into his sleeping bag and sat up fumbling for his book. He sighed contentedly. 'This all takes me back a bit. Living next to nature, that's the life for me.'

'Yes, I think we shall all enjoy it.' She glanced round the tent. 'You know, I can't help thinking that if Richard and Valerie had decided to sleep in this tent we might have had a job dividing it off. There wouldn't be much room.'

'Yes, it is a bit smaller than I remember it. I'm glad now that I persuaded them to stay with the Roots.'

Elizabeth smiled. 'Goodnight, Simon.'

'Goodnight, Elizabeth, sleep well.'

He sat up reading his book, gradually getting more and more drowsy.

It was about two o'clock in the morning, the rain was falling fast and beating a loud tattoo on the tent. Now and then the sky was split by a searing flash of lightning, followed by a deep growl of thunder.

In the Hallett tent the hurricane lamp still burned and in the gap between the two camp beds a small stream of water flowed impudently through the tent. Elizabeth was curled up in her camp bed fast asleep and Hallett was also asleep but still sitting up. His book was floating on the stream, his chin was on his chest and his spectacles had slid to the end of his nose. Slowly and limply, his left hand slid off the bed and splashed into the water. He stirred uneasily. Never a light sleeper, it took more than the ducking of his hand into cold water to awaken Hallett.

One night at home Elizabeth had woken with a headache and had tried to awaken her snoring husband to ask him to get her some pain-killing tablets. She called his name loudly, she shook him until his head lolled around on the pillow. He muttered incoherently, snorted and slumbered on. In desperation she tugged at his hair and pulled his ears. The snoring stopped, he smacked his lips and slept on. Elizabeth was now desperate to wake him and she seized his nose and shook his head from side to side. This had the effect of making his face wobble and she then found that by placing a finger at each corner of his mouth and moving upwards she gave him a grin that was quite comical. The effect so amused her that she found herself laughing out loud and realised that, because of this unusual therapy, her headache had gone. She had returned to bed still smiling and slept soundly.

In his bed, Hallett slept on, still in his sitting position, his hand growing colder and colder. He stirred uneasily then lifted his hand from the water and tucked it into his sleeping bag. As the water seeped through the leg of his pyjama trousers he shuddered and pulled his hand free again. Once more it flopped into the water and this time he grunted. His nose began to itch and swiftly his left hand rushed to alleviate the discomfort but carrying with it a palmful of water. As the cold water dashed against his face Hallett grunted again and indulged in a few moments of lip-smacking. He then sleepily realised that his back was cold and wet, his face was streaming with water and his left hand was wet and almost numb with cold. He stirred, removed his reading glasses and looked around him.

'My God,' he cried. 'Elizabeth, wake up, we are being flooded.'

Elizabeth awoke at once and as she opened her eyes she found herself looking at a copy of "Why Rommel Failed" floating by her bed.

'Simon, what on earth is going on?'

'It's the rain, of course. The whole field must be flooded. I can see now why that rascal of a farmer rents this at such a low price. Just wait till I see him.'

She looked at the damp, depressing scene. 'Just listen to that rain, Simon. Oh, I do hope this tent will be all right.'

'I really don't think we need to worry ourselves over this. Whatever peril that farmer has landed us in, I am confident that our tent will be secure against the rain. After all, I took the trouble to tighten all the guy-ropes.'

'I know, but I still think that David said to slacken them. I believe it's to stop the canvas being stretched and then splitting.'

'Now look, you must admit that with my experience…'

Before he could present his argument, there was an ominous ripping sound, the tent split just over the top of him and he was deluged with driving rain.

'Oh really, this is too much. What on earth has happened to this tent.'

As he spoke he was struggling out of his sleeping bag and trying to get along his bed to the entrance flap. He lifted it and looked out.

'Clearly, we can't repair the tent. We must make for the car.'

He looked back at Elizabeth who, after a little rummaging in her bag, produced an umbrella.

'Elizabeth, I am going to open the car door. I will take the bags with our clothes, you follow when I turn on the headlights.'

He searched in his carrier bag until he found his car keys, then he squeakily pulled on his canvas shoes and picked up the bags. Ducking through the flap, he hurried out into the pouring rain.

Through the wet grass, Hallett squelched his way to the car, unlocked it and jumped in. When he turned on the headlights, Elizabeth came hurrying from the tent to the car where Simon had opened the door ready for her. She was carrying an umbrella and wearing a plastic raincoat over her dressing gown. On her feet she wore a pair of wellingtons. The umbrella, raincoat and wellingtons were last minute items that she had included just before the packing was completed. The choice of these items, though, had brought scornful comments from Hallett. As she scrambled in, she neatly folded the umbrella as she closed the door.

Hallett switched off the headlights and they sat there in the darkness listening to the patter of the rain which was now slowing down. After a few minutes it stopped. The clouds rolled away and a pale moon looked down on the sodden scene. In the back of the car they found an old towel and were trying to dry themselves a little. Abruptly, Hallett stopped his drying and peered through the windscreen.

'Elizabeth, look over there by Roots' tent. There's a light'

Together they stared in the direction of the Roots' camp and, indeed, there was a faint light by the Roots' tent and, after a while, they realised that it was the interior light in Fred Root's car. Next the sidelights and headlights appeared and the car began a careful journey across the field towards them. Hallett switched his lights back on to show their location and a few minutes later Fred Root, dressed in pyjamas and a raincoat, drove alongside. They wound windows down.

'Hello, squire, saw your lights. Had a bit of trouble?'

'Yes. The tent seems to have developed a structural fault and started to let in the rain so we moved in here.'

'Well, you can't stay in there all night. Look, you follow me back over to our place and we'll talk about what we can do over a cup of hot tea.'

Hallett felt a little irritated to be caught out like this, but his whole being cried out to him to accept the offer if only for the promise of a hot drink.

'Right, thank you. I'm ready when you are.'

They drove slowly over the field back to Fred's tent and then squelched across the wet grass into the frame tent.

Hallett was astounded. He had never realised that the interior of a tent could be this luxurious. They were standing in a big space on a dry floor covered with a strong ground sheet and curtained rooms were situated all round.

'I must say, Fred,' said Elizabeth, looking round at the tent, 'this is all very nice. It was very good of you to come and rescue us. I can't think what it would have been like to spend the night in the car. Thank you.'

'Yes, of course, thank you. We're both very grateful to you.'

Fred smiled. 'My pleasure, squire. Now, how about that tea?'

Soon they were all sitting round sipping hot tea. Hallett was wrapped in a multi-coloured blanket and wearing a pair of Fred's plimsolls. After a short discussion and a little reorganising by the partitioning of a room Hallett and Elizabeth were provided with a place to sleep. They agreed that they would look at the tent in the morning to see what could be done.

The following morning was so sunny and pleasant that it seemed almost to have been offered as an apology for the bad-tempered storm of the previous night. Everywhere the land looked green and healthy.

In the Roots' tent breakfast was being tackled with great enthusiasm by everyone and, between mouthfuls of ham and eggs and fried bread, suggestions for the day's activities were being discussed.

'First thing,' said Fred, slicing through a fried egg and watching with childlike pleasure as the deep yellow yolk flowed smoothly over the fried bread, slowly sinking in and making it, for him, a gastronomic delight; 'first thing is to examine your tent and see what can be done.'

Hallett shook his head. 'Precious little, I should think. There's a slit in it about two feet long. Apart from which it must be thoroughly soaked both inside and out.'

'Well, it won't hurt to have a look at it,' said Fred, finishing the last of his fried bread, now soggy with egg-yolk.

They continued with breakfast and eventually rose from the table, all feeling that they were ready to face whatever the day would bring.

Elizabeth still wore her night-dress and dressing gown and had borrowed some sandals from Gladys. Hallett had brought their plastic carrier bags with them and was relieved to find that the clothes were still dry.

'What a good job you thought to put the clothes away safely, Simon.'

He shrugged modestly.

Soon they were dressed and ready to go.

Hallett and Fred walked over to the scene of last night's mishap and found the tent looking limp and soggy. The split in the side had lengthened and the surrounding area was muddy. Inside the tent, the scene was desolate, with Hallett's copy of "Why Rommel Failed" now a soft, pulpy mess at the back of the tent.

Together they looked at the scene, then Hallett spoke. 'As I said it's a complete write-off. I'm afraid that this means the end of our camping holiday. Pity, really. I was just beginning to take to the life.'

'If you will let me, squire, I can help. Do you remember when we first spoke about a camping holiday I offered you the use of another smaller tent I had.'

'Yes, I do recall that.'

'Well, as I told you when you were thinking about going camping, we did a package deal which included two tents and all the necessary gear some years ago. But, we only used the large tent once. So, I decided that it wouldn't do any harm if we brought along the small tent just in case. Sort of belt and braces approach. Anyway, it's yours for the holiday if you want to stay.'

Hallett found that he could find no words to express his feelings. He was unable to recall any occasion in his life and particularly in his Army days, when anyone had looked out for him to this extent. To think that they had bothered to go out of their way and quite possibly inconvenience themselves by bringing an extra tent.

'Really, I don't know what to say. I am more than pleased to accept your offer, but also I am deeply touched that you have been so considerate as to bring the spare tent with you. Thank you, we are most grateful.'

After a brief discussion, Hallett was persuaded to move from his site under the trees and the tent was erected on a site quite close to Fred's tent. The site was chosen by Hallett after some skilful guiding by Fred.

The spare tent having been erected, the damaged tent was dismantled, hung up to dry then the sleeping bags and beds were put out in the sun.

Hallett and Elizabeth moved into their new home with their

belongings and in no time they felt comfortable and once more looking forward to their holiday.

They were sitting comfortably in folding chairs outside their newly acquired tent, satisfied for the moment, just to sit and enjoy the sunshine.

'You know, I must say that I am really grateful to Root for bringing this tent. I would really have been most reluctant to go home at this juncture.'

'So would I.' She smiled. 'It's funny but last night now seems like a bad dream. I can hardly believe it really happened. At one time I must confess that I was very frightened but once you started to get us organised, I could see that we...' She looked across at her husband. He was fast asleep.

Later that day Fred called on them. 'Everything OK, squire. All comfortable now?'

'Absolutely. Do you know I even managed a short nap earlier on and I feel ready for anything now.'

Elizabeth smiled at his claim that he *even* managed a short nap. Naps of varying length had long been second nature to him.

'Well, if you're fit for anything, that fits in nicely with the reason for my visit. We are just trying to arrange a not very serious game of cricket. Would you like to join us?'

'I would be delighted.' He turned to Elizabeth. 'And it will be something for you to watch.'

'No spectators allowed, squire. Everybody joins in. How about it, Elizabeth?'

'Well, I don't know quite what to do, but I'll certainly be glad to give it a try.'

'Great I'll give you a shout when we're ready.'

'In the meantime, Elizabeth, perhaps we had better get changed into something more suitable for cricket. Something casual and comfortable.'

A little later Fred returned, just as Elizabeth came out of the tent. She was wearing a crisp, white, short-sleeved blouse and a well-fitting pair of powder blue shorts which revealed a pair of long, shapely legs. Fred whistled appreciatively and she smiled. A few seconds later and the tent flap was drawn aside once more. Hallett emerged in his casual and comfortable outfit. He was wearing an off-white sun hat with a floppy brim, a very loose khaki shirt and a pair of long and generously cut khaki shorts. These finished well below the knee and looked as if they had sufficient material in them to make a decent safari suit. On his feet he wore his plimsolls which were looking a little stained after their encounter with the uninvited stream last night. To complete his casual ensemble, he sported a pair of grey socks with vivid red diamonds.

'All set for the game, squire?'

'I most certainly am. Is everyone else ready?'

'Here they come now.'

They all trooped over to the field of play and organised themselves into teams. Fred, Elizabeth, Gary and Richard won the toss and Fred, as Captain, decided to bat first. This left Hallett, Gladys, David and Valerie to bowl, keep wicket and field. It was natural that Hallett should have chosen to be Captain and he elected himself as opening bowler. He put David to keep wicket and Valerie and Gladys were sent to act as fielders and they moved into a position one on either side of the pitch. Their Captain studied his fielders for a moment then called to Gladys.

'Would you go a little deeper, please.'

'Pardon, love?'

'Deeper, would you go a little deeper, please.'

She looked at him rather uncertainly then advanced on Fred was who the batsman. 'No, no. Deeper, Please go the other way.'

Gladys nodded and advanced on Hallett.

'No, stop. Just turn around and walk away.'

She did this and landed in a position hitherto unmarked in diagrams of fielding positions.

'All right, that will have to do. Just stop there.'

He looked at his fielders then walked back about twelve paces. He tossed the tennis ball casually in the air, caught it, and prepared for his run-up.

What shall it be, he thought, a fast run up then deliver a slow curling ball, or perhaps a googlie. No; how about a ball delivered quite fast and with plenty of spin. Then he wondered how much spin he could impart on a tennis ball. Never mind that, just give it plenty of wrist, pitch it just short of a length, then watch it zip under his bat and onto the wicket. Yes, that was it. Well, it wasn't much use depending on his fielders. With a final glance round the field he started his run-up, gaining speed until, with the baggy legs of his shorts flapping hysterically, he arrived at the single stump which marked the bowling end. He swept his arm over and delivered the first ball of the match. It turned out to be a full toss straight at the batsman! Fred had no idea what to expect after the bowler's frantic gallop towards him and so the full toss, normally an easy ball to play, took him by surprise and he swung at it. The ball flashed back up the wicket straight at Hallett who threw out a hand to defend himself. He felt a stinging sensation in the palm of his hand and when he looked down he was holding the ball. There was a silence round the field for a moment then he threw the ball casually from hand to hand.

'Next one in, please.'

Elizabeth was next in. She took the bat from Fred and stood awkwardly at the crease holding the bat near the top of the handle. Hallett decided that this called for one of his slow ones. He walked back a few paces, trotted up to the stump and sent down a lazy slow ball which Elizabeth lashed at with a wild, flailing stroke. The ball soared high into the air and both Valerie and Hallett ran forward to bring off a catch. 'I've got it, Valerie, I've got it,' shouted Hallett as he ran to get under the ball. It fell quickly towards his outstretched hands then passed in front of the sun. He lost sight of it but continued to hold up his hands hopefully. The ball rushed past his waiting hands, bounced off the bridge of his nose and straight into the hands of Valerie. Through eyes that were rapidly watering he could just see what had happened and, blinking away the tears, he caught the ball thrown to him by Valerie and looked at Elizabeth.

'Next one in, please.'

Gary walked in, collected the bat, and set himself in a very efficient stance to receive the first ball. Down came Hallett, pounding along his run, and flung down what he hoped would be a yorker. Gary leapt down the pitch and swung his bat smoothly enough to send the ball to the other end of the field, but something went wrong and the ball bounced off the side of his bat and into the waiting hands of wicket-keeper, David. Gary looked round, smiled then shrugged and walked away.

Last man in, Richard, walked in and collected the bat from Gary. He quickly took his stance and the whole field wondered what variation Hallett could now bring to his bowling. He stared steadily at Richard for some seconds in an effort to unnerve him then he suddenly turned and walked back at least twenty paces. The general feeling among the players was that he had forgotten something and was going back to the tent to get it. At last he stopped, turned and started a spirited gallop towards the bowling stump. Bent slightly forward, his arms working across his chest like pistons, he started to swing back his arm to deliver a sizzling ball. At the last moment he realised that he had seriously mis-timed his run and could not hope to deliver the ball effectively and so cantered on down the pitch. He had almost reached the baffled batsman before he could apply sufficient braking power to pull up and, as he did so, the legs of his baggy shorts surged forward then flopped back. He gasped for air and found that he had no breath left to explain to Richard what had happened. So, with a curt nod, he walked back up the pitch and decided that a slow ball might be more advisable under the circumstances. He turned and pitched the ball casually towards Richard. It hit the ground, ran under the bat, hit the wickets and dislodged a bail. Such was Hallett's fatigue that, much as he would have liked to, he could not even give a scream of 'howzat'.

Richard walked away.

Fred walked out and clapped Hallett on the shoulder. 'Great stuff, squire. You certainly know your cricket.'

'Thank you,' he panted, 'sorry it had to be so devastating for you.'

'That's all right. Our turn next, eh?'

'Yes. I shall open the batting as soon as I catch my breath.'

It took Hallett a little longer than he had anticipated to get back to a fairly normal rate of breathing. When he felt fit to start he signalled Fred who then marshalled his team. As he did this Hallett was practising his batting stance and glanced from time to time at the field positions adopted by Fred's team. He decided that his team tactics would be simple. Hit out at anything you can reach and he would first demonstrate what he meant.

He waited patiently while Fred walked a few paces away from the wicket, casually tossing the ball from hand to hand. He came trotting back and delivered a slow ball which hit the grass and bounced a little. Hallett bent one knee, scythed the bat across the grass and swept the ball in between Richard and Elizabeth. Each thought the other was going to retrieve the ball with the result that both stood watching it roll away. By the time they sorted that out Hallett had scored four runs. The next ball was fairly easy and was aching to be hit for six. Hallett lashed at it, caught it on the edge of the bat and Gary as wicket keeper, brought off a skilful catch.

Gladys was next in and, much to Hallett's amazement, scored fourteen. David got twelve and Valerie scored four off the first ball then spooned an easy catch to Fred.

They walked back to their tents feeling the healthy glow that a spell of pleasant exercise brings.

Soft drinks all round were served by Elizabeth, and Hallett raised his glass to toast the losing team.

'Cheers,' said Fred, in reply. 'Well, we can say that we were well and truly beaten today.'

Hallett thought for a moment. 'Perhaps if we play again sometime, I shall not have such a generous helping of luck. Your very good health, everyone.'

CHAPTER THIRTEEN

It was late afternoon and most of the two families of campers had reached that stage in the day when the need for a rest had overtaken them and were sitting or lying about in various attitudes of relaxation.

Hallett was stretched out on an airbed, the off-white sun hat lay flopped over his face and from his heavy breathing it was clear that he was fast asleep. From time to time he would grunt, smack his lips and settle down again. Elizabeth and Gladys were sitting at a table near the Roots' tent and Elizabeth listened with genuine fascination as Gladys recounted her early days with Fred when he had his stall. Richard and Gary were playing a leisurely game that seemed to be a cross between tennis and badminton. Fred was calling out the score as fast as he could work it out from the set of complicated rules that had been improvised. A ball sent over the shoulder high rope stretched between two trees and not returned counted three. If it was returned under the rope it scored one. If a ball hit a tree it counted as one point for the receiver if he could shout out that he claimed the point before the ball touched the ground. There were many other variations and Fred's ingenuity was taxed at times when he had to give a ruling on a complex situation. His good humour helped things to go smoothly as he joked his way through the game.

At a table outside the Halletts' tent Valerie and David sat playing cards. The game was not very serious and frequently it was interrupted as they found yet another subject for conversation. They were discussing sport and all was going well until they came to the subject of women in sport. David had just said that there were many women athletes he admired and how some of them had put up performances almost as good as a man. Valerie's eyes narrowed a little and her ready smile started to fade.

'How did you mean that exactly; almost as good as a man?'

David was looking at his hand and wondering if he should call hearts for trumps when he only had three low ones. Consequently, he missed the signs of approaching frost.

'Well, you know what I mean. No matter how hard they try they can't really compete with men in sport and sometimes it's just not fair on them.'

The lovely green eyes narrowed a fraction more and the last traces of the smile faded as completely as if it had never existed. The voice now had a brittle edge that had not been there before.

'Why is it just not fair on them?'

'Because they are females,' said David, in a tone which suggested that this condition alone explained their shortcomings. 'And it's just not fair to expect that class of performance from a girl.' He looked up and smiled. 'Hearts are trumps.'

'Are you saying that women are only second best?'

He looked startled. 'No, of course I'm not. I'm merely saying that there are things they are good at but generally they are at a disadvantage.'

He looked at Valerie and now he could not fail to see that her expression was icy and her normally attractive mouth was set in a thin line.

'I didn't mean that quite the way It sounded,' he added quickly, 'after all, they do some things extremely well.'

'You mean like washing, ironing and having babies, I suppose.' Her voice and the expression on her face together now showed a barely restrained anger.

David realised with an awful clarity how the things he had said must have sounded to Valerie. 'No, that's not what I meant. I only meant that women are, that is, considering their natural disadvantages – no, I didn't mean that. I mean, when you look at their physical, er, well, there are nurses of course who we couldn't do without and there are even women doctors. I didn't mean *even* doctors,' he added, hastily, 'as if I was implying that it was unusual or anything, I meant that, well, where would we be without… er. Can you beat the seven of hearts?' he asked timidly.

Without a word, Valerie laid the eight of hearts, took the trick, laid the ace, then the king followed by the ace and king of diamonds, not one of which David could even look like beating.

'I'm glad that we females can do something right, even if it's only to win at cards,' she said, coldly. She stood up.

David leapt to his feet and caught her by the elbow as she started to turn away. Her eyes flashed as she glared at him. 'I do not like women to be described as second-rate citizens. I think that we are as good as men in some respects and better in most. And please let go of my arm.'

'Val, please. I didn't mean it to sound like that. I like to see women take part in sport and things, really I do.'

'Well, thank you, that's very generous of you to allow us.'

'Look, this is silly. I know that I'm not expressing myself very well, but can't we just forget it all and start again?'

'I am not silly,' she said, raising her voice a little, 'and will you please take your hand off of my arm.'

Angrily he released her and they stood glowering at each other both lost for words.

David thought fiercely that of all the fiery, quick-tempered females he had ever had the misfortune to meet, this one was certainly the most... lovely and bewitching creature he had ever met. He pulled her to him and for a moment her startled face looked up into his. Then, before she could protest, his lips were pressed to hers in a breathless kiss. They drew apart a little and she looked at him with eyes that had lost their fire and were now wide with wonder.

'What made you do that?' she said, her voice barely audible.

For an answer he pulled her close to him again. 'Because I've wanted to do that from the moment I first saw you.'

His head moved closer until their faces were inches apart; then closer until their lips touched. There was, as yet, no pressure, merely a feeling of exquisite bliss as their lips remained in a contact of tantalising lightness. Slowly the pressure increased and David moved his arms round Valerie, drawing her closer to him. They remained in that rapturous embrace and when they parted, neither could have given any idea, if asked, just how long it had lasted. Such experiences are not measured in mere minutes and seconds. They smiled at each other as they came back to earth and both could be forgiven for wondering what had happened to the celestial choir which, a moment ago, had been in full and beautiful song.

'Would you like to go to the local town with me tonight? We could see a film or have a drink or perhaps just talk.'

Valerie nodded and gave him a radiant smile. 'I'd love to David. And I'm sorry about my temper.'

He laid a finger on her lips. 'Please, Val, not another word. We'll put it down to my male ignorance and forget it. I think as a species, you're marvellous.'

She laughed, they linked arms and walked towards the Roots' tent.

Fred had just shouted to the boys that their score was fourteen each and was adjudicating on a claim by Gary that the score was fifteen to fourteen in his favour when he saw Valerie and David walking onto the site. He took in at once the linked arms, the easy smiles and the shining eyes as he walked across to meet them, leaving the two boys to sort out the score for themselves.

'Hello there, you two. Had an interesting chat?'

They smiled and nodded.

'I'm taking Valerie into town tonight, Dad. Do you think I could borrow the car?'

'Course you can. I hope you both have a nice time. Are you staying here for tea?'

David glanced at Valerie. 'No, I don't think we'll bother, thanks. We'll get something in town. See you all later.'

'All right, then, off you go. I'll explain to the others where you've gone.'

He fumbled in his pocket and handed David the car keys. As they ran off to the car laughing and shouting he looked wistfully after them. He thought back to the time when he had first asked Gladys to go out with him. They had met in the Unicorn Café where Gladys worked as a waitress. He had asked her for a date, she accepted and that was the beginning of a long and happy life together.

'Where are they going, Fred?'

Fred spun round. 'Hello, Glad. Didn't know you were there. They're going into town together.'

'Oh, I'm so pleased. They make a nice couple, don't they?'

'Nice couple? Now steady on, Glad; you'll have them in church and married off before long. They've just gone out for the evening together, that's all.'

'Like when we went out for the evening together, you mean?'

He laughed and put an affectionate arm round her shoulders. 'OK, you win. Perhaps they will go on seeing each other like we did.' His arm squeezed her closer. 'Well, if he's as happy with her as I have been with you, he'll do very well.'

'Fred Root, you only get sentimental like that when you want to borrow something. What are you after, I should like to know?'

He grinned. 'Make us a cup of tea, Glad.'

Laughing together they went to their tent, playfully arguing about whose turn it was to make the tea.

Over by the trees the two boys continued their improvised tennis/badminton game and soon, Elizabeth was persuaded to join in and was trying to pick up the increasingly complicated rules. Gary was acting as umpire and was now trying to adjudicate on a claim from Richard that his return shot was legal even though he had kicked the ball back instead of using his racquet. Gary had observed that the ball, on its kicked return had whistled past Mrs Hallett at about waist level and, although kicking the ball had not been specifically ruled out at the beginning of the game, it was not the sort of thing to do, especially if you came close to winding your mother in the process.

However, the answer to this interesting sporting question was held in abeyance when Elizabeth saw Fred and Gladys walking towards them. Also she had seen David and Valerie drive out of the field a while ago. She handed her racquet to Gary and suggested that they play the point again.

She met the Roots and from their expressions she guessed the news that they were about to tell her.

'They'll be two places less for tea, Elizabeth. Valerie and

David have gone into town for the evening.'

She smiled. 'That's nice. I often wondered if they would get together sometime.'

It was Fred's turn to smile. 'That's funny, so did we.'

There was a lip-smacking, grunting sound followed by the start of a snore which never managed to get itself launched.

They all looked towards the airbed where Hallett still lay dozing in the sun. As they walked towards him they could see that he was nearing the end of his nap. He grunted, the sun hat slid slowly off his face and with a good deal of face twitching he awoke. He lay still for a few moments then slowly he sat up and said what he always said, as a kind of justification, whenever he awoke from a daytime nap. 'That's better, I'm ready for anything now.'

He blinked and looked around him. 'Hello, there. Have you all been busy with something, then?'

'Hello, squire. Yes, we all found something to do. And there will be two less for tea because David and Valerie have gone into town for the evening.'

They were not sure what Hallett's reaction would be but they were not ready for the dark frown that crossed his face. 'Really,' he said sharply, 'and whose suggestion was that?'

'Why should it be anyone's suggestion, Simon? They arranged it for themselves,' said Elizabeth, looking puzzled at the way her husband had received the news.

He replied with an impatient snort. 'I see, so that's the way it is.'

There was an uncomfortable silence for a while then, as Hallett bent to pick up his sun hat, Elizabeth looked at Fred and Gladys and nodded towards her husband in a way that said quite clearly, 'leave this to me'.

'Well, squire, we must be getting back. See you later.'

There was a grunted reply and they made their way back to their tent.

Elizabeth stood with folded arms. 'Simon, do I understand from your attitude that you are not pleased about Valerie and David?'

He straightened up and turned to face Elizabeth. 'Well, now

that you ask me; no, I am not pleased and I find it difficult to believe that you are.'

'But why shouldn't I be? David is an extremely nice boy.'

'That maybe so, but niceness is not the only quality I would look for in a potential son-in-law.'

'Son-in-law? Oh, really, I don't think it's that serious just yet.'

'Not at the moment perhaps. But later, who knows what might happen. It might become serious.'

'But what's wrong with that?'

'What's wrong with it? Elizabeth, you astound me. Young Root might be nice as you call it and his father has managed to accumulate some money and is a quite a reasonable neighbour; but that does not change the basic facts.'

There was a silence between them which lasted so long that Hallett began to fumble with a button on his shirt pocket with the sort of intensity that springs from embarrassment.

Finally, Elizabeth spoke. Her voice had an unfamiliar edge and was colder than he could ever remember it. 'By the basic facts, do you mean that David Root is not good enough to go out with our daughter?'

He cleared his throat in fussy manner and seemed to be engrossed in fastening his shirt pocket. 'Well, you know what I mean. After all they are they are in trade. Well, in a way, that is.'

The icy edge was still evident in Elizabeth's voice as she replied. 'Simon, I do not normally dispute points with you, but one thing that does upset me is when you forget who we are. Perhaps you have forgotten who I was before you married me.'

'That is entirely different.'

She shook her head and her expression softened as her flash of spirit faded. She took his hand away from his shirt pocket and fastened the button. 'No, Simon, it's not different at all. My father drove a delivery van for a laundry and we lived in a semi-detached house close to the laundry. But I'm proud of my family and so should David be. And, if you think back for a moment, your grandfather was a waiter in a London hotel and for over fourteen years your father worked in a shop.'

'It was not a shop, it was a department store,' he said with

193

some dignity.

Elizabeth smiled then spluttered into laughter.

Hallett frowned as he added 'And what's more it was in the table-ware department.'

Elizabeth laughed again. 'Oh, Simon, can't you see how funny this all is?' She swayed forward and kissed him lightly. 'They are nice people and that is what really counts isn't it?'

'Nice or not, I fail to see the relevance of the fact that my daughter is being taken out by someone whom I do not regard as a suitable match, and the former employment of some of my family.'

Elizabeth smiled. 'Simon, what would you say if Richard came to you one day and said that he intended to marry the daughter of a laundry van driver?'

'Well, I would say that er...look, it's not exactly the same sort of...well, things are different because...anyway, it's not a fair question.'

He put her hand gently on his arm. 'Please try to answer it for me, though.'

He looked baffled as he strove for a suitable answer. He sighed a heavy sigh. 'Oh well, if you insist on putting it that way perhaps we had better see how things turn out.'

'Of course. And when the time comes I am sure you will be able to handle the situation.'

'Naturally I will. You can safely leave these sort of things to me.'

'I'm sure we can.' Her face radiated a smile. 'Now that's settled, how about us inviting the Roots to tea for a change?'

'If you think we must. What are we having?'

'I thought we might have something simple like a fried meal.'

He nodded his approval. 'Good, good.'

'I'll get the portable cooker ready.'

Hallett stared disapprovingly at the cooker. 'I still say that that is not my idea of camp cooking.'

'I suppose not. But unless you can provide a reasonable alternative, the portable cooker it must be.'

'Of course I could provide an alternative. I could cook a

meal without the aid of cookers and bottles of gas and all that stuff.' He waved a derogatory hand at the cooking area.

'Cook a meal, Simon; you?'

'And why not?' he said, calling once more on his dignity.

'No reason. It's just that I can't imagine you cooking, that's all.'

'Very well. In that case I shall cook the tea.'

Elizabeth could see he was serious and tried not to smile.

'All right, Simon. Here's the food and the pots and pans are there.'

'As I just said, I shall not require the use of cooking utensils, thank you.'

Elizabeth was looking mystified. She shrugged. 'Just as you say. Shall I wait or would you prefer me to get out of your way?'

'If you wish, you can visit the Roots and I will let you know when I have finished.'

'Call me if I can help.'

'Thank you, Elizabeth, I don't think that will be necessary, but I shall, nevertheless, bear it in mind.'

She walked across to see Fred and Gladys and await the preparation of what promised, one way or another, to be a fairly memorable meal.

Hallett looked around him and wondered if he had been a little too hasty. Surely it would have been far easier to have claimed that there was a distinct difference in the taste of food cooked in the traditional camping style to that cooked over a slick and fancy portable cooker. He reflected that he could, for instance, have suggested that the technique involved in camp cookery was perfected only after many years of patient study and practice. He could then let a satisfied smile play round the mouth to suggest that he had, of course, mastered the technique, but not to say so in precise terms.

However, it was too late to think of that now. He had better have go at remembering some of the things that the cook corporal used to do when they were on military exercises. Things, that is, apart from his despicable habit of introducing herbs and other rubbish into almost every dish unless he was forcibly restrained. He had always suspected him of having foreign blood ever since the greasy little swine had put garlic in with the liver and onions. Hallett shuddered at the memory. However, there was no time to dwell on that now, he must make a start.

He thought carefully. 'Let me see, he used to dig a fire trench I think he called it. Yes, that will do to start.'

He found something to dig with and soon finished up with a trench about nine inches wide and ten inches deep at the back, sloping up to ground level. He found some stones to line the trench then carefully laid his fire. After a brief search he found his matches in his pocket. He paused and put them back in his pocket. Surely, though, he was not expected to rub two pieces of wood together now and somehow light the fire from them? He frowned as he debated with himself whether it would be cheating to use a match. For a start, he had never fully understood the principles involved in lighting a fire with just two pieces of wood. It involved friction. Well, obviously it involved friction, everyone knows that, he thought, angrily. The question is, at what stage does the flame appear and where? He snorted and took out the matches. I really see no point in ignoring an extremely useful invention just for the sake of emulating a caveman. He struck a match and soon a fire was crackling in the trench, helped at times by a down draught from the fanning of a floppy sun hat.

When the fire had settled to a steady glow, Hallett found some strong twigs and wiped them carefully on a cloth before laying them across the trench. He unwrapped a packet of bacon then gently laid some rashers across the twigs. While he waited for that to cook he unwrapped the rest of the packages that Elizabeth had left and found some sausages and tins of spaghetti. Hallett frowned and tutted a few times. He disliked spaghetti and particularly spaghetti out of tins but he decided that he would cook it anyway. Now, how do we open the tin and how do we get it warmed through? He thought hard for a while then the obvious solution came to him. Aunt Roberta's knife! She had given the knife to him on his fifteenth birthday when he was dreaming of joining the Army. Aunt Roberta had told him that the knife would be very useful for removing stones from horses' hooves and thus presented him with a muddled idea of how soldiers spent their time. He congratulated himself on having the foresight to bring a knife on a camping holiday, forgetting that it was on a key ring which held his garage keys and which would have made it difficult to leave it behind.

He quickly found the knife and tried to locate the tin-opener. He first of all found a screwdriver, then severely bent his thumbnail opening what he thought was the tin-opener but turned out to be the gadget for removing stones from horses' hooves. Then, taxing his thumbnail to the limit, he opened one more blade that turned out to be the tin-opener. Holding the knife like an old time assassin, he plunged it into the top of the tin of spaghetti. There was an immediate spurt of savoury tomato sauce, in which the spaghetti was said to be suspended, and this made its way smartly onto Hallett's shirt front.

'Oh blast,' he said, trying to wipe it off and succeeded in making a smear down the front of his shirt.

He managed eventually to open the tin, but left a lethal jagged edge round the lid that defied all his efforts at removal.

Gently he settled the tin on the twigs then tried to fit the sausages in between the rashers of bacon which, by now, were dripping fat into the fire. A glance at the fire convinced him that it was burning too low to be effective and he found some more twigs. He arranged these carefully on his trench fire but was totally unprepared for what happened next. The fire hardly stirred for a minute or so then it caught the drips of bacon fat on the dry twigs. It crackled merrily as the flames rose higher and higher then with a spiteful roar, it ignited the twigs across the trench. Hallett made a gallant effort to save the meal but feared for his fingers on the jagged edge of the spaghetti tin. Then, with a loud crackling noise, the whole thing collapsed into the fire. In a few seconds there was a roaring, sizzling sound as the bacon and sausages added yet more fuel and the spaghetti oozed out into the fire where it bubbled merrily causing the strands to move like the tentacles of some multi-limbed monster.

There was really only one thing that Hallett could say on an occasion like this. He said, 'Damn and blast the thing.'

Slowly he collected the packages together and examined

them. There was still more than enough for a decent meal if only he could cook it. The fire had died down by now and he hooked out the blackened tin of spaghetti and dumped it sadly into the refuse bag. Perhaps I should have used green twigs across the trench, he thought. As he turned back to his fire he found Gary waiting by the tent.

'Hello, young man. Are you looking for Richard?'

Gary had never spoken to Hallett on his own before and was a little uncertain as to how to address him. 'No, Colonel, I came to return his tennis racquets. He's gone off looking for birds' nests, but I'm not very keen on that.'

Hallett was pleased at his polite approach and the use of his rank. He felt quite amiable towards the boy. 'Thank you, I'll make sure he gets them.'

Gary glanced down at the trench fire from which all traces of bacon, sausage and spaghetti had now disappeared. 'Gosh, are you going to cook on an open fire?'

Hallett hesitated before replying. 'Er, yes, as a matter of fact I volunteered to cook the tea today.'

'Could I stay and watch, please?'

There was another pause while Hallett thought quickly. 'Of course you can.' He smiled. 'In fact you can help, if you wish.'

'Thanks, Colonel, that's super.'

They soon had the fire going well and were ready to start cooking the food.

'Well now, the first thing we need is something to put across the trench to lay the bacon and sausages on.'

Eager to please, Gary hunted round and came back with some spikes, which had been packed with the tent pegs.

'How about these?'

'First class. Just wipe them clean and lay them across the trench.'

Gary solemnly wiped each one and laid them carefully across the trench. They now had a serviceable grill on which to lay out the food.

'Shall I lay the food on here, now?'

'Very well, let's see how you manage under my guidance.'

Gary glowed. To be shown camp cooking by a real soldier,

this was what camping was all about.

With great artistry he arranged the bacon and sausages on the improvised grill. Meanwhile Hallett went to the tent and brought back two tins of baked beans. He produced his pocketknife with a flourish and opened the tin-opener blade. Having learned a little from his earlier tussle with the spaghetti, he managed to open the tins with a fair degree of expertise. Gary watched fascinated.

'Excuse me, Colonel; when this food is cooked, how are we going to keep it hot while we lay the table, make some tea and butter the bread?'

This problem had not even presented itself to Hallett and he knew he had no answer to it.

He looked at Gary. 'Well, young man, how do you suppose it is done?'

Gary thought hard. 'Well, I suppose that we have to improvise an oven, don't we?'

'Good, good, go on.'

'How about if I dig another trench with a small fire and set a biscuit tin or something on its side over the trench?'

'Good boy. Your resourcefulness would serve you well in the Army.'

Without knowing it he had just paid Gary the highest compliment that he could give.

Swiftly, Gary set about preparing his camp oven pausing occasionally to inspect the cooking and turn the bacon and sausages over with a carefully wiped tent peg. Already the beans were beginning to warm through.

Over at the Roots' site, Fred, Gladys and Elizabeth sat talking.

'You know, Elizabeth,' said Fred, 'we're really pleased about those two going out together. She's a lovely girl.'

'I know she thinks a lot of David and I'm sure they'll get on well together.'

'I'm sure they will.' He paused and sniffed. 'That smells good. It seems like the Colonel has the tea well under way.'

A little later, after Gary had been across to borrow some extra cutlery and plates, a shout from Hallett's tent informed them that tea was ready. They looked at each other in a puzzled way, then stood up and walked to the Hallett site.

The Colonel and Gary each holding a cloth were standing by the two tables that had been pushed together and set for six. As soon as they were seated, the two cooks went to their field oven and soon, everyone had in front of them a hot plate of delicious-looking bacon, sausages, beans and fried egg. This last item had been a suggestion by Gary. Each egg had been broken into a tin lid then cooked on their grill. As the plates were set in front of the hungry campers their faces showed their amazement at this accomplishment. As the meal began Gary lost no time in giving credit where he firmly believed it belonged.

'Guess what, Dad. The Colonel taught me to do camp cooking over a trench fire and I cooked all this with his help.'

'Well done, Gary, this is really delicious. I've got to hand it to you, squire, your pupil does you credit. Thanks.'

'Oh, think nothing of it. The lad is very quick to learn. However, I think that for the rest of the holiday we will rely on the ladies to prepare the meals; agreed, ladies?'

There was some good-natured chatter round the table and Gary felt as if he was the guest of honour at the Lord Mayor's Banquet. After the meal the two ladies washed up and for a while they still talked about how Hallett and Gary had managed to cook such a meal over an open fire and without pots and pans. From where he was sitting Hallett could hear snatches of the conversation and he smiled contentedly. Yes, this was the life.

Later that evening David and Valerie drove back into the camp, parked the car and walked over to the Roots' tent where the two families were spending the evening playing some games under the awning.

Fred had just reached the point where he was wondering whether it was worth putting a couple of houses on Park Lane and Mayfair or whether to pass "Go", collect his two hundred pounds and put them on at his next turn. Their game of Monopoly was left for a few moments when the young couple came in. Fred darted an anxious glance at Hallett to gauge his reaction on seeing them together. He need not have worried. Hallett was in a jovial mood and he smiled at David and Valerie as they stood together, obviously so very happy in each other's company and their faces beamed this message to their families.

'Hello, you two, had a nice time?' said Fred.

They both said 'yes' together and laughed. Then David spoke. 'Yes, thanks, Dad. It's quite a nice little town.'

'Good. We must all try to get down there sometime. There's some coffee there if you two would like to help yourselves but I must have my go and see what property I can buy next.'

The remainder of the evening passed pleasantly then Hallett and Elizabeth announced that it must be time to be getting off to bed. There was the usual exchange of 'goodnights' and, as they strolled across to their tent, Hallett, for the first time in years, walked with his arm round his wife's shoulders.

'They certainly looked happy, didn't they, Simon?'

'Yes, indeed they did. I still wonder just how serious it is.'

'It doesn't matter though, does it? If it is serious I'm sure they will suit each other. Personally, I think they will make a very happy couple.'

'Yes, you may well be right. We shall see.'

They walked on towards their tent.

The rest of the days went by quickly, the sun continued to shine and by the time the end of their holiday arrived, all the campers were looking fit and tanned. All agreed that the holiday had been great fun. Richard and Gary had become firm friends and Gary was more than ever convinced of the value of Army training. Hallett found himself feeling quite affable even at the thought of having David Root as a son-in-law and it seemed that this possibility looked more and more likely as the time went on. As for David and Valerie, they would have found it difficult to express their feelings in words but both felt that this had been the most wonderful holiday ever.

On the day of departure the two cars were loaded up and the families were having one more search over the site in case anything had been overlooked. The search party was the idea, and under the direction of, Hallett. He showed them how he wanted the area covered systematically, and finally, all was declared clear and the families climbed into their cars.

The journey home was uneventful and they managed to follow a fairly direct route. When they arrived at Forsythia Avenue they pulled into their drives and the men began the task of unloading the cars and Fred's trailer. Meanwhile, the ladies busied themselves in their houses opening windows and inspecting for dust and cobwebs. Elizabeth made the rounds of her plants tutting over a discoloured leaf and hooking an ivy back up over its miniature trellis. She nodded in a satisfied way as she noted the growth and progress of some of the newer plants.

Outside, the task of sorting out the cases, bags and bundles was about complete and Fred and Hallett were talking together.

'Smashing holiday, squire, but it's always nice to get back home, isn't it?'

'I'm with you there. An exhilarating experience and one that we're not likely to forget.'

'Perhaps we could try something similar next year, but there might be fewer of us.'

'Yes, I see what you mean. But I think that we could still have another go at camping. It has everything we need; excitement, fresh air and exercise. I tell you,' he said, inflating his chest and drawing in his stomach to the point where he risked losing his trousers, 'I tell you I feel ten years younger.'

Fred smiled. 'I think we've all done well out of this holiday. Roll on next year for another go at camping.'

'I am sure my family would agree with you. As far as holidays are concerned we will regard camping as *ne plus alter*, no, *plus ne*, er.'

'Do you mean *ne plus ultra*, squire?'

Hallett sighed, then he smiled. 'Yes, I have no doubt that is what I meant.'

CHAPTER FOURTEEN

'Good morning, Mr Hollett.'

Hallett straightened up from his rose bush to see who the hell was mangling his name and worse still, using it in that civilian way. He should have guessed. There was only one man who could be that thoughtless. He stared coldly across the hedge. 'Morning Padre.'

The Reverend Toby Pryde's expression tightened a little at being addressed in this military fashion but he forced a smile. 'Keeping busy as usual I see.'

'Well, you know what they say – the devil finds work for idle hands to do. And, incidentally, my name is Hallett not Hollett.'

Pryde peered over the top of his half-glasses. 'My apologies for that, I hadn't realised.' He smiled a little triumphantly. 'However, if you will excuse *my* correction, I think that you will find that the correct quotation is, 'For Satan finds some mischief still, for idle hands to do'. I trust you will forgive the correction.'

While Hallett was trying to think of a crushing response to this, they were joined by Fred Root. Fred smiled. 'Morning, squire.' He nodded. 'Morning, Vicar.'

'Ah, good morning, Mr Root. I was just commenting on Mr Hollett's commendable energy in his garden and we fell to discussing biblical quotations on idleness.'

Hallett's eyes rolled heavenwards at the Vicar's obvious inability to remember even the simplest name. Then he heard, to his delight, Root correcting the Vicar's quote.

'Yes, I heard you, Vicar, and, if you will forgive *my* correction that was not a biblical quotation. You were quoting from Isaac Watts. He wrote, "In works of labour and of skill, I would be busy too, For Satan finds some mischief still, for idle hands to do".'

'Yes, of course, Isaac Watts, quite so. Thank you.' He made no move to go and both men felt that their Vicar still had something else, apart from misquotations, to say to them. They waited. Suddenly, he smiled broadly. The smile was such that it gave the impression that a Great Truth had, at that very moment, been revealed to him. Hallett and Fred stood waiting.

The smile was still there as he spoke. 'I must say you both look bronzed and fit. A holiday, was it?'

'Yes, you're quite right, Padre. Both our families decided to spend a couple of weeks under canvas and it turned out to be a worthwhile experience for all concerned.' The Vicar's smile became broader. 'Ah, then perhaps you'll be able to help me. You see, all those I have spoken to so far seem to be planning holidays.'

Suspicion clouded Hallett's face. 'Help you? In what way, precisely?'

The smile was benevolent. 'The Annual Fete. You see I need volunteers to man the stalls and so on.' He beamed at them and he clasped his hands as if in prayer. 'Can I please count on you both?'

Hallett shifted his feet uncomfortably. 'The Annual Fete, eh? Well of course I'd love to help but I'm never quite sure when I'm likely to be...'

His voice tailed off as he looked across at Fred who was grinning at his discomfiture.

The Vicar turned to Fred. 'How about you, Mr Root?'

Fred nodded. 'You can put me down as a helper. In fact, you can include the wife as well.'

'Splendid. I am much obliged to you. Now, how about you, Mr Hollett?'

'Oh, very well. Put me down for a task of some sort and my wife also. And I'm sorry to have to remind you once more, Padre, the name is Hallett.'

'Yes, of course, foolish of me. Thank you, both of you. It really is most kind of you. You see, we are trying to raise funds for the new Church Youth Club building and it's proving additionally expensive because of legal difficulties over the rights of way and that sort of thing. But we are keen to get it started again in the new premises.' He looked at Hallett and seemed to be considering something; then he plunged in. 'I suppose I couldn't interest you in helping out with our youth work, Mr Hollett?' His tone was understandably doubtful.

The response from Hallett was so hasty that he neglected to correct the Vicar about his name. 'I'm sorry, I'm afraid I'm far too busy. My time is taken up with, with, er many other things.'

The Vicar did not look very surprised. The Reverend Toby Pryde was not unaccustomed to that form of reply. 'I see. Well, thank you again, both of you, for your offers of help. I will write to you.'

Hallett watched the Vicar as he pottered on down the Avenue. He snorted. 'So that was what it was all about. All that stuff about my commendable energy and how healthy we both looked. He was just lining us up as labour for his miserable fete and me for his youth work. I don't think the clergy should be allowed to be that devious, do you?'

'The way I see it, squire, sometimes it's the only way. And you must admit, it worked, didn't it?'

'Maybe so, but it still smacks of underhandedness.'

'Well, as our Vicar might say might say, "Needs must when the devil drives." '

'Is that also from Mr Isaac Watts?'

'Not this time. Unknown fifteenth century writer.'

There was a heavy sigh from Hallett. 'Now all we have to do is to start worrying about what sort of jobs we get landed with.'

They did not have to worry for long.

Two days later and Hallett was sitting after breakfast sorting his mail. He noticed a letter bearing a sticker which showed that it came from the Vicarage. He picked it up and for some seconds he sat tapping the letter on his left thumb. He slit it open with his miniature Nepalese Kukri knife, quickly skimmed through the contents then slammed the letter down on the table. 'What a blasted cheek. I rather thought that he would ask me to judge the roses or the home-made wines, but no, he's put me down to look after the White Elephant stall.'

Elizabeth looked up from her letter. 'Really? Well I think it could be quite good fun and at least it would be something new and challenging for you, wouldn't it?' She looked at him with that twinkle in her eyes that always made him wonder if he was being gently teased.

'Elizabeth, I'm not saying that I couldn't handle it; it's just that I feel I could be more usefully employed elsewhere. I merely think that Pryde could have been a little more sensitive in his choice of tasks and allocated them according to ability.' He hoped that this conversation would not develop into a discussion on how he would be employed because he was not quite sure what happened at a White Elephant stall. So before he could get involved in answering awkward questions he decided to take refuge in his garden. 'Think I'll just pop out and see how those new roses are progressing.'

As he was on the way to his new roses he saw Fred Root. He called to him. 'Morning, Root. Had your letter from the Reverend Pryde yet?'

'Yes, it came this morning. He's got me down to look after the Aunt Sally.'

Hallett had only a vague idea of what an Aunt Sally was but he thought that he ought to say something. 'I see. Had much experience of that, have you?'

'Not much, but who knows, it might be fun.'

From the look on Hallett's face it was clear that he did not share this enthusiastic approach.

The following week they were invited to a meeting of the fete committee to be held at the Vicarage.

Hallett was both surprised and pleased to see so many volunteers. This meant that the duties wouldn't fall on a few of them. They discussed the fete in detail and soon had a fair idea of what each person would be doing. When their plans were complete the Vicar said that he had an announcement to make.

'I have only today had this confirmed but I can now announce that we have a VIP who has agreed to open our fete.' There was a stir of excitement from the committee members and murmurs of approval together with one or two calls of 'who is it?'

Toby Pryde beamed at his committee. 'Any guesses?'

There were some suggestions of well-known personalities

each followed by a smiling shake of the head.

Hallett had an inspiration. 'Is it Major General Sir Aubrey Neville-Saunders?'

There was complete silence.

The Vicar stared. 'Who?' he said, his voice almost a falsetto.

'Who? Good grief, man, he's the best known military figure in this area. You surely must have heard of him.'

'I'm afraid not, Mr Hallett.'

'Well, if it isn't him, then who the dev... well who is it anyway?'

Pryde leaned back in his chair and steepled his fingers. He wore a benign smile. 'It's none other than Benny Benjamin.'

It was now Hallett's turn and he took full opportunity. 'Who?' he said, loudly.

'Come now, Mr Hollett, you must have heard of Benny Benjamin. He's very well known.'

'It's Hallett and I haven't. Who is he, what does he do?' He was still feeling irritated at the committee's failure to identify Neville-Saunders.

'He's a comedian and I hear that he's very funny. He used to have a radio show of his own called, "Never Fear, Benny's Here". I haven't actually listened to it myself but my next door neighbour speaks quite highly of him. But I must admit my neighbour is rather hard of hearing.'

To Hallett this did not sound too promising. The fact that he *used* to have a radio show was ominous enough, but the only available appraisal of his comedic abilities was from one man and he was partly deaf.

He stared at the Vicar. 'No, I can still say that I have never heard of him.' He muttered to himself, 'Nor do I wish to.'

There was long silence and it was easy to see that Pryde was disappointed that his surprise announcement had not met with unanimous approval. And, to judge from the expressions on the faces of some of the committee, he could not be certain that Hollett stood alone.

He declared the meeting closed.

Over the next few weeks the preparations for the fete were well on the way; then with unbelievable speed, the big day arrived. By then, with a well-organised committee and additional helpers, only a few minor tasks remained and these were soon attended to.

Hallett, now steeped in the functions of a White Elephant stall, had agreed to hold the items in his garage until the day. He was busily sorting through them to see if they would fit into the boot of his car when he heard Fred call.

'Busy, squire?'

'Not very. I'm just trying to get these into some sort of order and fit them into my car.' He frowned at his collection. 'Am I really expected to sell this sort of rubbish? Just look at it.'

Fred smiled. 'On the day I'll bet you'll be surprised just how busy it will keep you.'

As he steered his car slowly over the field chosen for the fete, Hallett tried to visualise the complicated stalls, tents and amenities map that the Vicar had prepared. He was just beginning to despair when he saw the Reverend Pryde waving at him and sweeping his arms in an exaggerated manner indicating where Hallett should pull in.

After he had successfully parked between two stalls, Hallett began the task of transferring his boxes of assorted rubbish, as he referred to it, to the stall. As he surveyed them he was convinced that the donors of these items were mightily pleased to be shot of them. He began to set them out and make the display reasonably attractive. This task, though, he considered to be only little less in difficulty than any one of the Twelve Tasks of Heracles.

In the Refreshments Tent Elizabeth was helping to complete the task of preparing teas, cakes and biscuits for the throng of people whom they hoped would be attending the fete.

Back at Hallett's stall he had completed his layout and found to his annoyance that he still had several boxes of items for which there was no room. He pushed them under the table and decided that he would display them when he had sold enough items to clear a space. He stared stonily at his display. He was so convinced of the utter worthlessness of the whole lot, he reasoned that the items stored under the table would probably never see the light of day.

He thought it would be as well if, despite his low opinion of his wares, he familiarised himself with some of them. He mentally waved aside the saucerless cups, odd glasses, cracked vases and concentrated on looking for something that might just be saleable and he added a deerstalker cap to his display. His appraisal of the items was still one of distaste until he found one repulsive item which elevated the remainder of his display to the level of respectability, almost desirability.

It was a desk lamp fashioned in the form of a young girl, completely naked. She stood with one arm thrust into the air and in her outstretched hand was the bulbholder which unfortunately was broken. This was, no doubt, the reason it had been donated. Hallett slowly shook his head as he looked at it and wondered what sort of person would buy such a thing, and more puzzling, have it on display in their home. After all, it was hardly a work of art. His silent contemplation was to be interrupted.

Without warning, there came a crackling sound then the strangely hollow voice of the Reverend Pryde bellowed from a loudspeaker, tied to the trunk of an adjacent tree. Hallett clapped his hands over his ears but Pryde's voice continued to echo in his head despite his covered ears. It stopped. But more was to follow.

Pryde had just introduced Benny Benjamin and now the guest of honour took over the microphone to speak to his assembled fans. He yelled out his delight at his being there then shouted to the crowd. 'Are we downhearted?' The resulting screams of 'No!' proved almost too much for Hallett. He was very near the point where he would go to the offending loudspeaker and rip out the wires with his bare hands.

Slowly he took his hands from his ears. Well, if that is their idea of a suitable person to open the fete, it is most certainly not mine, he thought. That's odd, he didn't formally open the fete.

As if in answer to this there came a loud crackle and back roared Mr Benjamin. 'Well, what do you know,' he bellowed. 'The Vicar's just told me I didn't open the fete. Well, I'll soon put that right.' Even louder than before he shouted. 'Benny Benjamin says this fete is bloody well open. All right?'

Hallett's aural bits and pieces plus his nerves were in a near state of shock. Apart from the coarse way the fete was opened, the volume had been unbearable.

He gave a sigh and decided that he may as well continue with his appraisal and was looking for something more suitable to replace that awful lamp. He was deciding between a gaudy vase and a rolling pin with one handle missing when the dreaded crackle sounded. Instinctively his hands were clapped over his ears. But he could still hear and it was Benny Benjamin once more.

He shrieked at the crowd. 'Never fear, guess who's here?' They roared back. 'BEN, BEN, BEN, BEN BENNY!'

Really, this was too much. He would have to find the Vicar at once. Leaving his white elephants to fend for themselves, he marched away.

He saw Pryde just leaving a marquee and hurried across.

'Just a minute, padre.' He trotted up to him. 'Look, you've got to stop the ghastly noises coming from those loudspeakers. It's unbearable.' He stopped. The Vicar's expression had changed and he looked as if Hallett had just struck him across the face.

Hallett was baffled then noticed that another voice was now wafting across the fete area. Turning slowly to face the dais he saw that it was Mrs Pryde, making an announcement about the ladies knitting competition.

He turned back. 'I'm most awfully sorry, I had no idea that it was your wife. I mean I wasn't referring to her when I mentioned the dreadful noise. I meant earlier on when you spoke. To introduce our guest,' he added hastily. 'That is, I mean, well the placing of the loudspeakers was not quite what it might have been and it…'

He stopped. The Reverend Pryde was looking more hurt with every sentence.

'Is there anything more Mr Hollet?' The voice was stiffly formal.

'No, not really. I was merely trying to point out the problems I was having with the… Well, I don't suppose it matters now. I'd better get back to the stall.'

'Yes, please do.'

Back at the stall there was no sign of any customers but he

could see plenty of people at other attractions. He started to fiddle about with the display, moving items from one place to another then he looked up and three young lads were peering at some of the items at the front.

The tallest lad stared for some time. 'Blimey, what a load of old junk.' He looked at Hallett. 'You don't expect to sell all this rubbish, do you?'

'Look, you don't have to buy it if you don't want to.'

'Don't worry, mate, we shan't.' Then the lad noticed the deerstalker. He seized it and put it on.

'Do you reckon this suits me?' he asked his companions. They both sniggered. 'Cor, you look a right poofter in that, Ginger.'

But by now, Ginger was quite taken with the idea of wearing a deerstalker. 'Well, I might just start a new craze with it.' He turned to Hallett. 'How much do you want for it?'

'The price is marked inside.' Hallett tried to put on a voice that hinted at authority but with a formal coolness.

Ginger handed the hat to Hallett who glanced inside. 'One pound, fifty.'

After a few seconds hesitation while he decided whether or not he was ready to start a new trend, he searched in his pocket and produced one pound and fifty pence. He handed this to Hallett who presented him with the hat. Ginger seized it and jammed it on his head. They ran off with shouts of 'Sherlock Holmes' and other remarks about Ginger's new headgear.

Over the next ten minutes or so there were no more customers and it was beginning to look like a boring afternoon when the Vicar arrived.

'Ah, Mr Hallett, how is it going?'

'Frankly, Padre, it isn't. No one seems interested.'

'But didn't I see a young lad just now wearing the deerstalker? Although one wonders why he would buy something like that. He didn't look the type to pay that much for a hat.'

'Really? But it was only one pound fifty, after all.'

Pryde looked stricken. 'One pound fifty? I donated that hat and it was brand new. The price at which it was fixed was only a third of the purchase price. He should have paid eleven pounds fifty.' He glared at Hallett who was now looking uncomfortable.

'Oh, I see. Eleven pounds fifty. I must admit that I only glanced at the price tag and I must have misread it. Sorry about that, but these things happen you know.'

It was obvious from the Vicar's expression that he accepted neither the apology, nor the explanation that 'these things happen'.

There was some shouting nearby and both men turned to see what was happening. They saw that Ginger and his mates were taking turns wearing the hat and jumping up and down to see who could make the earflaps move the highest.

Without another word the Reverend Toby Pryde walked away.

Hallett sighed and had just resigned himself to another period of inactivity when, walking towards his stall, he saw none other than Major General Sir Aubrey Neville-Saunders. What a pity, he thought, that they hadn't invited this distinguished former Army officer. It all could have been so different.

The distinguished former Army officer stopped at the stall and stared for some seconds at Hallett.

'Good afternoon, sir. May I welcome you to our church fete.'

The General continued with his steely stare. 'Do I know you then? What's your name, eh?'

'Hallett, sir. Lieutenant Colonel Simon Hallett, now retired. I was once in your Command,'

'Hallett, Hallett.' He looked thoughtful, his chin sunk on his chest. Suddenly he looked up. 'Hallett, I remember now. You appeared before a Board of Inquiry that I was chairing. It concerned some of your men who apparently rampaged through the local town creating havoc as I understood it.'

Hallett gave a light laugh. 'Well, hardly that, sir.'

'Hardly that, sir? It was worse than that, sir. Behaved like a bunch of lunatics. Said so at the time. Anyway, what are you doing here now?'

'I thought I'd lend the local church a hand so I volunteered to run this stall.'

'Stall? What stall? What are you talking about?'

Hallett waved his hand over his display of mixed items. 'This is what we call our White Elephant stall.'

'White Elephants? Just what is all this rubbish doing here, then?'

'The idea is, you see, that I sell it.' He added a dry laugh.

'Sell it? By the look of it you'd be bloody lucky to give it away.'

His eyes roamed over the table until he came to the desk lamp. 'Hello, what have we here?' He put on a pair of steel-framed spectacles and leaned forward to inspect the lamp more closely. 'By the left, Jeremy, she's a strapping young thing.' He turned the lamp slowly. 'Just look at the detail that's been included.' He peered more closely. 'They haven't missed anything out, what?' He gave a coarse laugh. 'I wouldn't mind this in my study, you know.'

Hallett pointed to the top of the girl's arm. 'My name is Simon and I think I should show you, sir, that the bulb-holder is broken.'

'Bulb-holder? Oh, I see, it's a lamp, is it? I hadn't noticed. But anyway, what are you asking for it; what's your price, eh?'

'It's priced at one pound seventy-five, sir.'

The General gave a sharp intake of breath. 'I expect you'll take a pound, though, won't you?' It was clearly not intended as a question. He bought out a handful of coins and tipped them into a small dish.

'Bound to be a pound there, probably more, I should think.' He leaned forward conspiratorially. 'Would you put her in a bag for me, Jeremy. I wouldn't want my better half to see her. I'm sure you know what I mean.' He gave a loud guffawing sort laugh. His guffaws were well known in many Army units and were much used in impersonations of the General by young subalterns.

Hallett sorted through the boxes and found a supermarket plastic carrier bag. He wrapped the lamp and handed it to the General who made no effort to take the bag.

'Perhaps you'd better keep her here for me, Jeremy and I'll call for it later. Thing is, I've just spotted the little woman approaching.'

Lady Marjorie Neville-Saunders was indeed approaching, but no-one with normal vision could possibly describe her as 'the little woman'. An ample frame on sturdy legs, she habitually wore tweeds and a felt hat pulled firmly onto her head.

'Hello, Marjorie, my dear. Seen anything interesting yet?'

'No I have not and I have rarely been more bored with any event.' The rich, plummy voice carried quite a distance. 'Come, Aubrey, we're going to have tea now.'

'Yes, of course, dear. By the way, this is Major Jeremy Hallett.'

'How do you do,' she said over her shoulder. She seized her husband's arm. 'Come along, Aubrey.'

'Yes, of course. See you later, Jeremy.'

'Actually, sir, the name is Simon.'

'Really? Jolly good. Well, goodbye Major.'

Together the General and his little woman strode briskly away.

Hallett stared after them feeling that his long-held respect and loyalty for senior officers had been badly dented. He picked up the small bowl and counted the small change left by the General. 'Seventy-five pence? Lecherous old fool,' he said, viciously.

There was a buzzing, crackling sound and as he clapped his hands to his ears, a stentorian voice boomed out that the Flower Show was about to be judged.

A few minutes later the Vicar visited the stall and with a relief for Hallett who then was free to visit the rest of the stalls and attractions.

At the Aunt Sally stall Fred had attracted a small crowd who were waiting their turn and being kept amused by Fred's friendly banter. He looked over the crowd and saw Hallett. 'Hello, squire. Sold out already?'

Hallett walked over. 'Not really. In fact, I've hardly sold anything. It's just that my relief has arrived. How are you doing?'

'Not bad. It's proving to be very popular. Want to give it a try?'

'Yes, why not? I might prove to be good at it.'

He paid his money and joined the queue.

When his turn came he took the six sticks and stood on the white line ready to throw.

He took his first stick and did a good deal of practising the throw, taking his arm back, swinging it gently forwards then stopping to align his arm with the wooden dolly. He did this a few times then smoothly swung his arm forward, released the stick and watched it sail over the top of the dolly, missing it by about four feet before it thudded into the padded board at the back. He did this four more times and his aim progressively improved. His last try called for the maximum concentration. Slowly, the arm was taken back, the arm aligned on what he now regarded as the Target, the last minute check that he was ready and the last stick was on its way. It hit the dolly a glancing blow causing it to fall neatly into the ring at the base of the stand.

'Perfect,' shouted someone from the onlookers.

Hallett felt inappropriately pleased with himself. He joined Root once more.

'Well done, squire, a good effort.'

'Thank you, I rather enjoyed that. I could almost consider putting something like it in my back garden. I think I could get to be quite good at it.'

'Good idea. My relief should be here any minute. Shall we visit the tea-tent? We could see how the ladies are managing.'

'Splendid idea. My treat.'

They seated themselves in the marquee and had tea and iced buns served by Gladys with her comment. 'No charge for workers.'

Fred looked round. 'The fete seems to be a fair success from what I've seen of it. Have you seen the Vicar yet, squire?'

Hallett was about take a bite of his iced bun but he paused. 'Yes, I have seen him but they weren't very happy meetings.' He explained about the misunderstandings regarding the Vicar's wife and the misreading of the price-tag on the deerstalker hat.

Fred sat, a stifled smile tightening his face. 'I'm sure you overcame greater problems than that in your Army days, didn't you?'

'Well, yes, but I do seem to have a certain propensity for putting my foot right in it this afternoon.' His face twitched a smile. 'I'm not making too much of it all, am I?'

'Course not. Come on, let's have a walk round.'

Later, when both men were back at their respective stalls, each was visited by Elizabeth and Gladys who were taking a brief break from the tea-tent. Both tried the Aunt Sally and both scored two. At the White Elephant stall, business had picked up and Hallett was down to selling the items in the last box.

Elizabeth looked over the display. 'Are all the items in this display supposed to be items of low value, Simon?'

'I must admit that is what I thought at first, but now I am not so sure. They all seem to be selling briskly and the items from the very last box seem to be quite saleable.'

'Good. Well, we'll leave you to it and see you later on.'

After they had gone, Hallett had another sprinkling of customers then things were quiet. He occupied himself by looking over the remaining items. There was an old and battered toffee tin containing a good quantity of pre-decimal coins. He picked out a few and was about to examine them when another customer appeared. He stood looking at the items on display. His appearance, though shabby, was clean and tidy. He seemed interested in the assorted paraphernalia of the White Elephant stall. He picked up one or two items to study them. He held out a glass paperweight. 'How much is this, please?'

Briskly Hallett took it from him and flipped it over. 'It's priced at one pound, fifty pence and well worth it I should say.'

The man gave a nervous laugh. 'Well, I expect you are far more experienced than I in these things and if you say it's worth one pound fifty, I'm sure it is. You must be very experienced.'

Hallett waved his hand to modestly dismiss this compliment. 'One gets familiar with these things, you know.'

The man smiled. 'The fact is I'm involved in a sort of charity work and I work closely with the Salvation Army. They have asked if I could help them raise funds for their activities and, because I believe it to be a worthy organisation, I have agreed. And since then, I have helped them to organise whist drives and bingo sessions. Mostly, they provide the prizes but I do like to do my share to help and that is why I like to browse over stalls like this.'

'I see. You are looking for inexpensive items to give as prizes. Perhaps I could stretch a point about the price of the paperweight. Let's say one pound, shall we?'

'That is most kind.' He handed Hallett a pound coin. 'Now perhaps I could look to see if I can find any other suitable items.'

As the man was speaking Hallett was taking the very last items from the box. That completed, he picked up the old toffee tin and picked out a few coins. As he replaced them in the tin and placed the tin on the table, the old man smiled. 'Oh dear; not quite what I was looking for, but I would like to show my grandchildren what pre-decimal coins looked like.'

Hallett waited while the man examined some of the coins. He looked up. 'Excuse me, but have you got a price for this?'

'Is there no label there?'

'None that I can see. But, would it be in order for me to make you an offer for the tin of coins – say two pounds?'

Hallett looked thoughtful as he took the tin of coins from him. 'I shall have to check with one of the organisers. It shouldn't take too long.'

At that moment one of the team of relief helpers was passing the stall and it was arranged that he would look after things while Hallett went to find one of the organisers.

Hallett went straight to the Aunt Sally stall where Fred Root was still doing a brisk trade. He saw Hallett and could see that he wanted to speak. Calling to another helper to take over, Fred joined Hallett.

'You got a problem, squire?'

'I think I may have, but I want to take things cautiously. At my stall there is a man who claims to be involved in charity work and seems to be looking for concessions when buying. I think, though, that he may not be all he says he is.'

'Really? What makes you think that?'

'First of all he was unable to conceal his excitement when I showed him a tin of coins and he offered me two pounds for the lot. I haven't been through all of them yet but I did notice some pennies from eighteen eighty-four in very good condition. They must be worth ten or twelve pound each, possibly more.'

'I didn't know you were interested in coins, squire?'

Hallett gave a quick shrug. 'It was merely a passing interest of mine once. But with this man, there's more to it than just the coins. He claims to be working with the Salvation Army arranging whist drives and bingo sessions and, while the Salvation Army provides the prizes, he likes to provide them himself at his own expense when he can afford to.'

Fred looked puzzled. 'Is there something wrong with that, then?'

'Well, at first I didn't see anything wrong with it, but I started thinking and remembered that the Salvation Army does not approve of gambling and that includes such things as raffles and bingo.'

'Yes, come to think of it, I have heard that about the Salvation Army and gambling. Well spotted, squire. I think you're right, he sounds a bit iffy.'

'Iffy?'

'Sorry. Iffy is doubtful, questionable or suspicious. And he sounds all three so let's go and have a chat with him.'

They walked to the White Elephant stall where the man was chatting amiably with the helper.

Fred nodded a greeting but his expression was serious. 'Understand you're interested in coins and you're offering two pounds for this tin of coins. Is that right?'

'Yes, that's correct, that is what I offered. But I really don't know much about them.'

'But don't you think that two pounds is a bit over top for a tin of copper coins?'

The man was biting his lower lip now. 'Well I thought that they might possibly be, well, sort of…' he paused, 'I thought that they would make a good prize, wouldn't they?' he finished weakly.

'Funny sort of prize I should have thought. What do you think the Salvation Army would say?'

He shook his head. 'I don't know. In the past they have always relied on me to choose the prizes.'

'You also don't know that the Salvation Army does not approve of gambling and that includes bingo. Yet you claim to supply prizes and organise bingo sessions for them. I find that a little strange, don't you, Colonel?' The use of his Army rank was deliberate.

'Very peculiar I would say,' said Hallett with solemn dignity. 'In fact, I would say that is virtually akin to criminal deception.'

By now the man was perspiring and fidgeting uncomfortably. 'Look, perhaps I was wrong. Let's say no more about it and I'll be on my way. All right?'

Fred and Hallett looked at each other and nodded. Hallett held out his hand. 'I'll take another fifty pence for the paperweight, please.'

Hurriedly he handed over the paperweight. 'Here, take this and we'll call it quits.'

He turned and scuttled away.

Both men smiled and thanked the helper as he left.

Later, when Hallett had had once more assumed command of his stall, the Vicar arrived in a fluster. 'Mr Hallett,' he said, gasping for breath. 'There has been a ghastly error. You will recall that I mentioned our difficulties with the building of the Church Youth Club?'

'No, I can't say that I do. Why?'

'Oh come now,' his tone had become sharp, bordering on the recriminatory.

'You must remember my saying that extra costs would be incurred because the original site we had chosen had difficulties with the rights of way and our second choice would cost more than we can afford at the moment.'

'Yes, I do believe I can recollect you saying something of that sort.'

'Good. Well, the lady who is insisting on the rights of way, Mrs Agnes Mattingley, is here. She says that she told her housekeeper to sort out some items for our White Elephant stall and among them is something of great sentimental value to her. I just pray,' he glanced heavenwards, 'that we have not already sold it.'

'Might have done, we've cleared a fair amount of items. What is it?'

'It's a tin of old copper coins.' He couldn't keep the hopeful, almost pleading note out of his voice.

Hallett picked up the tin. 'You mean this one?'

The Reverend Pryde seized the tin and clasped it to his chest. 'Oh you marvellous man. How very splendid. I am told that Mrs Mattingley, as well as owning the right of way over our original choice, also owns that site and the site of our second choice. Goodness knows what she would have said if these coins had been sold.' He hurried away.

The remainder of the afternoon went by fairly smoothly and Hallett managed to sell most his stock. He was left with an old flat-iron, some faded place mats and a few items whose immediate future looked like their being dumped in the nearest skip.

He was agreeably surprised to find that he had quite enjoyed the experience and was about to start tidying up when he noticed the package that was supposed to have been collected by the General. He decided that the old fool had forgotten it, then he saw him approaching.

'Ah, there you are, Jeremy. I expect you thought that I had forgotten my little purchase. No chance of that, eh?' Guffaw, guffaw. 'Is she still wrapped up for me?'

Hallett nodded. 'I'll get it for you now.' He started to turn when he saw Lady Marjorie swiftly but silently approaching the General from behind. He slowly picked up the package and handed it to its jubilant owner. He said loudly. 'There you are, sir. I hope that she graces your study beautifully.' He observed that all of this had been taken in by Lady Marjorie Neville-Saunders.

'Not much doubt about that, Jeremy.' His guffaws had taken on a coarse note.

'What have you got there, Aubrey?'

He froze then slowly turned round. 'Oh, hello, dear. Er, nothing much, just a desk lamp.'

'Show me!' It was not a command to be questioned.

He held out the package.

'You will unwrap it.'

Reluctantly, he unwrapped his purchase until she was revealed in all her nakedness.

'What does this mean, Aubrey?' Am I to understand that you have actually purchased this lewd and disgusting article?'

'Well, you see dear, I just thought…'

'Enough!' She pointed to the unsold flat-iron. 'You there. How much?'

Hallett picked it up. 'It's just one pound fifty.'

'Pay it, Aubrey.'

He fumbled in his pocket and produced a five pound note, handed it to Hallett who began to sort out some change.

'He will not require any change, thank you. Please donate it to the church.' She turned to the General once more. 'Aubrey, pick up that flat-iron.'

He reached out and picked it up.

'Now, you will use it to smash that obscenity.'

'Look, dear, it's only a lamp and…'

'NOW!' Her volume almost equalled that of the fete loudspeaker.

He raised the iron and smashed it down on the lamp reducing it to fragments. He stood there, still grasping the iron. Lady Marjorie took it from him and placed it back on the table. 'You may sell that again if you wish. And as for you,' she glared at her husband, 'we will continue this discussion at home.'

As he watched them stride away, Hallett gave a slow smile of satisfaction. He gathered up the takings and walked across to the marquee to hand them in.

Inside he saw the Vicar talking earnestly to a small, grey-haired lady and on seeing Hallett, the Vicar beamed and threaded his way towards him.

'Mr Hallett, I really must apologise to you. I have been talking to Mr Root and he has told me about your astuteness in dealing with that dreadful little man this afternoon and saving Mrs Mattingley's coins. Naturally, she is most anxious to meet you. Would you please follow me.'

They wound their way through the throng of stall-holders and other officials and the Vicar introduced Hallett to Mrs Mattingley.

'I'm very pleased to make your acquaintance, Ma'am.'

She waved a grey, gloved hand. 'Please call me Agnes. And,

Toby, if you have nothing to do, please find some seats for us.'

Still beaming, the Vicar hurried away to find two chairs and soon Mrs Mattingley and Hallett were seated at a small table.

She looked up at the still hovering Vicar. 'Perhaps a little tea, Vicar, please.'

'Of course, Mrs Mattingley, of course. I'll see to it right away.'

Mrs Mattingley leaned back in her chair. 'The Vicar has just explained to me how close I came to losing these coins, but, thanks to you, I still have them. Thank you very much, Colonel.'

'Not at all. I'm very pleased to have been able to help. I understand that they are of some personal value to you.'

Agnes Mattingley's normally composed expression softened as she smiled wistfully. 'It all seems rather silly now, but many years ago, my husband and I decided to start a coin collection. We had only just begun when, quite suddenly, he died. I didn't feel much like continuing with the collection, but I couldn't bring myself to get rid of it. And, of course, my housekeeper didn't know that when I asked her to sort out some items for the Vicar's fete.' She put her hand into the tin of coins and stirred them round. 'It's funny how many memories these bring back to me.'

She withdrew her hand. 'But I mustn't go on. Thank you again.'

'I'm happy that it all ended well for you.'

'Hello, Agnes,' came a familiar voice. Hello, squire.'

Mrs Mattingley looked up. 'Hello, Fred.'

Hallett stared. 'You two have met?'

'Yes. As soon as I saw the Vicar with the coins, I was able to explain what had happened. All fixed up now, Agnes?'

'Yes, thank you, Fred. The Colonel and I were just chatting about it.' She looked at her watch. 'I really must be making a move. Thank you again, both of you.'

The Vicar arrived with the tea for two.

'Thank you Toby. You can have my tea, Fred.'

They finished their tea then helped the Vicar and others with the clearing up.

It was a few days after the fete and Hallett was reading the morning paper when the telephone rang. 'Hello, Simon Hallett here.' He listened intently.

After the call he went into the kitchen to find Elizabeth.

'Who was that, Simon?'

'It was the Vicar. He called about the fete. Apparently, Mrs Mattingly was so pleased about those coins that she has decided to waive the right of way she has over the original site for the Youth Club. Also, she has reduced the asking price, so naturally, the Vicar is delighted.'

'Oh, that is good news. Now he can go ahead with his fund-raising.'

'Yes, of course.' He looked at Elizabeth and sighed. 'What on earth do you suppose he can get me involved in now?'

CHAPTER FIFTEEN

It was Sunday morning and Hallett was lounging in his easy chair reading the Sunday papers and catching up on one or two of the daily papers he had not yet found time to deal with.

From time to time his newspaper would rustle and at times, vibrate; powered by his indignation at various items he had encountered. These, in the main, concerned the antics of some foreign government or the meting out of what he called ridiculously lenient sentences to criminals.

Eventually, he reached the local paper in which was reported their church fete. He read through the report, nodding occasionally. 'I must say this report is quite well done. An observant reporter, no doubt.'

Elizabeth looked from her book. 'Yes, I read it. I expect that the Vicar is quite pleased.'

In the article the reporter had described their efforts and, when he gave the name of the volunteer who ran the White Elephant stall, he not only spelled it correctly, he also gave details of his military background. This was not entirely due to the reporter's powers of observation. Hallett had 'accidentally' met him in the tea-tent and they chatted together.

Idly he flicked through the pages. He stopped at one small paragraph. 'Elizabeth, have you seen the entry in this week's Gazette about road repairs?'

Again she looked up from her book. 'No, I can't say that I have. Is it something special, then?'

'What it says is that the Local Council representatives are to start inspecting this area looking for roads and paths in need of repair.'

'Is that important, then?'

He rustled his paper impatiently. 'Have you forgotten how

many times I have written to that Council complaining about that huge pot-hole in the road?'

'Oh, that. Yes, I think I remember you mentioned it once or twice.'

'Mentioned it once or twice? I did more than that. For a start I said to...He paused as he realised that he was again being gently teased. 'Well, it's about time that they got on with it,' he finished gruffly, and continued to read his paper.

Even after two interruptions Elizabeth knew that a third, fourth or even a fifth was not out of the question. She had accepted for some time that during her husband's combat with controversial or disagreeable items in the papers, he needed not only an audience, but also a sounding board.

'Elizabeth, have you seen this?' Without waiting for a reply, he continued. 'A man has pleaded guilty to breaking into several houses and stealing valuable property. He openly admits this and was told he would have to serve thirty hours' community service. And that, as far as I can see, will probably amount to pushing a broom along some pensioner's path. It's wrong, it just will not do.'

Elizabeth put aside her book. She had a fair idea of what was to follow and this would be his regular tirade against the police and the judiciary. She waited with commendable patience. But the normally spirited attack did not appear. He looked thoughtful and a little troubled. 'I suppose it makes it easier for the criminals if we leave a clear invitation to a burglar by sloppy security.'

'I didn't think we did that, Simon.'

He was indignant. 'We do not. But I have always found that it pays to be both secure and vigilant.'

'Oh, that reminds me,' she said, in the tone she sometimes used to correct him gently, 'you said you were going to do something about the faulty lock on the porch door.'

The delay of a few seconds before he replied told Elizabeth that she had scored a direct hit.

'That lock is not faulty. It's just that you have to understand the knack of locking it.'

Patiently, Elizabeth replied. 'But it's not the locking that's the problem. The problem is that if you press the door-handle up and down rapidly, the door unlocks itself.'

Her score of two-nil showed on his face. 'Yes, very well. I will look at that very shortly.' He thought for a moment then his face brightened. 'As a matter of fact, I have just decided that I will carry out a complete security check of the whole house and that will include your porch door. In fact, I'll start now and I'll begin with house keys. First I will find Valerie and Richard.'

'Why Valerie and Richard?'

He smiled. 'Because we all have our own set of keys and I want to do a surprise check to see if they know where their keys are.'

He marched briskly out of the house to find Richard. He would put to the test his theory that his insistence on each member of the family knowing the whereabouts of their set of keys was now being disregarded. He saw Richard sitting in the back garden reading. He strolled over.

'Ah, Richard. Can you tell me where your house keys are right at this moment?'

'Yes, Dad, you've got them.'

This was not a good start and he searched for a suitable reply. 'I have them?' He tried to claim, by the rising inflection of his voice, that this was most unlikely. 'How could I have them?'

'It was yesterday, you remember? You saw me on the way to the swimming baths and asked for my keys because you said you had left yours on your desk. You said you were on your way home.'

'Yes, of course. That is quite true and at least you knew where they were.' He found himself floundering as he searched for a dignified way out of this. 'I shall, of course, let you have them back at once.'

Hallett decided not to continue with his survey of various locations of house keys and, to save further embarrassment, he must not fail to return Richard's keys. He picked them up from his study when he went for the garage keys which, for some forgotten reason, were also in his study. His next priority must be a security check of the house. He went outside, walked to the gateway and stared at the house. All seemed well. Then he walked to the rear of the house. All was not well.

A ladder was leaning against the wall underneath his study window. He tutted to himself as he remembered that he had put the ladder there just over a week ago. It was when he had to cut away some twigs that irritatingly tapped on the window when the wind blew.

'Blast,' he muttered to himself, 'I meant to put that away.'

But, more was to follow.

The handle of the up and over garage door was locked but the catch had not clicked into place and the door could, therefore, be lifted up. He asked himself how that could have happened, particularly as he was the last one to use and then lock the garage. This was worrying. It was more worrying when he walked to the back of the garage and saw that the window on the back wall of the garage was open. Even worse; it was obvious from just a casual glance that it had not been closed for quite some time.

Well, he thought, let us put that right straight away. He wrenched at the handle and tried to force it into position but, after its many months of freedom, it was reluctant to return to its rightful place. After a heart-pounding session of pushing and wrenching he conceded a temporary defeat.

He was now forced to admit that, while his home was his castle, it was definitely not the fortress he had always believed it to be. Obviously, something must be done and fairly urgently. He must now speak to Elizabeth and explain what he intended to do.

Later that day after making some notes, he went to explain to Elizabeth that his survey had shown some grave weaknesses in the security of their house but that she need not concern herself as he would be attending to it right away. He thought it best not to mention his security lapses.

She listened attentively then said. 'Simon, this all sounds very technical. Why don't we ask someone to give us an estimate of the cost of putting it right?'

He shook his head. 'No, I really don't think it will be necessary to call a man in. After all, I have some experience in security matters and if I take it slowly and carefully, I think I can make us secure against intruders.'

Elizabeth tried to show no sign of the mild panic she always felt at his taking on such a task as this. She consoled herself with the thought that whatever he did could be undone, but how many middle of the night false alarms must we get before he would concede defeat?

Hallett went to his study and laid out a collection of pens of various colours, a ruler and some sheets of white paper. First, he thought, I must identify the area in which I think we are most at risk. That's it, look for chinks in the armour. Burglars? That could be my first area of concern. What about a burglar alarm? Good thinking! That must be the first job I tackle. He stopped when he realised that their installation involved wiring and drilling through outside walls. Yes, perhaps that could be left until later when one had become more proficient at this sort of task.

But, better make a note or two and lay out a plan of campaign. He wrote 'burglar alarms' then in red he wrote "defer". He then made notes of the sort of action to be taken on the sounding of the alarm. Next came an item headed, "Items Connected With the Installation of an Alarm". This would involve the installation of a bedside telephone, a torch to be placed by the telephone together with a reminder that the torch must be checked at regular intervals. He continued with his notes until he was satisfied that he had included all the important items.

He now felt more qualified to decide where he should start and what better place to start than those items he had noticed on his initial walk-round survey. He regretted that he had not made a note at the time but he was sure he could recall some of them.

For a start there was that small window on the back wall of the garage. That needed seeing to and that, surely, was within his competence. As he headed for the garage he noticed that Richard was no longer there but he had left his book on the chair.

He picked up the book. 'I suppose if it rains I will be responsible for that,' he muttered. 'It will be left to Father to think of things like rescuing books from the rain.'

He placed the book in the garage and went to the rear of the garage. He studied the window and its recalcitrant handle.

Obviously it had not been closed in months and it was also obvious that any intruder could easily gain entry to the garage and the contents were then theirs for the taking.

Right, he thought, I shall soon put a stop to that. He went inside the garage and, with some difficulty and a fair amount of ear-piercing, screeching noise, pulled the window to a closed position. Now to secure it in place. He gripped a determined fist round the handle and began a steady pull that increased in force as he met a creaking resistance. The almost silent struggle went on with neither side willing to give in until sheer exhaustion made Hallett submit. But, he told himself with racing heart, this was not a defeat, it was merely a strategic withdrawal. If victory was to be his, he must adopt a different approach. So, instead of that energy-wasting pull, he would apply a sudden and powerful jerk and this should move the handle and secure the window. He grasped the handle, adjusted his stance and took a deep breath. Then suddenly he tugged his arm backwards with all the force he could muster. His arm jerked taut as a bowstring and a white-hot lance of agonising pain shot up to his shoulder. He cursed and let go at once, his face a mask of suffering. Frantically he massaged his arm, quietly cursing as he did so, then walked outside to see if he could do anything there to help matters.

He couldn't.

However, there was no questioning Hallett's determination to secure that window; but with his arm aching like fury he was forced to accept that physical force was not needed. What was needed now was a military tactical approach. Back inside the garage, he searched round all the shelves until he found an aerosol of oil that he could use to spray on the window handle and hinges to try to ease them. Determined and now fully armed, he advanced on the window. Taking careful aim he blasted the catch with numerous clouds of oil droplets then turned the aerosol onto the hinges. He retired and waited for it to take effect as it soaked in. When he considered that it had taken long enough he prepared himself for another tussle with the window, but this time, it would not be quite so one-sided.

He grasped the handle once more and tugged, gently at first, then gradually increasing the pressure until he was at full stretch;

then the window moved. It screeched its protests as it was finally re-acquainted with the window frame then with a final screech, the handle was pulled into place. Hallett stood back and looked at his victory. Right. One down, several more yet to go.

What next? Of course, the ladder standing against the house. He admitted that it was negligent of him to have left it there and it must be moved.

He walked across to the ladder and slid the top extension down. It was now ready to carry but he soon found that moving an extension ladder, whether carrying it vertically or horizontally can be a tricky task. He decided, on the horizontal approach and, having got it onto his shoulder with some difficulty, weaved his way across the lawn towards the garage. He was about to put it in its usual place on the floor by the garage when a thought struck him. What was to stop an intruder from taking the ladder and using it to gain access to the upstairs windows? No! It must be locked away.

He held the ladder horizontally, gripping the rungs so that he could walk crab-wise round to the garage door. Now he must guide this inside and find a convenient place to put it. Preferably off the floor. He steered the ladder inside and at once could see that the logical place to keep it, was one end on the bench and the other onto that convenient hook. It looked straightforward, but experience told him that there would be hidden snags. What had to be done first was to swing the front end of the ladder up onto the bench. This proved to be fairly easy; now all that remained was a muscular push upward and secure the other end onto the hook. That also looked fairly easy. But it was not.

There was no time to be timid about this; just grasp the ladder firmly, take a deep breath and push upwards. He did, but even at full stretch, he was still a fraction of an inch short. Red in the face and on tiptoe, he continued the struggle but still could not link the ladder onto the hook. By now, he was gasping but refused to give in. He stretched as high as he could and gave a last thrust upwards. Fiendishly, the end of the ladder resting on the bench started to slide as Hallett gave an almighty heave. Then came the sound of breaking glass as the ladder smashed its way through the window and a faint, metallic click told him that the window catch had sprung loose. The window was now open again.

There was an eerie silence broken only by the tinkle of glass falling onto the concrete path but from Hallett there was no sound but heavy breathing. He stared at the ladder which he was still holding as it lay with its feet through the window. He gave a fierce tug and pulled it back through the broken pane onto the bench once more. He lowered it gently to the floor and walked quietly out of the garage.

He felt irritated and saddened at the way things just seemed to act against the normal laws of behaviour. Perhaps a strong cup of tea might help. He sighed a deep sigh as he walked towards the house.

He was met in the doorway by Elizabeth. 'Simon, you're just in time. Would you like some tea?'

'Thank you, Elizabeth, I would like that very much.'

As he sat wearily on a kitchen chair Elizabeth looked at him. 'Are you feeling all right?'

'Yes, thank you, I'm all right. It's just one of those days when very little seems to go to plan.'

She knew better than to press for details. 'Valerie and I are just going to that new Garden Centre. Would you like to come along?'

Slowly he shook his head. 'Thank you, but no. I still have things to do.'

Elizabeth placed a cup of tea on the table in front of him and kissed him lightly on the forehead. 'We'll see you later and please don't overdo it, will you.'

'No, of course not. See you later.'

Left alone, Hallett sat thinking dejectedly about whether or not he should, after all, call someone in to advise him on security. A part of him was still fiercely determined that he could, and should, continue; but a smaller voice persisted in reminding him of his earlier folly with the garage window. He sipped his tea and by the time he had finished, his mind was made up. He felt better now; in command once more. After all, anyone could have had that sort of problem with a weighty ladder and particularly with a window so close at hand. Even so, he thought that it might be tempting fate to have another try so soon. After all, there was the problem of the porch door to tackle yet. It surely wouldn't hurt to take a look at it and, as this was just in the nature of a preliminary reconnaissance, there was no need for tools or other equipment. This meant that he wouldn't be tempted to tinker with something and possibly cause it to malfunction, particularly when he considered how things had gone thus far.

He walked to the front of the house and decided to view the porch as a potential burglar would see it, then decide which parts, if any, needed attention. He strolled to the gateway, turned and looked hard at the porch. It seemed sound enough, but now he would tackle the problem of the lock at close quarters.

He walked into the porch and closed the door. The first thing he noted was that the key had been left in the door. He made a mental note to include this in his survey. The practice of leaving the key in the door must cease and it must be taken into the house until it is time to lock the door again. It might be an even better idea for the door to be kept locked at all times and everyone to have a porch key to be kept with other keys they carried. Yes, that was worth considering; although the memory of his recent experience of standing in the pouring rain waiting to get into his own house made him want think about it a little more.

Meanwhile, he wanted to examine the lock and test Elizabeth's claim that the door unlocked itself. As he remembered it, she said that when the door was locked, it was only necessary to press the handle up and down and the lock would spring open. He firmly believed that it wasn't as bad as that. It was just an exaggeration to ensure that the lock was examined. He locked the door and gently pressed the handle down. So far, so good. He was looking forward to telling Elizabeth that he had found the lock in perfect working order and he grasped the handle firmly then pressed it up and down a few times. There was a click and the door was unlocked. He frowned. The first thing a miscreant would do if intending to enter the house uninvited, would be to see if the door was locked and to do that he would press the handle up and down a few times. Then he was free to enter. He ignored the fact that this would give him access to the porch only, but decided that this must be put right and he wondered why he had never been told of this earlier.

However, there was no point in worrying about that now. He must get back to his study and make some notes on what he had found so far. He grasped the door-handle firmly and pressed it down only to find that the handle had slipped off its shank. Really, was there no end to these failures of security items? He was beginning to think that nothing could be relied upon and he thrust the handle back onto its shank. At least, that was his intention. Instead, he succeeded in pushing the shank backwards until it disappeared into the door and there it stayed, the end of the shank, level with the surface of the door. He was about to give vent to his annoyance when his position became clear to him. Although the door was unlocked, he could not, without turning the handle, open the door. He still held the handle in his hand, but without its union with the shank, it was useless.

But of course, there was the front door right behind him. As he turned he remembered his instruction to the family regarding the front door. He had said that unless this door was actually in use, it must be locked. But today, everyone would know that he would be in the house and thus there surely would be no necessity under these circumstances to keep the door locked. He reached a hand, pressed the handle down and gave a gentle push. It did not yield an inch. The front door was locked and Lieutenant Colonel (retd) Simon Hallett was trapped in his own front porch.

Right, he thought, I have to consider what to do; so perhaps my Army training may be of some help. First task; sum up the situation. This, though, was not as easy as it appeared because, to sum it up as 'You have just trapped yourself in your own porch', seemed not only curt but downright unhelpful. True though it may be; it was not conducive to constructive thought on extricating oneself from this embarrassing situation.

First, everyone was out of the house, so there was no help there. Who would be the first to return? As I do not know where Richard has gone, I am in no position to even guess when he might return. As for Elizabeth and Valerie, their visit to the new

Garden Centre would not be complete until they had inspected and assessed every department. His situation report did not cheer him.

He peered through faintly tinted glass but could see no-one. He sighed heavily and was about to accept temporary defeat when he saw a movement on the opposite side of the road. He stared. Yes, it was Mr and Mrs Meakin evidently going out somewhere. Mr Meakin closed and checked the front door then they both climbed into their car. Let me see, now, he thought, if they are going to see her mother, they will turn left and that will give me a chance to signal Meakin. The car edged down the drive then stood indecisively by the curb for few seconds. Then a left signal.

As they turned, Hallett frantically waved his handkerchief but it seemed that Mr Meakin was in earnest conversation with his wife. They had just started to pull away when Mrs Meakin tapped her husband on the shoulder and pointed to the porch where Hallett was still waving hopefully. Both the Meakins smiled and waved as they drove away.

Hallett slumped. 'Well, what else would you expect from a Chartered Accountant?' he said, bitterly. He considered sitting on the floor but decided that it was, perhaps, not a very good idea. There was still just a slight chance that he might attract the attention of someone. Preferably someone with just a smidgen more comprehension than the Meakins: and that, surely, should not be too difficult.

He stared gloomily out of the window hoping to see someone, anyone who could be of assistance to him. He was inclined to include in this list, Jehovah's Witnesses, double-glazing salesmen (not much chance of that on a Sunday) and people seeking subscriptions to local papers. In fact, anyone with the slightest grasp of the English language and a IQ of about ten and upwards. Why is it, he asked himself, that when I am trying to get on with my gardening, I am pestered by every one passing by? But now, when I need someone, I might just as well be on a desert island. He gave another sigh and resumed his moody surveillance. His thoughts strayed and as they did he came, as he usually did, to the Army.

The Army. Surely there must have been something in his career that he could compare with this. Of course, there was that time in married quarters when he unfortunately found himself locked in the toilet. But that was different. At least there was someone else in the house and, after Elizabeth had managed to stifle her giggles, she had pushed a small screwdriver under the door and was able to remove the lock. That situation wasn't of much use to him now, though.

There must be another way, I must get out of here soon. An uncomfortable thought struck him. What if I have a call of nature? It would be more than just a little embarrassing. What about a signal of some sort? He looked around. There was nothing except his handkerchief and that had failed him lamentably with the cretinous Meakins. Another sigh and he slid down the wall and sat on the floor.

He was almost on the point of nodding off when he heard a familiar sound. It was someone whistling. But not just anyone. It was Richard. No-one could whistle off-key like Richard.

Hallett scrambled to his feet and waved at Richard and was relieved as he saw him stop, then approach the porch. He gestured towards the handle and Richard pushed the shank back into its position and opened the door.

'Ah, thank you Richard. As you can see I was slightly disadvantaged there because I was checking the lock when the handle came adrift and I couldn't open the door. Silly thing to happen but there it is.'

'I'm glad I came back then, because I had intended to call and see a friend of mine but he wasn't in. How long have you been in there?'

'I don't know. It seems like hours.' He gave a dry laugh.

'Couldn't you get in the front door?'

Hallett looked confident. 'I think you'll find, Richard, that in accordance with my wishes, the front door is kept locked.'

Richard nodded. 'Yes, I see.' He looked puzzled. 'Dad, why were you checking the porch door?'

'It's quite simple. It's part of a plan I am carrying out to check the security of the house.'

'I see. Is that why you asked me about my keys earlier on?'

'Exactly. I wished to ensure that everyone still had their own keys, or knew their whereabouts. And that reminds me,' he added quickly, 'I remembered to get your keys from my study.' He produced the keys. 'Here you are and thank you.'

Richard took the keys and stared at his father with a very puzzled look on his face. Instantly, Hallett realised his blunder. He could have used Richard's keys to let himself in by the front door.

He could think of nothing to say that would, in any way, exonerate him from the ridiculous action of locking himself in the porch, while holding the keys that could release him. In defeat, he stared at Richard. 'I think I'd better fix that handle on the porch door and make it safe.' He went off in search of a small screwdriver.

With his screwdriver he soon had the handle fixed and, after subjecting it to a series of tests, he decided it was safe to use.

As he finished, he walked out onto his drive, almost savouring his freedom. He idly glanced across the road at the Meakins' house and was turning away when he was almost sure he saw a curtain twitch and he remembered that they had both gone out. It was just possible that they had returned while he was sitting on the porch floor, but no, there was no car there.

That's odd, he thought, there's only the two of them live in that house now their son has gone to Canada. Also, he remembered seeing Arthur Meakin check the front door before he left and he would hardly do that if there was someone left in the house. He continued staring then saw someone in the main bedroom walk swiftly by the window. Hallett's hands gripped into fists. Someone was robbing the Meakins and he must do something about it. He looked across his drive and saw Fred Root coming out of his kitchen door.

He waved and beckoned energetically for Fred to come across. Fred stopped and stared in a puzzled way then, seeing the urgency on Hallett's face, he hurried across.

'Problem, squire?'

'There's not much time to explain, but I believe that someone has broken into the Meakins' house.'

Fred wasted no time in asking questions. 'Right, I'll call the police.' He ran back into his house leaving Hallett to keep an eye on the house.

A few minutes later he returned. 'They're on their way.'

'What do you think we should do now?'

'I think we should wait for the police; there's not much else we can do.'

'But what if they get away over that back fence?'

Fred nodded. 'Yes, you could be right. Perhaps we ought to keep an eye on them. Let's creep round to the back of the house and all we will do is to observe. And, if they leave before the police arrive, we will just get a good description of them. But no heroics.'

'You may depend upon that.'

Quickly they crossed the road, crept down the side of the house and into the garden keeping cover in the bushes. Hallett pointed to a broken kitchen window then to the patio door that had been forced and was opened a few feet. He nudged Fred. 'Means of escape?' he whispered hoarsely. Fred nodded. 'Got it in one.'

They crouched together, their eyes never leaving the place they now believed to be the escape route. For a while nothing seemed to be happening then there was a movement in the sitting room and they could see two men struggling to lift something between them. Fred quickly realised that they could never have intended lifting something of that weight over the garden fence. He glanced down the garden and nodded as he saw that the door was hanging by one hinge.

Fred tapped Hallett on the arm and whispered. 'I'm just going out to the front to see if the police have arrived and I'll tell them about that broken door in the fence. Keep your eyes peeled for anything happening, but don't try anything on your own.' Hallett nodded. As Fred made his way silently to the front of the house, Hallett kept his eyes on the patio door. He had been watching for a minute or so when he saw one man slide back the door and beckon to his companion in the room. It looked as if they were preparing to move. He felt helpless. He knew that to tackle the men himself was to risk very serious injury, but he felt that he should do something and do it quickly. His mind raced as he tried to think what he might do. Suddenly, he startled himself with the action he took.

'Get ready men, they're coming out. Stand by to release the dogs.' Hallett was surprised at the strength of his voice and how steady it had sounded. He really had not planned this, it just burst out. He saw a face peer from behind a curtain.

'Hold onto that dog, Sergeant, and wait for my order.'

The face was quickly withdrawn.

There was still no indication of when the police might arrive and Hallett wondered how long the criminals would wait before they realised what was happening. He peered cautiously over the bush but, unfortunately for him, it was at the same time that one of the criminals looked out of the door. For a moment they stared at each other then the man grinned unpleasantly. He and his companion walked out into the garden towards the bush. Seeing them coming, Hallett stood up and stepped from behind the bush.

'Just what do you think you are doing here?' His firm voice held no trace of fear.

The taller of the two men looked at his companion. 'Hear that voice, Greg? He's the one who's been shouting about letting the dogs loose.' He glared at Hallett. 'It was you, wasn't it.'

'Yes, it was, and I think you ought to realise that you are in very serious trouble.'

'Not nearly as much trouble as you're in right now. Get 'im Greg.'

They rushed forward, but before they could start an attack on Hallett, three policemen, followed by Fred Root, sprinted across the lawn and quickly overpowered them.

As the policemen led them away Hallett and Fred stood watching.

'What were they saying about you and setting dogs loose?'

Hallett smiled. 'Just a little diversion to keep them busy until the police arrived and I was very pleased they turned up when they did.'

Fred looked impressed.

They crossed the road and as they reached Hallett's drive Fred stopped. 'Tell me, squire, how did you manage to spot them in Meakins' house?'

'Oh, that. Well, it's rather a convoluted story but it was mainly concerned with security. You see, I was making a check of the house and garage to highlight any security weak spots and I suppose I had security on my mind and...' His voice tailed off. He smiled. 'I think that when the police have finished with us, I had better tell you the whole story.'

A little later Elizabeth and Valerie returned from the Garden Centre. Elizabeth was pleased that the boot of the car held so many exotic additions to her collection of houseplants. She saw Hallett standing in the drive when she drove in and she climbed out to greet him.

'Hello, Simon. We've had a very interesting time; that new place is certainly well stocked.' She smiled. 'Well, it was when we arrived there but it's a little diminished now.'

She lifted the boot-lid and Hallett glanced at the type of plants he regarded as being on the very fringe of horticulture. 'A very well-chosen selection,' he remarked.

'Have you been busy while we've been away?' asked Elizabeth she as searched around in the boot.

'Yes, a little. But I've decided that I will probably call in a man to have a look at our security.'

'What a good idea. I'm sure you've made the right decision and now I expect you're ready for a cup of tea if I know you.'

They were soon in the kitchen with their tea and Elizabeth had walked into the hall to call upstairs to ask Valerie to join them when the front doorbell rang.

Slightly puzzled at who could be calling on them, Elizabeth opened the door and wondered why on earth Mr and Mrs Meakin had decided to visit them for the first time ever.

'Oh, good afternoon. Is anything wrong?' she said, immediately feeling foolish asking this when it was so obvious that the Meakins were both very pleased about something.

'Not at all. We would just like to thank your husband for what he did. May we see him?'

'Yes, of course. Please come in.'

As they walked to the kitchen Elizabeth was wondering what Simon could possibly have done for the Meakins. They entered the kitchen.

The first thing that Elizabeth noticed was the rather guilty look on her husband's face.

Arthur Meakin walked to Hallett and held out his hand which Hallett shook briefly.

'Please let me offer you our grateful thanks for your actions today. If it had not been for you, goodness knows what would have happened to our possessions. We could have lost everything. You are a very brave man, sir. It must have taken a lot of courage to face those two dangerous criminals; you could have been badly hurt. We are both indebted to you.'

It was the turn of Mrs Meakin to step forward. She laid a hand on Hallett's arm and gazed into his face. 'You are a truly gallant gentleman and we count ourselves fortunate to have you as a near neighbour.'

Hallett was finding Mrs Meakin's intense stare a little disconcerting and he was feeling rather uncomfortable. His voice was subdued. 'It was nothing really. One does what one considers necessary in the circumstances.'

After more effusive thanks and good wishes the Meakins left and Elizabeth saw them to the door.

Alone in the kitchen Hallett knew that he should have explained to Elizabeth what had happened and he knew that she would now be very worried. She entered the kitchen and sat opposite Hallett. For a few seconds no-one spoke. Then Elizabeth said in a quiet voice. 'What happened while I was away, Simon?'

'I was going to tell you, of course, all in good time. But what happened was this.'

He explained simply what had happened and when he had finished, Elizabeth sat very still, her hands clasped tightly in her lap, her trembling lips told of approaching tears.

'You could have been badly hurt or even worse.' The tears now welling up in her eyes. 'Didn't you think for a moment about your family or about me?' Her voice rose. 'Don't you see what you risked? I just can't bear to think what might have happened if they had…' The rest of her sentence was lost in her tears. Her shoulders shook as she sobbed quietly.

Hallett felt helpless. It was true that he had given no thought to his family and the effect on them if he had been badly hurt or worse. He found it difficult to explain his actions; he had acted by instinct.

He stood and put an affectionate arm round his wife's shoulders. 'Elizabeth, my love, please understand.' His voice, slow and tender. 'It wasn't something I set out to do; I had to act under the circumstances as I saw fit. In fact, I don't recall making a decision to do anything. Things just seemed to happen. But I am terribly sorry that I have upset you like this and, of course, I should have told you about this much earlier. I'm really sorry.'

Elizabeth looked up at him with an expression of tender affection. 'No, Simon, it is I who should apologise. I was being selfish there for a moment but I really couldn't help it.' She smiled at him. 'I never knew you could react so aggressively in a situation like that. Really, I am so very proud of you and Mrs Meakin was right. You are a truly gallant gentleman.'

He folded his arms around her and they stood together quietly.

By that evening, Hallett's encounter with the two house-breakers was well known and Richard was particularly interested. 'How did you get onto them, Dad?'

'It was simple observation, Richard and I consider that I was fortunate. I think, though, that it would help if we all took notice of what is going on around us and report anything suspicious. I certainly intend to be more vigilant from now on.'

'Right, Dad, I'll remember that.' The normally placid Richard looked at his father with obvious admiration.

Next morning Hallett and Fred were discussing yesterday's events.

'There is one thing about yesterday's happenings, Fred,' he had never used Root's first name before, 'it has proved to me that I should pay someone to advise me on the security of my house and I would like it done as soon as possible.'

'Why don't you telephone the police and ask to speak to the Crime Prevention Officer. He will come out or send someone out to give you advice.'

'First class idea. I'll do it right away. Have you done it yet?'

'Now that you mention it, no, I haven't.'

'Then I shall ask him to include both of us.'

'Right, squire, you're on.'

Hallett clapped his hands together. 'Right, that's that fixed. Oh, and one other thing; having seen this sort of incident at first hand, I have asked my family to keep a sharp lookout and let me know of anything suspicious.'

A few minutes later Richard appeared looking flushed and excited.

'What is it, Richard, have you found something?'

'First of all, my library book has been stolen and someone has tried to break into your garage and they've broken a window.'

CHAPTER SIXTEEN

'If I drive over that blasted pot-hole many more times I shall damage the suspension on that car.'

Hallett was in his 'What's Wrong With The World' mood.

Elizabeth looked mildly surprised but was rather more interested in the shopping that Simon had been to get. 'What pot-hole?'

'What pot-hole?' He was nearing his exasperation point now. 'Why, that gaping hole in the middle of the road out there. It's dangerous and it shouldn't be allowed. Surely you remember that I mentioned it when I read in the paper that the Council were looking at the necessity to repair paths and roads.'

'I can't say that I've noticed it myself,' she said, ignoring his impatient snort at this admission. She looked into the carrier bag. 'Did you manage to get the potatoes for me?'

Hallett looked down at his carrier bag which contained only carrots and runner beans. He cursed to himself as he remembered that he went to get potatoes. Elizabeth had asked him to go down to the shops and get five pounds of potatoes, but at the time of asking, he was engrossed in his gardening magazine. And, as the article dealt with pests on carrots and runner beans, the result was the sorry mix-up he was now looking at. 'I have no clear recollection of your mentioning potatoes, none at all. However, if you are now sure it is potatoes that you want, I will go down to the shops again.'

'Thank you, Simon. And I'm sure that the other vegetables will come in handy.'

As he strode from the kitchen, Elizabeth smiled. She knew that if she *had* made a mistake with her shopping requirements, he would have made much more fuss about having to go out again.

As Hallett strode towards his car he realised that Elizabeth had not commiserated with him over his teeth-jarring thud into that confounded pot-hole. Typical of her, he thought, if it had been one her house plants it would have been a different story.

About twenty minutes or so later he walked back into the kitchen carrying another colourful carrier bag depicting several impossibly healthy vegetables and bulging with potatoes which he dumped on the table with some force. He then stood with fists on hips, mouth compressed into a tight line and breathing noisily through his nose.

'Thank you, Simon.' She looked at him. 'What's the matter, having you been running?'

He ignored that. 'Would you believe it, I have just driven into that confounded pot-hole again?'

'Oh dear, that's not very nice for you.'

'Not only that, it made me bite my tongue.'

Elizabeth fought back a smile as she pictured the scene and the reaction with its snarl of agony and the flow of chosen words. As she looked into the bag she was pleased to see that she had at least ten pounds of potatoes there. Although she felt that there was not much else to say about the hole in the road, it was obvious that Simon did not yet consider the subject closed. She looked thoughtful. 'Well, perhaps someone ought to do something about it.'

It was Hallett's turn to look thoughtful.

'You may be right.' He said slowly then slammed his hand on the kitchen table causing the carrier bag to slump sideways and the contents to tumble onto the table. 'Dammit, you *are* right. We should all be doing something about it. And about that tree that overhangs the road at a dangerous height and those three street lights that have not worked for over a year. Not only those things but a great many more besides.'

He paced up and down. Suddenly he stopped, turned and brought his fist down on the kitchen table causing some the potatoes to leap from the pile onto the floor.

'What we need is a Residents Association.'

Elizabeth looked dubious. 'Do you really think so?'

'I'm convinced of it. In fact I shall start by canvassing the neighbours.'

'But isn't that what our old neighbour used to do? You know, Aubrey the Sanitary Inspector.'

'Nonsense. What I am doing is a studied attempt at improving community facilities: what he was always doing was getting great masses of signatures on piffling petitions about saving the starling population or some other inconsequential nonsense. And all of which came to nothing. Something will come of this, though, you'll see.'

He walked out in the brisk manner he adopted when dealing with a new idea.

Elizabeth watched him go and smiled to herself. At least it would keep him busy for a while and, who knows, he might even get some things fixed in the Avenue.

'Mother, do you think that these shoes go with this dress?'

Valerie had come into the kitchen and was looking down quizzically at her shoes as she compared them with her attractive blue dress.

'I think they suit you beautifully, and they go very well with your dress. You look lovely.'

'Oh, thanks. David is taking me to the theatre next week and we are going to see that new musical that's just opened.'

'That's nice for you. Where was it you went last night?'

'We had a go at ice-skating. I thought it was great fun and thanks to David, I didn't fall over many times. Sometime we are going swimming at the big Sports Centre.'

'You certainly seem to get on well together.' Elizabeth paused and smiled at Valerie. 'You like him very much, don't you?'

For Valerie, the word 'like' now seemed so inadequate. She found herself thinking about David constantly. She discovered that she could always visualise his face perfectly; she could remember little things he said and she experienced that electric thrill every time she saw him. Most important of all, she could think about the future only if David was included in her dreams.

Her face aglow, she nodded, not wishing to betray her feelings, but as she looked at her mother smiling, in that knowing way that only mothers have, she let her feelings pour out in a torrent.

'Oh Mother, I think he's just wonderful. He's so thoughtful and attentive, he makes me feel so marvellous when we're together and when we're apart I find myself thinking about him all the time. He always seems to say just the right things and I really think that I am…' She stopped.

'What is it you think, angel?' said her mother softly, using a term of endearment she had not used since Valerie was a small child.

Valerie answered in a very quiet voice. 'Mother, I think I'm in love with him.'

Elizabeth looked at her daughter, now so suddenly grown into a woman. She put an arm round her shoulders and, with a voice not as steady as usual, she said. 'You know, I think you're in love with him too.'

Valerie threw her arms round her mother then surprised herself by bursting into a flood of tears. Elizabeth hugged her and patted her shoulder.

'There, there, angel. I think I've known for some time how you felt about David. It was just a question of time and I'm sure now that you'll both be very happy.'

Valerie lifted her head and rubbed the tears from her eyes. 'I don't understand it, though. I feel so happy and yet all I can do is to cry like a baby.'

Elizabeth again smiled her knowing smile. 'There are tears of happiness as well, you know. There are times when you feel so full of emotion for someone, that for we women, the only thing we can do is to let it all out in our own way. It's something that men don't always understand.'

Valerie sniffed and fumbled for a handkerchief. 'I'd better get changed again,' she said, and walked towards the door. At the door she stopped and turned. 'Thanks, Mother. You're wonderful.'

They both smiled and Valerie walked up the stairs to the accompaniment of the now familiar celestial choir.

Outside the door of number fifteen, Forsthyia Avenue, Hallett was awaiting the reply to his solo on the doorbell. Abruptly, the door was flung open and he was confronted by

Timothy Lurker, a small, rather officious civil servant who worked somewhere in the bowels of the Inland Revenue.

'Yes? What is it? What do you want?' He spoke with the staccato delivery of a machine gun.

'Ah, good morning, Mr Lurcher, I'm sorry if I have disturbed you.'

'Lurker.'

'I beg your pardon?'

'Lurker, my name is Lurker. And yes, you have disturbed me. What do you want?'

Hallett managed to force a smile. 'My apologies for disturbing you and for misunderstanding your name, but the purpose of my visit is to ask if you might be interested in helping to form a Residents Association in Forsythia Avenue.'

'For what purpose?' he asked, sharply. It was clear from his tone, that whatever microscopic amount of patience he had when he started this conversation, it was now in serious risk of running out.

'Well, in order to get things done. Like, for instance, that pot-hole in the road and that tree that overhangs the road at a perilous height and many more things besides.'

Timothy Lurker drew himself up to his full height of five feet two inches. He was a dapper little man with very dark hair on which he regularly lavished generous helpings of hair-cream. His voice was brittle and deceptively calm. 'I was under the impression that there are paid officials whose job it is to see to such things.'

'Yes, no doubt there are, but the problem is getting them to do it. You know what these jumped-up jack-in-offices are like. All paper-work and no action. Everything has to be in triplicate before they will even look at it. My intention is to get them up off of their shiny seated trousers.'

The instant he had finished this attack Hallett, realised that it was, perhaps, not the most tactful approach to make to a civil servant steeped in administrative traditions.

Lurker's voice now fairly crackled with indignant wrath. 'Really? Well, firstly, the expression "jack-in-offices" is incorrect. The correct plural is jacks-in-office and I stand amazed that you were unaware of that. Secondly, it is my opinion, sir, that the sort of troublesome meddling you propose can only lead to chaos and anarchy. Good day to you.'

He stepped back smartly inside and slammed the door.

Hallett glared at the sickly green door with a ferocity that almost cracked the idiotic little triangle of glass that this fussy little gnome had seen fit to set in his door. He snorted furiously and stamped up the path reflecting bitterly that this was the sort of person who had the audacity to sign himself, "your obedient servant". He opened the gate and stamped viciously on some weird looking shrubs as he went out.

Outside he came face to face with a large, fair-haired man dressed in rough tweeds and wearing a pair of enormous brown brogues.

'Hello, Simon. Been getting some free advice on your income tax then?'

Hallett scowled. 'No, I have not. I have just had a rather unpleasant meeting with that nasty little ferret of a man.'

'You mean old Lurcher?'

'Lurker.'

'Eh?'

'His name it seems is Lurker.'

'Really? Isn't it funny, I've lived next door to him all these years and I didn't know that. But, whatever his name is, he's a difficult blighter to deal with. Had the cheek to complain about my trombone again last week.'

Charles Oliver Grenally was a veterinary surgeon and had a passion for brass instruments. He loved not only to admire them, he liked to play them. His favourite was the trombone which, like all the rest of them, he played with more enthusiasm than skill. Although Hallett was pleased to have Grenally's support in his dislike of Lurker, he could not help feeling that in the case of a prolonged recital by Charles on the trombone, some sympathy was surely due to anyone within earshot. He thought it prudent, though, not to make this known. He nodded. 'Yes, typical of the obnoxious little bureaucrat.'

'Was yours a social visit then, Simon?'

'No, not really. I was merely trying to get his views on

forming a Residents Association in the Avenue to get some action on things that need doing.'

'Residents Association, eh? Damn good idea. Who's organising it?'

'Well, I got the idea this morning and I was just making some preliminary enquiries.'

'Good man. Put me down for whatever it is and we'll show these petty little bastards what's what.'

Charles Grenally had never been a man to mince his words.

He clumped off down the path towards his gate waving to a woman passing in a large car. She was one of his better clients and was in the habit of calling him out to her house regularly to tend to the almost non-existent illnesses of her three Pekinese dogs.

Hallett stood for a few moments feeling rather better now that he had found someone else who favoured a battle with the local authorities. Looking further up the path he could see Fred Root working in his garden. Perhaps he might be interested.

'Morning, Fred. Keeping busy I see.'

'Morning, squire. Just a bit of weeding, that's all.'

'Tell me, have you ever noticed that nasty pot-hole in this road?'

'Yes, I have. When I'm in the car I always take care to steer round it.'

Hallett had also tried to do that but had often failed to judge it correctly or was too late to even try.

'Yes, me too. But the fact is, it should be filled in. Also there are many other things that ought to be attended to in this Avenue and I am proposing to form a Residents Association.'

'Not a bad idea. If I can help, let me know.'

'Good, good, thank you. I have already won the support of Charles Grenally. Unfortunately, though, our diminutive civil servant colleague was not interested.'

'Timothy Lurker? I didn't think he would be. You could have saved yourself a journey there.'

Hallett was mildly irritated to be given this 'wise after the event' advice and also to find that Fred Root not only knew that his name was Lurker, but he also knew his first name.

'However, I still feel that many people would be interested in an association pledged to working on their behalf.'

'You're right there, squire. Why not call a meeting to see who's interested?'

Hallett thought this over swiftly. 'Yes, I was thinking along those lines. I'll see about arranging it. Let's see, it's Saturday now, I'll fix it for next week.'

So saying, he walked briskly back to his house drafting the notice of the intended meeting even as he strode along.

On the following Wednesday evening an assortment of the residents of Forsthyia Avenue sat in the living room of the Halletts drinking coffee prepared by Elizabeth. At one end of the room a table had been arranged with three chairs one of which was occupied by the figure of Charles Grenally. He shuffled a few papers around then banged on the table to get the attention of his neighbours. The murmuring stopped and attention was turned his way. He rose, leaned forward and placed his large scratched and scarred hands on the kitchen table which tonight served as the Chairman's bench.

'Ladies and gentlemen, most of you know me, and tonight I am acting as temporary Chairman and opening this meeting merely because someone has to get proceedings under way. The object of us all meeting together,' he paused and looked towards Elizabeth, 'and here I must thank our hosts on your behalf for the generous use of their home,' there was a mild ripple of applause. 'The object is to see if we think that we can organise a Residents Association.'

A tall, thin man uncoiled himself from his armchair. 'I'd like to put a question, please.'

Grenally looked over his spectacles and recognised him as Bruce Simmons. It reminded him that he must ask Simmons sometime how his labrador was progressing with those pink tablets he had prescribed.

'Yes, Mr Labrad, er, Mr Simmons,' said Grenally, still thinking about those pink pills. 'What is it?'

'Well, I'm not quite sure what a Residents Association is supposed to do.'

'Thank you for your question, Mr Simmons,' said Grenally.

'To put it briefly, we hope to get some action on various matters such as those street lights that have not worked for ages and that pot-hole in the road.'

At the mention of the pot-hole there were cries of assent and general agreement that something should be done about it.

Grenally waved them to silence again as Bruce Simmons sat down.

'It seems that we are in agreement about that, then. But, in addition to the business of getting things done, I hope that the Association will bring us all together socially.'

There was a good deal of hear-hearing and nods of assent at this idea. Grenally glanced at his notes. 'First, ladies and gentlemen, I suggest that we elect ourselves a Chairman. I think that it should be someone who has influence, someone who can get results, someone who can be persuasive and has shown the ability to lead and make progress. Can I have a nomination, please?'

Several pairs of eyes turned in the direction of Hallett who seemed to be lost in thought, but before anyone could speak he stood up. There was an expectant hush as they waited to hear what he had to say.

'I have noted the remarks made by our transient Chairman and I heartily concur. Therefore, I have no hesitation in nominating,' he paused and looked round the room, 'my very good neighbour, Mr Frederick Root.'

There was silence for a moment in the room then calls of 'yes' and 'aye' started to make themselves heard.

Charles Grenally accurately judged that there would be no more names forthcoming and with a final glance at his friend, Simon Hallett, he banged his fist on the table. 'Thank you, ladies and gentlemen, I have great pleasure in declaring Mr Root as your first Chairman.'

Fred got to his feet. 'Thank you, everyone. I'm very flattered to be chosen like this and I'm sure I will do my best to get results for you.'

He sat down to a fluttering of applause and they continued with the election of a Secretary, Treasurer and Action Committee.

When the meeting broke up and people drifted away to their

various abodes in Forsythia Avenue, Fred crossed the room to speak to Hallett. 'Thanks for that, squire. I must say I expected you to be asked to fill that position. Nominating me like you did sort of stopped anyone putting your name forward.'

Hallett waved a dismissive hand. 'Nonsense. I meant what I said.'

Fred looked at him for a few moments then held out his hand. 'Thanks again, I appreciate it. This Committee business is bit new to me, though. I hope you won't mind if I lean on you sometimes for a bit of guidance.'

'Not at all, feel free at any time. My experience is at your disposal.'

They shook hands, and when Fred and Gladys left, Elizabeth busied herself tidying up and plumping up the cushions. She picked up a couple of ashtrays and walked to the waste-paper bin.

'I heard what you said in there, Simon. Why did you do it?'

He looked slightly embarrassed. 'Well, I thought about what Grenally said and I considered that, of all of us, the one man who measured up to those requirements and was most likely to get results was Root. That is why I proposed him for Chairman.'

Elizabeth knew that Simon must have originally planned to lead the Association himself and she could find no words to express her feelings for her husband's act of honesty.

She laid a hand on his arm and looked him full in the face. 'I'm sure he won't let you down.'

He smiled and said quietly. 'No, I don't think he will.'

CHAPTER SEVENTEEN

In the foyer of the Embassy Theatre, Valerie and David were being jostled by the homegoing crowd as they tried to make their way to the doors. When they eventually found their way onto the pavement outside the theatre, they stood for a moment.

'Fancy some coffee, Val?'

'Love some.'

'Great, there's a place over here.'

They ran dodging through the thinning crowds into the dimly lit restaurant and were soon comfortably seated at a quiet table. David expertly caught the eye of a passing waiter and a few minutes later two cups of coffee were set down in front of them.

'Did you enjoy the show?'

'Oh, yes, David, it was great. I shall be singing and humming those songs for weeks. It was such a happy show. You enjoyed it, didn't you?'

David nodded but he looked very serious as he unwrapped his usual two cubes of sugar and dropped them into his coffee.

'Val?'

'Yes?'

He looked flustered. 'Er, the meeting about the Residents Association was on for tonight, wasn't it?'

She smiled and looked puzzled, 'Yes, it was.'

He nodded. 'Yes, I thought so.'

They lapsed into silence.

'Val?'

'Yes?'

David folded the sugar wrapper with unnecessary precision and then looked as if he didn't know what to do with it. He dropped it in the ashtray. 'Look, I don't know how to put this, but there's something I want to say.'

She noticed the tense look on his face and the tiny beads of perspiration on his forehead. He reached out casually, unwrapped two more cubes of sugar and dropped them into his coffee.

'What is it you want to say, David?'

'I've been thinking,' he said, stirring his coffee vigorously. 'About us; you and me.'

'What about us?' she asked, with just a slight tremor in her voice.

'Well, I thought that if I earned more money, or to put it another way, if I had a different job or promotion, maybe I would be in a position to, er, well, you know, I could...' his voice trailed off and he reached towards the sugar basin and unwrapped his third pair of sugar cubes.

'David,' her voice had lost its tremor, 'what are you trying to tell me?'

He looked her full in the face and took a deep breath. 'Valerie, I love you. I love you more than I can ever tell you. I'm not sure how you feel about me, but,' the perspiration on his brow was now clearly visible, 'will you marry me?'

For David it seemed that the whole world had stopped revolving while he waited for her answer. His eyes searched her face for some clue as to her feelings. Oh no, now she was crying; he had upset her with his clumsy proposal and it was clear that she didn't feel the same way he did. But wait, was she going to say something?

'Oh David, you've made me so happy. Yes, of course I'll marry you and we'll be the happiest couple who ever lived,' she said, as the tears streamed down her face.

It would have been difficult to have measured the brief time it took David to get to Valerie and take her into his arms for what was to be a long and memorable kiss. Only when they parted did they become aware of the laughter and quiet applause as their fellow diners enjoyed the spectacle of uninhibited young love.

They smiled and sat down at their table where David cheerfully unwrapped his fourth pair of sugar cubes and plopped them into his cup. He stirred the coffee, then lifting his cup he smiled at Valerie.

'Here's to us'. He drank about half a cup.

It says much for the power of love and impending marriage that the effect of drinking a toast using something approaching concentrated syrup was almost lost on David who merely glanced at his cup and set it down. They just sat there each having eyes only for their future partner and both lost in their own private world.

In the kitchen of the Halletts, Elizabeth had just finished drying the last of the coffee cups and was folding the towel to place it on the rail when she heard voices. She glanced at the clock and realised that it must be Valerie returning from the theatre with David. The kitchen door opened and in they walked looking radiantly happy.

'Hello, you two. Did you enjoy the show?'

'Hello, Mother. Yes, it was the most beautiful and wonderful show ever.'

Elizabeth was mildly surprised to hear this because Mrs Grenally had seen it and thought it was a bit plodding and stodgy.

'I'm glad you both enjoyed it. Would you care for some coffee? It won't take long.'

'Thanks all the same,' said David in a very serious voice, 'but I'd like to speak to the Colonel first if I may.'

Elizabeth glanced quickly at both of them and wondered if she was reading the signs correctly. Did they both look even happier than when they went out? Wasn't Valerie holding David's arm just that bit tighter?

'Yes of course; he's in the sitting room. Come on through.'

They walked into the sitting room where Hallett sat engrossed in his latest book on heraldry. He looked up mildly surprised. 'Hello, there. What's this then, a deputation?'

David stepped forward, swallowed hard then looked directly at Hallett. 'Colonel, I want you to know that tonight I have asked Valerie to marry me.'

He hesitated as there seemed to be no more to say unless he was expected to seek formal approval.

Hallett looked from one to the other, put down his book on a side table, removed his spectacles and stood up. He walked forward and stood facing David. He held out his hand.

'Congratulations. Look after her carefully, won't you.'

Eagerly David shook his hand. 'I certainly will that. I promise that I'll always take good care of her.'

'Well now, I suppose that I should be asking you if you are in a position to support a wife, shouldn't I?'

The question was put briskly but he had a twinkle in his eye as he spoke.

'I have my plans for that, Colonel.'

David turned to Elizabeth who was looking on quietly. She smiled happily though her eyes seemed to be brimming with tears. She kissed him lightly on the cheek.

'Welcome to the family, David.'

'Look here, young man, er, David. Why don't you use that telephone and ask your parents to come round. Then we can celebrate this properly.'

Valerie and her mother sat chatting happily while David made the call.

A few minutes later the two families stood in the Halletts' living room raising glasses and proposing toasts of health and happiness with the occasional tear rolling down female cheeks. Fred looked contented as he stood by the happy couple and he raised his glass once more.

'Here's to both of you and if you can be as happy and well matched in your married life,' he looked across the room, 'as the Colonel and Elizabeth so obviously are, then you're in for a great time.'

The bridegroom-to-be felt that he ought to say something in reply and as he stood up he gave a quick nervous smile to Valerie. 'Thank you all for your good wishes and I think I can say that if Valerie and I have happy dreams about what married life is like, then it must be because of the good examples shown by the two couples in this room.'

The two couples received this sincere tribute and tried to look suitably modest as they exchanged smiles.

Next morning, Fred had finished his breakfast and was in his garden inspecting the rockery to see if his new plants had established themselves. He saw David crossing the lawn towards him, looking a very serious young man to the happy, laughing person of last night.

'Can I have a word with you, Dad?'

'You can have more than one if you like.'

'I'm serious, I want to talk to you.'

Fred nodded. 'All right, let's go and sit down.'

They sat on a rustic bench and as Fred leaned back at his ease, David crouched forward, his hands gripped into fists.

After a few seconds of silence, Fred thought that he had better help him to start. 'What's on your mind then, David?'

He sighed. 'It's about that job of managing a fruit shop.'

'What about it?'

He knew what was coming next but he thought that he should let David put it into words.

He straightened up and turned to face his father. 'Look, Dad, I'd like a chance at managing a shop for you. I'm not looking for any favours or special treatment. I just want a chance.'

'Well, I'm glad you're not looking for favours because I'm not offering any. All the managers have to produce results for me and so would you.'

'I understand that. All I want is a chance to show that I can do it.'

'All right, David, I always said that there was a place for you and I'm pleased to welcome you into the business. How does getting up at four in the morning appeal to you?' He smiled at David's expression. 'Not every morning, but you'll find that it will often be necessary at certain times of the year.'

'If that is what's needed I'll do it, I know I can.'

'I know you can, son. Give me a few weeks and I'll sort something out.'

'Thanks Dad.'

David stood up, looked around, took a deep breath and marched confidently across the lawn and out on his way to work.

Fred looked at his son's departing figure and murmured to himself. 'You'll do it all right, I know you will.'

He sat on the bench for a while thinking about their conversation and of plans for the future.

Later, Fred saw Hallett pottering about in his garden. He

noticed that he had adopted his floppy sun hat from their camping holiday and wore it constantly in the garden.

He strolled across to the fence. 'Morning, squire.'

'Morning, Fred. You're out and about early.'

'Not really; just pottering about. Just planting something are you?' said Fred, looking at the small pink plants Hallett was carrying in a wooden tray.

'Yes, I'm rather pleased. A friend gave me these rather attractive little plants. I intend to put them in my rockery.'

Fred pursed his lips and slowly shook his head.

'You don't advise it?'

'Well, they look like asperula suberosa to me.'

'Yes, that's what he said they were, asperula suberosa, an evergreen herb.'

'Very nice, squire; but I think you'll find that if you put that on your rockery it might just take over and it's very difficult to get rid of.'

He looked disappointed. 'I see. Very well, I suppose I shall have to get rid of them.'

The statement was clearly intended as a question.

'No, you don't have to do that. Why not put them in that little tub you've got over there. Then, if you ever get fed up with them, rip 'em all out.'

'Yes, of course. That sounds like common sense. I'll fill the tub now.'

He turned away then turned back. 'Do you think that sandy soil would be all right?'

'Try equal parts of loam, leaf mould and sand. Put it facing north or protect it with something. Remember to cover it with a sheet of glass from October to the end of March. And, by the way, the stem is very brittle so it needs handling with care.'

'Thank you,' he said, now regaining his usual confidence, 'I usually manage to handle plants with a fair degree of delicacy.'

'Good for you,' said Fred, just as Elizabeth stepped out of the back door.

'Morning, Elizabeth,' he said cheerfully. 'Nice morning.'

'Good morning, Fred, yes, it looks like a beautiful day.'

'See you later, squire.'

'Yes, of course,' said Hallett, now busily evicting several families of wood lice from his tub.

'Did you plant those asperolas, Simon?'

'No, I didn't. As a matter of fact, Fred tells me that they are better off in a tub and I am about to prepare the sort of mixture I think they would grow well in,' he said, reluctant to let Fred Root take all the credit for the well-being of his plants.

'He's very well informed, isn't he?'

He nodded. 'Yes, in some matters he certainly has a fair knowledge.'

'I think he's a very pleasant man and a good neighbour, don't you?'

'Yes, I don't think I would argue with that.'

'There is one thing that puzzles me, though. Why does he always call you squire?'

Hallett looked thoughtful. 'I think that the explanation must stem from his beginning. He has always had to be subservient to his customers and so he is aware of the importance of correct address. I think that it was natural when we were first acquainted for him to choose an appropriate mode of address for me and he automatically chose squire. I think I can see the reason for this and he has maintained it ever since.' He smiled modestly. 'Nothing odd about it, really.'

As he spoke he was idly watching the milk float pull up on the road outside the gate. As usual, the milkman leapt out before it had stopped, seized a small crate of milk bottles and strode up Fred's drive whistling with an ear-piercing noise that had irritated Hallett ever since this cheerful milkman had started on the round about two months ago.

He stopped at Fred's back door and expertly changed three empty bottles for three full ones then he turned to leave. He saw Fred standing near his rockery. 'Morning, Mr Root.'

Fred looked round to see who had spoken and his reply drifted back to Hallett loud and clear.

'Morning, squire.'

Elizabeth smiled, looked at her husband and waited for the reaction that she knew must come.

Hallett gave an impatient snort.